As the Fire DIES

VANESSA ROSE

author.vanessa.rose@gmail.com

Printed in the United States of America

First Printing, February 20, 2026

https://www.facebook.com/groups/vanessaroseromancereads

Edited by Amanda Brown

Cover Design by SWEET 15 DESIGNS LLC.

DEDICATION

To all who believe that love never dies.

Acknowledgements

I would like to say thank you to some wonderful people who supported me through the process of creating this story. While the story told itself, these wonderful friends aided in making it flow and feel as amazing as possible: Aaron Jones, Summer N. Dawn, Celeste Kaide, Tamsyn L. Key, Melissa Poster, and Lillian Elizabeth. I also would love to show appreciation to all of the baristas, coffee shops, game stores, and other people and places that put up with me loitering while I pounded out the words. None of them laughed at me for crying either.

There are so many amazing musicians and bands that were also a huge inspiration for me. Their songs are a staple in my life, and often their music pulled me out of some of the darkest moments of my life. Even now, when the weight on my shoulders becomes too heavy, it is the music that pulls me out. This book, and all the ones to follow are a love letter to all the incredible artist who have given me my voice again and shown me back to the light. I will forever be thankful.

TRIGGER WARNINGS

Just a note to my readers. This book takes you on an emotional journey, and with it we delve into some themes that may be difficult to read. These themes include loss/death, cancer, drug abuse, recovery, and relapse, surviving domestic violence, death of a parent, teen pregnancy and alluding to abortion, depression, grief, abandonment, and suicidal thoughts. While this story does not have a happily ever after, it is the catalyst that brings about the joy and happiness for the rest of the series. Without this story, none of the others would be possible. There can be beauty in sadness, and the goal of this story was to show that even short-lived love can last a lifetime.

If any of these themes will affect your mental health, please put down the book. I care more about your health and well-being than anything else.

Otherwise, happy reading!

Prologue

Hannah

This isn't my story. It isn't even his story, though we were lucky enough to be a part of it. No, this is her story, the story of a beautiful woman who lived a not so beautiful life. While she suffered through pain and darkness, often all alone, she lived unapologetically. She lived strong and fierce right to the end. Growing up, my whole goal in life was to be her, though not because her life was perfect. No, it was far from it. I wanted to be her because no matter what happened, she kept fighting. She kept living. She kept smiling.

My mother, Alanna Grace Merrick, never had it easy, but I don't think she would have been the woman she was had she lived any other life. Hopefully, I can be that for my own daughter. Of course, this story, Alanna's story, certainly changed everything for my little girl. So, no matter how sad I feel when I think of her, I am thankful for everything. She gave me and my girl the best life either of us could have asked for. While I will always miss her, I know she guided my path and, to this day, gives me strength when I feel like giving up.

Alanna

"Sounds like a you problem," Keith said, pushing her back as he tried to get away.

"How is this a me problem? I'm pretty sure you were just as involved in the getting me pregnant part of this," Alanna yelled, going after the man who seemed all too content to be done with her. "This is happening whether you like it or not."

"It doesn't have to happen," Keith snapped back, his face stern and cruel. She knew what that meant, and she would never think of doing that.

"It's happening," Alanna replied, her tone hard and unwavering. "You know what, don't worry about it. I don't fucking need you. Never did."

"Good, now fuck off!" Keith answered, throwing his fingers up in the air and walking off toward his beaten-up Pontiac.

Alanna didn't respond. She had her own problems to deal with, and Keith was just another obstacle she was getting out of the way. As she pressed a hand to her still very flat stomach, it was strange for her to think she was carrying a life inside of her. Had she not taken a test, no one, including her, would have been able to tell. She still looked like her, but now she was so much more.

Taking a deep breath, she snatched up her backpack and threw it over her shoulder. Her dirty blonde hair was swept to the other side and flowed in messy waves down to her waist. She had worn her favorite pair of low-cut black jeans and punk T-shirt to school today. Her makeup was dark and had smudged down her cheeks from the roller coaster of emotions raging through her all too hormonal body.

Sixteen. She was only sixteen years old. How was she supposed to have a baby? Why did she let a dick like him convince her that giving up her V-card was a good idea? Deep down she had known it was a mistake, yet she went along with it. God forbid she be uncool. Well, she certainly wouldn't be getting invited to a lot of parties now that she had a baby on the way.

She took the long way home, needing that extra time to get her head together. The idea of facing her mother was difficult most days, but telling her she was about to be a grandmother was not a task Alanna wanted to deal with. Maybe the woman had a good day and would be more welcoming to the news. Not likely. The moment her house came into view, Alanna could feel bile start to rise. It could be the baby, but she knew it was more than likely anxiety.

Beverly Merrick was a practical woman who wanted her daughter to grow up and have a comfortable life. It didn't matter that Alanna loved music more than anything in the world. To Beverly, it was more important to start your 401K the moment you entered the workforce and to slave away for a comfortable retirement. Alanna had long since given up on talking to her mother about her desire to become a singer. She wouldn't listen, so it didn't matter. Now Alanna was starting to think her mother had a point. Being a starving artist was one thing, but being a starving artist who was also a mother was another. She no longer had the luxury of thinking only of herself.

"You're late!" Alanna's mother called out from the kitchen.

"You're early," Alanna grumbled under her breath as she went to set down her backpack. Pulling out the little stick that showed the proof of her transgressions, she took a deep breath and went to get the inevitable over with.

Beverly was leaning over the counter chopping vegetables for dinner. Her gray hair was pulled back in a severe bun, and she was still dressed in her slacks and collared shirt from work. For as long as Alanna could remember, her mother had been a secretary. While the offices changed from time to time, her mother had stuck with the same career, and she wanted Alanna to take the same path. So much so that Alanna had gotten a summer job being her mother's assistant the year before. Alanna had hated it.

"Why are you late?" Beverly asked, not even looking up from her task.

"I had to talk to Keith before I left school, so I missed the bus and had to walk," Alanna answered.

"Why did you have to talk to Keith so badly after school, and why didn't he just give you a ride home? He doesn't seem to mind picking you up all the time," her mother asked.

"He didn't bring me home because we got in a fight and broke up," Alanna answered. It was the truth.

"Oh good. I never did like that boy. He doesn't have your best interest at heart," Beverly said, finally looking up. "But I'm sorry. I'm sure you're a little sad about it."

"No, not really," Alanna said and walked closer to the counter.

"What's going on? You're worrying me, Alanna. What's that in your hand?" her mother asked, her brow creasing. It was rare for Alanna to see her mother falter from her usual stern demeanor.

The words got stuck somewhere between Alanna's throat and lips. Panic set in, and before she knew it, she was slamming the pregnancy test down on the counter as she rushed out of the room to be sick. Alanna had just fallen back from the toilet to lean against the tub when her mother showed up at the door. Tears streamed down Alanna's face, and she wasn't sure if sadness, anger, or just being sick had brought them on.

"How did this happen?" Beverly asked, holding the stick between her fingers.

"I'm pretty sure you know how things like this happen, Mom," Alanna answered. "I'm sorry."

"Well, nothing we can do about it now, and don't think this means you are quitting school. Hell, you need an education more than ever now. We will figure this out," Beverly said.

Alanna wanted to believe that the woman was being caring, but her tone had been more practical than anything. At least she wasn't getting kicked out of the house. Of course, she had thought she would at least get yelled at.

"I know. I'm going to do everything I need to. I messed up, but that isn't this, ummm, baby's fault. So, yeah," Alanna said.

Her mother just turned away and went back into the kitchen to finish cooking. Alanna pulled her knees up so she could rest her chin on them as she cried. No, it wasn't the baby's fault. It was her fault, and with that, the last shred of her dreams for her future fell like rain from her eyes. She would do anything to give her child the best life possible. Anything.

Abel

"The state of California charges you with first degree assault, possession, and probation violation. How do you plead?" the judge asked, looking at the stack of papers that made up Abel's file. He had been lucky to get probation in the first place. How had he managed to fuck that up? What was wrong with him? Years of being in and out of jail and getting into trouble were starting to catch up with him and becoming more and more difficult to run from.

Abel swallowed hard and did what his lawyer advised. He looked directly at the judge as he sealed his fate, "Guilty."

"So noted. Please put in the record that the defendant, Abel Sharp, has pled guilty to the charges," the judge said, turning his attention to the court record keeper. Once they finished typing, the old man turned back to Abel. "You have been in a lot of trouble over the years. It is getting difficult to look the other way. I'm afraid you have left us with no other choice. You are sentenced to three years. Hopefully you will use that time to think about your life. You're twenty years old and far too young to be throwing it all away."

"What the fuck? I thought you said if I pled guilty, I would get a lesser sentence," Abel whispered to his lawyer.

"That is the lesser sentence. Sorry," the lawyer said in a droll tone. Apparently, he was just as through with him as everyone else.

Already his body was shaking. Need. Deep-seated need coursed through him with every pump of his heart. He had to get out of here, but it was too late. Two officers came over and locked his wrists behind him before escorting him out of the courtroom. A couple of his friends had come to support him, but they couldn't save him. His muscles ached with a desire to fight back, but that would only get him in more trouble. Three years. How the fuck was he supposed to go away for three years?

The next couple of hours came in a blur of information and paperwork, most of which he couldn't even remember. The longer things went on, the more the need rose in him. The demons inside screamed at him. *Run. Fight. Feed us!*

"Are you listening to me?" the man on the other side of the desk asked, slamming down his hand to get Abel's attention.

"Fuck! No. I have a headache. I can't see or think straight," Abel answered. The room felt like it was spinning, and he was pretty sure he was going to be sick. He sat with his long legs stretched out in front of him as far as they would go. His long black hair fell forward like curtains on either side of his face. Tattoos covered each arm, his chest, back, and up his neck. They had already made him change into one of those stupid jumpsuits, which helped hide the marks that traced up and down his veins.

"You will be getting treatment while you are in prison. Abel, you are twenty years old. You still have time to get your life fixed," the man said. Abel wasn't sure what the officer's name was, nor did he care enough to learn it.

"Looks like it's going just about right to me," Abel answered sarcastically.

His parents had been drug addicts. His sister had died of an overdose when he was eighteen. Drugs were the only comfort anyone in his family had ever known. When acting out didn't seem to get anyone's attention, Abel fell right in line with everyone else. If you can't get the love from others, get the love from the only thing that feels good.

It started slowly—alcohol, weed, pills, but those things didn't do enough. He could still remember the first time he shot up and the rush it sent through his body. It was the best high he had ever had in his life, and he had been chasing it ever since. Nothing ever felt like that first time again.

He spent a few weeks in the county jail before they shipped him off to prison. His friends and band mates had all but abandoned him to go chase the dreams they had once shared. With each passing day, he saw his future slipping away. Surprisingly, it was almost easier to get drugs in prison than it had been outside, but that only got him in more trouble. No, that almost killed him... again.

Forced into treatment, Abel followed the steps and did what everyone told him to—not because he actually wanted to do them but because he wanted out of the hell he had found himself in. Shaking, vomiting, head pounding, he fought it all, and he wrote down his experiences. He turned his hell into hope, and he knew this was just the beginning. He refused to let this bump prevent him from making it. Fuck them. Fuck everyone. One day, everyone would know his name.

Days passed into weeks and then into months. Page after page was steadily filled with the words, poems of his pain, his anger, his desire, and his promise to himself. By the time he was stepping out of those walls, he had everything he needed to start again. This time, it would be on his terms. His once friends may have left him to rot, but there were always others hungry for a chance at the spotlight. He would get the best—the best musicians, the best producers, and the best manager. He would settle for nothing less, and one day, crowds of people would be screaming his name.

THE LETTER
24 YEARS LATER

*D*ear Abel,

You don't know me. Hell, you will probably never even read this letter, but I had to write it. For myself, if nothing else. You are my mother's favorite singer, and her favorite band. So much so that for years she performed in a tribute band that exclusively did your music, but this isn't about that. No, this is just about her. See, I can't let her die without sharing her with you. I feel like you deserve to know about her. If nothing else, this is one last thing I can do for her.

My mother is a very beautiful woman who has lived a not so beautiful life. Through all of the pain she has gone through—the abandonment, the abuse, the loneliness—she was always able to smile. My mother hid so much from me that I am just now finding out about. She never let me know when she was hurting. She never let me see her cry. Though her life was hard, she made sure my life was amazing.

Whenever she felt sadness or darkness, I would find her singing and dancing. She used your music to heal from the things she always kept hidden from me. I think deep down, she relates to your music and your story more than she could express to me. Unfortunately, now, she is lucky if she can get through one song. I'm slowly watching her waste away, and there is nothing I can do about it. She sits and listens to music, and she fights for her life, but I think she is only doing it for me. I see hopelessness behind her eyes that was never there before. She has always been a fighter.

See, it has been just me and her for as long as I can remember. My grandmother decided my mother made too many bad decisions and left. It's been ten years since I saw that woman. My father abandoned me before I was even born. My mom dated off and on while I was growing up, but about ten years ago she got into a relationship with a man who promised her the world. Or at least her dreams. That is when she started the band. How was I supposed to know what was really going on? I was just a child.

Lately I have found myself listening to your music as well. I'm older now, and I see what my mother got out of it. I feel what she felt. Feels... she isn't gone yet.

The doctors say she waited too long. Had we brought her in when the symptoms first started, maybe we could have saved her. Maybe it wouldn't have spread as far as it has. It is eating her away, and there is nothing I can do but sit back and watch death come for her. It is lurking in the shadows, and I'm so afraid. I don't know if I can live my life without her. If only I had pushed her to go to the doctor when the weakness started. When the dizziness came. When she complained about pain she had never had before. If I had made her go, maybe I wouldn't be losing her now.

I'm not asking anything from you other than the hope that you will read this letter and learn about someone you brought peace and love to in the hardest moments of their life. When she sings your songs, she smiles. She becomes another person. It is like watching an angel burst out of the shell of the body my mother inhabits. I hear the passion in your music, and I feel it come from her. My friends used to beg her to sing at school functions, but she always said the music she sang was not appropriate for school, and she refused to soften herself for anyone. She never cared about singing in front of me. I remember being in the car as a small child watching her rock out as if she were a star and the world was watching, even though it was just me and the other cars around us.

When I say my mother performed your music, I don't mean she sang like some weak karaoke imitation. No, she belted it with every ounce of emotion and depth within her. I honestly think you would have been proud of her had you ever seen her. It didn't matter if she was on stage or cooking dinner. She sang, she screamed, she roared, and I loved every moment of it because I saw the powerful strong woman that no one else believed in.

My grandmother always told her music wasn't a real career. My mother was sixteen when she got pregnant with me. Luckily my grandmother made sure she finished high school, but she never went to college. She ended up working customer support jobs, becoming a zombie to the man to provide for me. She put all of her dreams to the side because no one believed in her, and her spirit had been beaten down so much that she stopped believing in herself. So, when she finally started doing music, she never pursued more than a few festivals and local shows. It made her happy, but she could have been more. She could have been great.

I know this letter is long, and it is probably rambling. I know there are splotches where my tears have fallen. I'm sorry for that, but if you ever do read this, I hope you know one thing. My mother, Alanna Grace Merrick is a beautiful woman with a not so beautiful life, and you made it just a little bit better. She may just be another fan in a long line to you, but you for her, well, you saved her life. You gave her an outlet. You made her smile.

The doctors have given her six months or less to live. She is doing treatment, yes, but I know it is only so she can live longer for me. I honestly believe that if my daughter and I were not factors, she would just let the cancer take her. I have enclosed some pictures of her as well as a small drive that has a copy of her performing her favorite of all of your songs. That video was taken three days before we found out she was sick, yet she still performed like the world was hers and you were speaking through her. That is what she used to say. That she was just a vessel for you to speak through. She is weird that way. That video is not my favorite performance of hers, but it is the only one I have of her performing that song. And since it is her favorite, I wanted to share it with you.

Again, I know you probably will never read this. I wrote this for me, but I am still going to send it to you anyway. If you do ever happen to read it, I hope you find comfort in knowing that though you may have touched many lives with your music, this life was special. This life was beautiful. This life's light is going out having been touched by you.

With my broken heart,

Hannah Merrick Reading

Chapter One
Abel

"Abel, I think you should read this," Mason said, walking into the green room and handing him an envelope. Inside was what Abel could only assume was a letter, some pictures of a pretty woman, and a USB thumb drive.

"What the fuck is this?" he asked with a shrug.

"It's a fan letter. Well, not exactly. It's the daughter of a fan letter," Mason answered.

"I don't have time for this," Abel groaned and tossed the envelope down on the table.

"Make time. I really think you should read this one," Mason said, his voice serious.

Mason was never serious. They were always joking around and being idiots. It helped break some of the stress of being on tour all the time.

With a deep sigh, he picked up the envelope and twirled in between his fingers. Abel went to sit down on the couch and pulled out the letter, reading it completely once before he looked up at his friend, "Is this for real?"

"Seems to be. I looked up that Hannah girl. She has a pretty decent social media network and YouTube page. She's been posting videos about her mom for years now. In the last few months, though, it has all been about that," Mason answered.

Abel looked at the pictures again. The woman in them looked like a rock star. She was singing into a microphone, and her face expressed the same passion he felt when he was on stage. "Did you check out the drive?"

"No, I was worried it might have a virus, but the YouTube page has performances," Mason explained.

"Let me see," Abel said, getting up and going to his computer. He wasn't sure what was coming over him. It was like something itched at the back of his brain. Sure, he got letters from fans all the time telling him their sad stories and how his music had helped them, but this one felt different. Abel couldn't put his finger on it, only that it did.

Mason typed at the keys until he brought up the site. The girl in the videos didn't look like the one in the pictures. She was younger and had darker hair than the woman in the photos. Of course, the letter had told him it came from the daughter. Mason went to click on the most recent upload of the woman performing, but Abel stopped him. "Give me some privacy please. Go tell the band to get ready. I'll be out in just a few minutes."

Mason gave him an awkward smile and left the room. Instead of clicking on the performance, Abel clicked on the latest video the girl had posted.

"Hey guys! I can't express just how much your support and love has meant to me. We just got back from the doctor, and Mom is really tired. She is out in her office sitting and listening to music. Brandon has wired the whole place, so I'm doing my best to muffle the music in here, so I don't get a copyright strike. Anyway, I just wanted to give everyone an update. She is still fighting and smiling. I even caught her singing a little bit ago but wasn't fast enough to record it. I will post one if I catch her again. So, yeah, thank you again, and I will give all of you an update as soon as I have one." He assumed the girl was Hannah.

The video was really short, but he could hear the quiver in her voice and feel the pain she was in all the way through the screen.

With a deep breath, he then clicked on the upload of the last posted performance.

"Hey, everyone! So, my mom is doing a performance tonight. I decided to record it for you in case you weren't able to make it. I know it's been a while since she performed. Ever since John left the band things have been a bit on the rocks. Anyway, she is singing her favorite Louder in Silence song tonight. So, I'm excited to share it with all of you," Hannah explained before turning the camera toward a stage.

They were in a bar and standing in the spotlight was the woman from the pictures, only she looked thinner. Her eyes were deeper, tired. Even if he hadn't already known the truth, he would have known something was wrong. She wore a beautiful silver dress that fell all the way to the floor. Her hair was done with braids from either side, with the rest flowing in beautiful dark blonde waves down to her waist.

She was stunning. A man sitting at a piano started to play. Abel didn't even realize he was holding his breath until it quivered out of him. He watched in awe and amazement as the woman sang a song he had written during one of his darkest moments. It was about wanting to give up, wanting to die. She sang it like an angel, each word stabbing into him as it built from something soft, almost broken, to something powerful and full of anguish. That woman felt those words, just as much as he did when he sang them. It wasn't a song he often did on stage. Honestly it hurt too much to perform.

His eyes stayed glued to the entire performance, and he gasped when he saw her stumble. She took several deep breaths and steadied herself without missing a note, and when she got to the end of the song, she looked directly into the camera. He felt like she was staring into his soul, and a shiver ran down his spine. Who the fuck was this woman? For several long moments he sat there in stunned silence. Hearing other people sing his songs often felt cheap and awkward, but not this woman.

Abel picked up the letter again and read the name. Alanna Grace Merrick.

The doctors say she waited too long. Had we brought her in when the symptoms first started, maybe we could have saved her, the letter had said.

His head screamed back and forth in a roar of indecision. Part of him knew he should put it away and ignore it. Surely nothing good would come from him responding. He couldn't save this woman. He certainly wasn't a doctor. Yet another part of him really wanted to meet her. Maybe he could give her a moment of happiness. Her daughter had expressed that she'd had a hard life. He could relate to that. If he could make this woman's last few days on this Earth happier, maybe it would go a long way into making him feel more worthy.

"Dude, we got to get on stage!" Derrik, his drummer, yelled from the door.

"I'm right behind you," Abel answered, exiting the website and shoving the letter and pictures back into the envelope. He put the letter in his bag so no one would run off with it and grabbed his hat before he headed to the stage. Maybe the show would provide clarity.

More than twenty thousand people were waiting to hear him perform. He had come a long way from addiction, prison, and a life of poverty. He had made his dreams come true through blood, sweat, and grit. Pulling his locket out from under his shirt, he opened it and kissed the picture of his daughter inside. Without her, he may have relapsed back into oblivion, but she made him want to be better every day.

"Love you, Briar," he whispered a moment before he stepped out onto the stage to a roar of screaming fans. Fire burst out all over the stage in a spectacle of pyrotechnic glory. No expenses were spared when it came to him putting on a good show.

"I have two days off here. If I fly in, and that Hannah girl can pick me up at the airport, I can spend a day there and then make it back in time for the Oklahoma City show," Abel pointed out going over his schedule. The tour was jam packed, but he always put in time for him to fly home and see his daughter. He was sure she would understand if he didn't make it one time.

"Are you sure you want to do this?" Mason asked, arching a brow in Abel's direction.

"No, I'm not fucking sure of anything, but I think I need to do it," Abel answered.

"Well, do you want to make the call, or do you want me to do it?" Mason asked next.

"I'll do it," Abel answered, taking Mason's phone and dialing the number listed. It didn't occur to him that it was after eleven at night, and normal people tended to go to bed before then. His mind had been set, and he wanted to do this before he lost his nerve.

The phone rang three times before a woman's voice answered, "Hello?"

"Hey, ummm, yes, is this Hannah? I'm trying to reach her about a letter she sent me," Abel asked, realizing he was probably just going to get hung up on.

"Who is this?" the woman asked in a hushed tone as she yawned. He could hear fabric rustle and movement. Had he gotten her out of bed?

"This is Abel Sharp. You wrote me a letter about your mom," he answered.

"You can't be serious. Look, I don't know who you are, but my family is going through enough right now," she said and hung up.

"Fuck!" Abel yelled.

"Here, try this," Mason said. He handed Abel the letter and had him hold it up in front of him with one of the pictures of her mom in front. Then he had him stand in front of a calendar and point at the date. Mason took a picture then texted it to the number.

"This is stupid. There's an address on the letter, I can just show the fuck up," Abel said when no reply came.

"You could, but you are talking about Alabama. A strange, heavily tattooed man walking up on someone's property there is asking to get shot," Mason joked.

"You're an idiot." Abel laughed and then jumped when the phone rang.

Thankful the picture had worked, he pressed the button to answer the phone, and brought it up to his ear. "You're really him."

"Yeah, I am. So, I wanted to see if we could work out a time for me to come see your mom," Abel explained.

"What? You would do that?" she asked, her voice giving away her shock.

"Yeah. I've been thinking about it all night. Sorry it took a while to respond. I only got the letter a few hours ago, and then I had a show," he explained. "I have some time off scheduled in a couple of weeks. Usually I go visit my daughter, but I think I can make an exception and fly down there. Do you think you can pick me up at the airport?"

"I'll make any arrangement I need to. You have no idea how much this would mean to her," Hannah answered. "I really didn't expect you to respond."

"I know, but I did. I'm going to give you to my friend Mason. He will be your point of contact while everything gets set up. But, hey, let's keep this between us. I would like it to be a surprise to your mom," he said. "How is she doing, by the way?"

"She had a good day today, but she goes in for treatment tomorrow. Every day is, well, a day," Hannah answered. "But right now, she's holding on and being a trooper."

"That's good to know. Hey, if anything does happen, reach out, okay. Sorry I can't get there any sooner, but you know, I'm working," Abel explained.

"Like I said, I didn't expect anything. I just wanted to tell you about her. She's a pretty awesome woman, and I'm not just saying that because I'm her daughter," Hannah answered.

Mason took over the call from there. Abel felt exhausted, his head spinning. It was much earlier in California. His daughter stayed up late, so he decided to call her and let her know the change in his plans. "Hey, Dad! How was the show tonight?"

"It went good. I'm just tired," he answered, lying back on the couch. "I need to talk to you about something."

"Oh, okay. What's up?" she asked.

"You know I was supposed to fly out in a couple of weeks. Well, I'm not going to be able to make it," he said.

"Why? Did they add a show?" She didn't sound upset, just curious.

"No, I just have something I need to do. I got a fan letter today, and well, let's just say it hit a chord with me. I'm going to go meet this lady," he explained.

"That's a little weird," Briar answered.

She was right. It was weird for him. He wasn't the type to run off to meet fans. While he loved meeting them at shows, it wasn't normal for him to take time out of his life to go and visit one.

"This is different. It's a bit complicated to explain, but she is really sick, and I just want to meet her."

"Well, if you think it's the right thing to do, I trust you. I'll see you the next time," Briar answered. "I mean, I've got school and stuff anyway."

"Thanks. How is school going?" he asked, always trying to stay involved in her life as much as he could. No way was he going to be an absentee father. She was nineteen, but he had done his best to always be in her life, right from the start.

"It's good. I like my classes," she answered.

Briar had started Berkeley that last fall having graduated high school. She had turned into the complete opposite of him, and he was thankful for it.

"Well, you let me know if you need me. You don't have any boys sniffing around. Do you?" he asked next.

"Dad!" Briar exclaimed and started to giggle.

"Oh, he better keep his hands to himself. I was a young man once. I know what they are thinking," he said, laughing a bit.

"Yeah, probably the same things you still think. Don't worry, I am not going to let anything bad happen to me. You taught me well," she answered.

"Good, and remember, I have been to prison. I'm not scared," he joked. He had been making that same joke since his little girl got her first boyfriend in middle school. Since then, angry dad mode had become a constant monster inside of him. It may have been a joke, but he would fuck up anyone who messed with his baby.

"I'm going to go. Have a good trip. You will have to tell me about it later," Briar said exasperated.

"Alright, well good night. I love you," he said.

"I love you too, Dad," she answered and hung up.

Mason had already left, and he assumed taken care of the first discussion. Drained from emotions and the physical exertion of the stage, Abel made his way to the bus so he could get some sleep. He wasn't sure what possessed him to do it, but he took one of the photos from the letter, folded it up, and put it in his wallet.

CHAPTER TWO

ABEL

The humidity was the first thing to hit him when he stepped off the plane at the Birmingham airport. It was almost summer, and the humidity in Alabama didn't seem to stay outside of buildings. It made him miss the dry air in California. With his bag flung over his shoulder, he made his way toward the exit where he was supposed to meet Hannah. Despite the weather, he had a hoodie and hat on to hide him. Not that he expected to run into a lot of fans at the Birmingham airport in the middle of the week. No one knew of his detour there, so all anyone seemed to see was some punk with black hair and too many tattoos.

At the exit, he saw her standing there holding a sign that said "Hannah" with an arrow pointing up at herself. A little girl was standing next to her, holding on to the bottom of her shirt. The girl couldn't have been more than four or five years old. Her dirty blonde hair was up in a high ponytail, and she was dressed in one of those matching outfits a lot of kids wore at her age. Abel didn't know who the girl was, but he figured she was Hannah's daughter, who was mentioned in the letter.

Hannah looked like he expected, having seen a couple of her videos online. Her dark brown hair was loose and rested on her shoulders. She had short bangs and was dressed in jeans and a green shirt. She was a bit curvy and looked like just a normal woman in her mid-twenties. Walking up to her, he gave her a smile.

"I'm guessing by the sign you're Hannah and my ride?" he said.

"I am. I thought it wouldn't be smart to put your name on the sign. I figured we are trying to keep your trip here out of the press," Hannah explained.

"You thought right. So, ready?" he asked.

"Do you need to get any luggage or anything?" she asked, looking toward the baggage carousel.

"I packed light. Everything I need is in my carry-on," he answered.

"Oh, okay. Well then, follow me. Come on, Lacey," she said and turned to walk out of the airport. The little girl took hold of her hand, and the three of them stepped out into the most blistering and suffocating heat he had ever felt. Sure, he had been to Atlanta and several other southeastern cities before, but this place was taking the cake.

"How do you live here?" he asked, trying to catch his breath.

"What do you mean?" Hannah asked, clicking her key to unlock the most mom-van looking vehicle he had ever seen. A tan minivan that had sliding doors on either side.

"You can't breathe here," he answered, going around to the passenger seat while Hannah buckled the girl in.

"I was raised here. You kinda get used to it. Sorry, it does suck, though," Hannah answered with a bit of a laugh.

Once he was in the car, he pulled off his hoodie and hat. Hannah slid in and turned on the van, letting a burst of air hit him in the face. It was hot at first but cooled off quickly.

"Mommy, that man drew all over himself," the little girl said, and he couldn't hold back a laugh.

"No, baby, that isn't markers. That is something called tattoos. They don't come off," Hannah explained. "I'm sorry. She hasn't met a lot of other adults in her life yet."

"I can tell," he said, then turned toward the little girl. "My name is Abel. It's nice to meet you."

"Mommy, is he a stranger?" the girl asked, not responding to him.

"No, baby, you can talk to him," Hannah answered as she merged into the traffic.

"Hi, my name is Lacey. Mommy gets mad at me when I draw on myself," the girl said next.

Abel reached back and shook her hand. She held on to him for a minute rubbing at one of the tattoos on his hand. "Yeah, they don't come off. You should listen to your mom. I wish I had waited to get some of these. Some of them are really bad, and I don't like them anymore at all."

"Well, you should have used water markers. Then you could take them off," Lacey explained as if that was the answer.

"I will keep that in mind for next time," he answered before turning back. "Mason didn't tell me you would have your daughter with you."

"I didn't tell him, and he didn't ask. I still can't believe that you're doing this. Keeping this from my mom has been torture," Hannah said.

"Well, hopefully it's all worth it. How is she doing?" he asked. In truth, he had messaged every day to ask not wanting to depend on any kind of update.

"She seems to be doing well this week. Even after treatment she didn't seem too bad. She even cooked some food for today, or is cooking. I'm not really sure," Hannah explained. "I told her I was bringing some friends over to go swimming."

"Right, is that something you often do?" he asked.

"Yeah, more often than you would think. When she is feeling up to it, she cooks. I did tell her one of my friends is vegan, so you should be good," Hannah said.

"How did you know?" Abel asked. Sure, he mentioned it now and then in videos and interviews, but it wasn't something he openly talked about all of the time.

"Are you kidding? My mom had a Louder in Silence tribute band. Obviously, she was fan enough to have caught a few videos where you mentioned it. She even thought about going vegan for a bit but couldn't stick to it," Hannah answered as if his question was stupid. It probably was.

Abel burst out laughing. He was nervous, but so far, the company wasn't bad. "Now that is a fan. Willing to change their diet in support."

"Mom has always tried to change things to get healthier. She worked out and tried to eat right. Water, lots of water. It's still so crazy to me that this is happening," Hannah said, and he heard a quiver in her voice.

"Your letter said you guys waited too long. What did that mean?" Abel asked.

Hannah glanced in the rear-view mirror, and he knew she was looking at the girl. Then she took a deep breath. "There were signs. She started to stumble now and then. She wasn't eating like she should, and she was hurting. But she would just say it was because of her getting older. Of course, her ex didn't help with that. I don't think she could tell the difference between what he did to her and what the, ummm, C word is doing to her. She just assumed a lot and didn't want to face it. She fainted at the gym one day. She had been going to try and work on her stamina and balance., and she just fell out. We rushed her to the hospital, but it didn't matter. They gave her six months with treatment, less if she decided not to."

Hannah sniffled a bit and blinked her eyes several times as if trying to will the tears not to fall. Abel didn't know what to say. He'd never had a good relationship with his parents. Silence fell over the car for a bit, and he looked out the window. There wasn't a lot to look at. Mostly trees and now and then small exits with a couple of gas stations. He didn't really know anything about where they were going other than it was outside of Birmingham.

"I watched some of your videos but didn't have time to watch a lot of them," he finally said, needing to break the deafening silence. "Your mom is very talented."

"Yeah, she's amazing. I used to ask her why she didn't do more with it, and she would always say that music wasn't a real job. I swear it was just my grandmother coming out of her mouth. She always looked so sad when she said it," Hannah answered. "The only time she really looked happy was on the stage."

"That's when I'm happiest most of the time," he answered. "I saw that you have a really long video on there, looked like a concert."

"Yeah, that was the last full concert she did. It was a two-hour set at the state fair, and it rained the whole time. She said it was the best night of her life, and I loved watching every minute of it," Hannah answered. "The doctors think she was already sick. If you watch, you can see her a little unsteady. My mom, man, she would dance, and when it hit the harder breakdowns, she would head bang just as hard as any man. She did not give a, ummm, well she didn't care what anyone thought. But that day, she had to stop and steady herself a few times. We blamed it on the rain. Oh, she was so mad about ruining those pants."

"What?" Abel asked, confused by her last sentence.

"She had saved up for these low-rise leather pants. They were, well, let's just say it was awkward as her daughter to see her in them and see all the guys looking at her in them. But she wanted to show off her stomach. She would wear these little like coin scarf things around her waist when she performed so you could really see her move. She knows how to belly dance and all that crazy stuff. So, as a fan of hers, she looked incredible. As a daughter of hers, I wanted her to put on more clothes." Hannah laughed.

Abel had to know. so he pulled out his phone. He loaded up Hannah's YouTube page and found the concert in question and watched in amazement as the woman he was there to visit walked out onto the stage. She had on a pair of leather pants cut so low that if she moved wrong, he was sure he would see everything she had hidden. A tasseled scarf was wrapped around where a belt would usually go. Little golden coins dangled from the tassels, and they accented every move she made. Her top was little more than a bra with gold embroidery. While she had on a long leather jacket, he could see the long expanse of naked torso that lay between her top and her pants. Her hair was already soaked and sticking to her, but she didn't seem to care as she lifted her hands up in the air and shot her horns to the crowd.

"Fuck, y'all! It's wet out here and not in the good way! You ready to have a good time!" she called out into the microphone.

The crowd roared, and the band started playing instantly. It was one of his older songs. He smiled hearing them play, and while the band wasn't as good as his, they certainly made up for it with their energy. A few moments later, Alanna started singing the playful words, and another roar erupted from the crowd. The band wasn't as good, but she was phenomenal. He was entranced as he watched her sing, dance, and then scream. It wasn't as harsh and rough as he could do, but it certainly wasn't just singing. He was thoroughly impressed. She put it all out there, and the crowd ate it up.

"She's a fucking rock star," he whispered, not remembering there was a child in the car.

"Mommy, your friend said a bad word," Lacey said from the back seat.

"Baby, it's not the first time you have heard that word and it won't be the last. What have I told you?" Hannah responded.

"Just because I hear it doesn't mean I say it," Lacey answered.

"Sorry about that. I'm not used to having to watch what I say," Abel said.

"Don't be sorry. Having been raised by that woman you are watching, trust me, I'm used to people not watching their tongue," Hannah answered.

Abel went back to watching the show, unable to stop until the car speakers started ringing. "That's my mom. Hold on," Hannah said. "Hey, Mom! What's up?"

"I just wanted to see if you were still coming over. I just got finished cooking, and you know I'm not going to eat all of this food," the woman on the other end said.

"Yes, I just had to run an errand. I'm about fifteen minutes away," Hannah answered.

"Hi, Grandma!" Lacey called out from the back seat.

"Hi, baby! See you soon!" Alanna said from the other side of the line. "Alright, well I'll see you when you get here. I'm a bit tired now so I'm going to go sit down and listen to some music."

"Okay, see you soon," Hannah said.

She managed to hang up the phone before Lacey called out. "We are bringing a friend for you, Grandma!"

Abel watched the concert the rest of the way to their destination. With each song, he became more and more impressed. She didn't just sing. She felt, and she sent that out to the world with every note and every move. Her face, her posture, nothing about that show said amateur. How badly he wished he had met her before she got sick. Maybe he could have helped her break into the business. Then again, he wasn't always seen as being nice and helpful. Without that letter, he probably wouldn't have given her the time of day.

The house was small and sat on a large, secluded plot of land. Most of the land was still full of trees, but enough had been cleared to make room for the house, pool, and another small building. There was a patio with a grill and some furniture, and more chairs were laid out around the pool. It looked like she used to take care of plants, but now they were either overgrown or dying. When he got out of the car, he was once again hit with the horrible humidity.

"Mom has a dehumidifier in her house and her office. The office is where she used to work before she got sick. It is also her music room," Hannah explained, pointing at the smaller building before leading him to the main house.

She didn't knock but instead walked right in. He could smell the food the moment the door opened, and it made his stomach growl. He had been filled with so much anxiety that he hadn't bothered to eat, and it was starting to catch up with him. They walked into a kitchen where several pans and pots were set up but covered. Plates, forks, and napkins had also been left out. A sign on the fridge said, "Help Yourself," and he chuckled.

From the other room he could hear her. She was singing a pop song that had been playing the entire time. He could hear it the moment he stepped out of the van, and it followed them through the house. He wasn't familiar with the song, but she sang it beautifully, even if it was weaker than when she was performing on the video.

"Mom! We're here!" Hannah called out. They didn't go past the kitchen.

A few moments later a woman walked into the room, but she did not look at all like the pictures or videos. Her face was gaunt, and her eyes were encircled with almost bruise-like discoloration. She was tiny and frail, and her clothes hung off of her. The beautiful dirty blonde hair she once had was thin and brittle. It stole his breath to see her. Then he realized she was staring at him. She had frozen in place and hadn't moved, her mouth slightly parted as if she had stopped breathing. He knew he should say something, but he had no idea what.

"Hannah, I thought you said friends with an s. This is not friends with an s. This is one person. I cooked way too much food," the woman said. "And since when are you friends with Abel Sharp?"

CHAPTER THREE
ALANNA

She thought she was going to be sick. Her head spun, and her heart was beating so hard it sounded like drums were pounding in her ears. As much as she tried to breathe, she couldn't make her lungs work. Shock. There was no other word for the wave of emotion that had paralyzed her to the spot. How she was still standing, she had no idea. Abel Sharp was standing in her kitchen, and she was in her pajamas with her hair a mess. This certainly was not how she had ever dreamed of meeting him. He still hadn't said anything, and the silence was making her feel uncomfortable. Someone needed to say something.

"We, ah, met a couple of weeks ago. Or well, we talked on the phone. Your daughter wrote me a letter, and I decided I wanted to come meet you," Abel said, taking a couple of steps forward.

Alanna was mortified. She knew what she looked like. Weak. Tired. Fragile. She was a shell of the woman she had once been, and knowing he was there out of pity made it all worse. "Why would you want to meet me?"

He sighed and looked behind him to Hannah who just shrugged. She would certainly be having a conversation with her daughter once whatever this was had ended. When Abel turned back toward her, he took another step closer. "Honestly, at first it was because of you being sick, but not anymore. Alanna, I've never heard anyone else sing my songs like you do."

"You heard me sing?" she asked, darting her eyes toward her daughter.

"I did, and you are incredible. Most people, they sing it like they are trying to be me. You sing it like you are me. Or well, you are you but know exactly how to feel those songs," he answered. He held a hand out to her and she could see he was shaking. Why was he shaking?

"Your music has always been special to me," she said and then reached out to him. The moment he took her hand in his she felt heat consume her. "It's an honor to meet you."

"Likewise," he whispered. "So, I was told there was food, and I'm starving."

Alanna couldn't help but laugh, and it broke away the rest of her nervousness. She walked further into the kitchen and started to take lids off of things. "Well, Hannah made it sound like it was a group of people, so I cooked a lot of food. But this pasta here is vegan, and then this dessert over here is vegan. She told me one of her friends was vegan, so I made sure to accommodate," she explained, glaring over at her daughter.

"Well, it wasn't a lie, and I appreciate it," he answered.

"So, I actually have to get Lacey home, but I'll be back in a couple of hours. You two good?" Hannah said as she made her way closer to the door.

"I guess. You know you could have at least told me to put real clothes on," Alanna sighed.

"You look fine. Now, have fun," Hannah answered.

"Oh, let me grab my bag," Abel said and walked out with Hannah. He returned a few moments later with a leather bag over his shoulder along with a hoodie and a hat. "So, I've never done anything like this before."

"I have to admit, I'm not an expert either. I can at least tell you that I won't be attacking you like a raving lunatic. I'm too weak and tired for that, but if you do feel the need, my car is out there, and the key is in it," Alanna joked, and Abel laughed. "I'm not allowed to drive anymore, so it's just out there collecting dust."

"I'll keep that in mind if I need to make a quick escape," he said, still laughing a bit as he took a seat at the stool by the counter so he could eat.

"Well, you might. I say I'm weak and all, but you know, adrenaline can kick in now and then," she said next, and he nearly choked laughing.

"Oh fuck, don't kill me." Abel coughed. Once he regained his composure, he set his fork down. "This is fucking good."

"I'm a Southerner. One thing we know how to do is feed the masses. Eat up because most of this will just go to waste," she said and went to sit down next to him.

"You aren't going to eat?" he asked.

"I don't really eat all that much these days," she answered.

"Will you eat a little at least? For me?" he asked, and the look he gave her made her melt. Most of the time eating made her feel sick. The last thing she wanted to do was throw up in front of him, but he had asked so nicely. She put a small portion of pasta on a plate and took a deep breath before taking a bite. It wasn't pleasant, but she forced it down.

"So, I assume Hannah told you I'm not doing so well. I had no idea she wrote you," Alanna said, still not sure what the hell she was supposed to do with a hot sexy rock star in her house. She lived alone and listened to music all day. It wasn't like she had things for them to do.

"She did, and she sent me some pictures and videos of you," he answered. He reached in his back pocket and pulled out his wallet. A moment later he unfolded a photo of her from when she was singing on stage at the state fair. It had been such a memorable day that always made her smile.

"Oh, I miss those pants. I loved them so much," she said, taking the picture and looking at it more closely. "You put it in your wallet?"

"Yeah, I liked it, so I wanted to keep it with me," he answered and then took another bite of food.

She didn't eat any more, but she pushed the food around on the plate to make it look like she was. "That day was amazing. It rained the whole time, and we were all cold and wet, but we had one hell of a time. Out of every show and performance I ever did, that one just felt like magic."

"I didn't get to watch the whole thing, but I plan to," he said as he finished off his plate. "I was surprised at your performance. You didn't just sing. You really got into it. And you know how to scream, too."

"I did. Not as harsh as you. I didn't want to risk my voice, but I could get some gravel up when I wanted to," she answered. Slowly the awkwardness started to fade, and it was like she was talking to someone she had known for a long time. "You want to see my music room?"

"Yeah, I would love that," he answered.

She slid off of the stool, and he reached out to steady her. She whispered thank you and swallowed back her embarrassment. Why couldn't this have happened when she wasn't staring death in the face? It wasn't fair. Of course, nothing in her life had ever been fair. Why should that change at the end of her life?

She led him back outside, and they walked by the pool toward the small office building she had set up. Alanna slid open the door and stepped inside then waited for him to join her. To one side was a desk with a computer and papers strewn over it. Behind it were several shelves of books. Reading was the only other thing she really enjoyed doing.

The other half of the room had her piano, guitar, and drums, though she only knew how to play the piano. The walls were decorated with concert posters and T-shirts she had collected from various shows she had attended over the years. In the center of the room was a recliner that Hannah's husband Brandon had brought in when she got sick. It faced a TV that had been mounted for when she was in the mood to watch something.

Abel moved around the room looking at everything as if trying to memorize it. "You've been to a lot of shows."

"Yeah, I worked to feed my concert addiction," she answered, standing there and watching him.

"This is from my last tour," he said, seeing one of her signed T-shirts. It was encased in glass to protect it. "I signed it."

"Yeah, I think I met you for all of thirty seconds. You signed mine and Hannah's shirts, took that picture and then we went on with our day. It was the only time I ever paid extra to go to the meet and greet. I've been to maybe five of your shows, but that is the only time I went backstage," she answered. Now that he was there, she decided she didn't count those few seconds as them meeting before.

"I don't remember you," he said as if he felt guilty for it.

"You meet thousands of people every day. I don't expect you to remember me. In fact, I would think it was weird if you did remember me," she answered and walked over to him. Slowly she put her hand on his shoulder. "But I remember it, and that is all that really matters. I was high on life for months after that. Well, until this happened really."

"This is not at all what I expected," he said then, turning to look at her. He reached up and brushed a strand of hair back from her face and she found herself stepping away. She lost her balance, and he reached out to grab her, so she didn't fall.

"What did you expect?" she asked. He at least knew it was happening; she was still pushing through shock.

"I don't know, but it wasn't this," he answered.

"Well, this is me. This room is my favorite room in my house, and it isn't even in my house. The only other place I really like is the pool," she said.

He started looking around the room again until he saw the picture of her on the wall. She was performing. It was another shot from the show Hannah had sent him. In it she was belting out a song while gripping the microphone stand. Her eyes were closed, and her mouth was open so wide it looked like she was going to swallow the thing. Her arm was in the air and in her mind, she could picture exactly what was going on. She was roaring out a note that was filled with a mixture of pain and frustration. Cathartic. It was one of her favorite songs to perform.

Abel moved closer and closer to the photo and then put his fingers on a section of her back. By that point of the show, she had given up the jacket weighing her down, heavy with water, and had thrown it off. There was discoloration in her skin, which she usually tried to cover, and a shiver ran down her spine as she watched him trace over it. "You have a bruise."

"I did," she answered, her voice shaking. "Look, I loved being on stage. It was the happiest time of my life. The rest of my life, well, it hasn't been so great, but I don't want to fill this day with a big sob story. I wear my bruises and my scars, and I keep pushing forward and will until the last breath leaves me."

She watched him. He didn't move for a second, and she saw his body tense in anger. It stole her breath. The emotion passed as fast as it came, but it took him a moment to turn around. "That is probably the best way to live. I've tried to do the same."

"I know. I sing about it all the time," she teased. Another silence fell between them before she got a crazy idea. "Do you want to go swimming?"

"I didn't bring a suit," he answered, and she couldn't help the huge smile that covered her face before she fought it down.

Before she could say anything, she started to giggle and then covered her face as she felt a blush threatening to set her on fire. He burst out laughing, too, as if he had read her dirty mind. She certainly wouldn't have complained about him not wearing a suit in her pool, but she would be damned if she said that out loud.

"I'm so sorry. I have been trying so hard to not fan girl out, but damn, I didn't intend for that question to make that thought go through my head." She laughed and ended up falling down into her recliner.

He laughed harder and came to kneel down in front of her. "You're fine. Don't be embarrassed. I get it."

It took her a second to catch her breath before she started giggling again. After several minutes, she was finally able to compose herself. "I have spare swimsuits and such. I keep stuff here all the time cause people are always wanting to go swimming when they come visit. I even have some with the tags still on that I got last year on summer clearance. I'm sure I have something that will fit."

"Okay, do you want to go swimming?" he asked, his smile bright and real. He wasn't just smiling to make her feel better. He actually looked happy.

"I love swimming," she answered.

"Then we will go swimming," he answered. "Point me toward a suit. If for no other reason, Hannah might come back."

He was teasing her, and she turned red all over again.

CHAPTER FOUR
ABEL

Once the ice was broken, he found himself having a good time with her. She was funny and didn't treat him like anything other than another human. Well, other than the giggle fest over the idea of him swimming naked. He had not intended to bring up that thought, but he gave her a pass considering how embarrassed she got after. It was strange, but he noticed when she started smiling and laughing, he didn't see her like he had the first moment he met her. He didn't see the fragility and weakness. He just saw beauty and passion. She was the woman from the photos.

His eyes looked over himself in the bathroom mirror as he inspected the fit of his borrowed swimwear. He tied the suit as tightly as he could. It was a bit big for him but would work. Either that or she would get her wish after all. He honestly didn't care. True to her word, the tags were still on them, so he didn't even feel awkward about wearing them. Given the heat, the idea of getting in the water was very appealing. When he headed back out, he found her sitting on the edge of the pool. She had on a tank top and a pair of shorts. Her hair was pulled up and she was singing along with the song playing as she kicked at the water.

"You don't have a suit?" he asked, sitting down next to her.

"I do, but it doesn't fit anymore. And I thought we decided we weren't going skinny dipping," she answered with a laugh. The embarrassment had worn off and instead she just flashed him an almost devilish smile.

"Fair enough," he answered and then slid into the water. "You getting in?" He held his arms out to her and helped her slide into the water. She felt so small in his hands. Not that he was a terribly large guy. He was an average build and only mildly tall, but she felt tiny. He could feel her bones, and it made him shiver. The doctor had given her six months, and at least two had already passed. Things were progressing, and he could feel an ache in his heart over the fact that this woman would no longer be in the world.

"You're thinking too much," she said, then splashed some water at him. It succeeded at pulling him out of his thoughts, and he splashed her back.

Before long they were laughing and playing as if they had been best friends their entire life. While he was mindful of her, he still splashed and pulled her around the water, letting it take some of the impact so she wouldn't be hurt. When she laughed, it took away all of the reality. She was just a woman. He was just a man. One of his songs started playing, and she turned toward the speaker as if trying to make it stop. "I have no idea where my phone is to change it."

"Why would you change it?" he asked, and then started singing along with it. He came up behind her and turned her toward him.

A wicked grin spread over her lips, and she joined in. They sang together, belting it out as they danced around in the water. He was surprised at how well she did, though he could hear her losing her breath at times. When the song was over, he ran his fingers through his hair to pull it back from his face, and he couldn't help but see her watching him.

She took a deep breath and then went to lean against the wall. "I'm getting tired. I'm sorry."

"Don't be," he said and went to stand with her. "You want to go inside?"

"No, but I probably should. Besides, it's past time for me to take my meds," she answered.

Suddenly reality came crashing back around him. Her having to take her medicine was just a reminder of what was to come. He didn't want to think about that. He wanted to spend more time with her. His brain was racing. This woman was special. Something had brought them together, and it wasn't a letter. No, something had made Hannah write that letter and made Mason read it and give it to him. Not that he really believed in all of that, but something like fate had pulled them together.

"Let's go inside. We can just hang out. You can tell me stories, and I'll do the same," he suggested.

Once they were dry, they sat together on the couch. Her living room had a mix of family photos, pictures just of Hannah at different ages, and more photos from her various performances. He was still stunned by every one of them. None of them had a man in them, though. It was just her and Hannah. "What happened to Hannah's dad?"

"Well." She sighed and leaned her head on his shoulder. He put an arm around her and waited for her to explain. "He got me pregnant when I was sixteen. You know, did the whole, 'You can't get pregnant the first time and I'll pull out' bullshit. But I was young and in love and felt invincible. When he found out I was pregnant, he disappeared, and I never saw him again. I didn't need him anyway. I did finish school, and my mom helped me get a job. I did everything I could to take care of that girl. She is my everything."

"What a dick," he sighed. "Briar is my world. I have no idea what would have happened to me had she not come into my life. I mean, her mom and I aren't together, but we did a good job raising her together.

Or at least I like to think so," he said about his only daughter. He pulled the locket out from under his shirt and showed it to her.

"You always seem like a good dad when I see videos of you two," she said, her fingers lightly touching the necklace as she looked at the picture of him and his daughter inside.

"I tried. I wasn't about to leave her like my parents did me," he answered.

"My mom stopped talking to me about ten years ago. She apparently was done with my poor life choices. I don't even know if she knows I'm sick," Alanna said next. "I honestly don't care. She made her choice. I just, well, I worry about Hannah. It's always just been the two of us, and sure she's married now, but that isn't the same. She's trying to hide it from me, but I think there are problems between her and Brandon. Not like bad ones, but I don't think they are going to be together much longer."

He didn't know what to say to that. So he just sat there in silence with her for a moment. Alanna breathed softly, and it appeared she felt comfortable just sitting there with him. It was nice to just relax, and he closed his eyes, taking it in.

"Why are you here?" she asked again, but this time the tone was sad.

"I told you. I wanted to meet you," he answered. It was the best answer he had. He certainly wasn't thinking with his head on this one.

"Yeah, you said that, but why?" she asked. "What are you going to get out of this?"

"Nothing really. I read that letter and saw your performance, and I just had to meet you," he answered and then turned to look at her. She shifted a bit so she could look up at him. "I have an idea."

"You do?" she asked, arching a brow at him.

"I do," he answered and smiled. It was a crazy idea. A stupid idea really. "I'm doing a festival in Florida in a couple of weeks. I want you to come."

She sat up and moved away a bit. He couldn't tell by her face what she was thinking, only that she was shocked. "I can't go to a festival in Florida. I can barely handle day to day here. Festivals are grueling when you're healthy."

"I know, but you would stay with me. I could even get you a wheelchair or something, and I'll take you to meet all the other bands. You can watch all the shows from backstage. If you get tired, you can go sleep in my bed on the bus. I'll take a bunk. Come on. What do you have to lose?" he asked, taking her hands in his.

"That sounds crazy," she said, but she was starting to smile.

"I get the feeling you like crazy," he continued. "Come on. It'll be fun."

"Have you lost your fucking mind! You can't take my mom to some festival in Florida. She needs to be close to the doctor," Hannah protested from outside.

Alanna had to go to sleep, the day having taken a lot out of her.

"I know it's crazy but think about it. It will be one last weekend of her getting to just be her. She will have all her meds. I'll have a chair and everything for her. I'm giving up my bed for her, and I can even get a nurse or something. Think of what it will mean to her," he explained, but Hannah was not having it.

"And what happens if..." she started to say but then turned away as her throat caught.

"It won't," he said, knowing he couldn't promise that but praying he was right.

"You don't know that. I just. I can't..." Hannah couldn't get her words out.

"I will take care of her the whole time. The only time I won't be with her is when I have to perform, and she will be just off stage with Mason. She will never be alone, and if anything happens, you will be the first to know, and I will make sure you get there." It was the best offer he had. "It's the only thing I can really give her that will mean anything. I'll get her some new clothes and have her hair and makeup done. I'll treat her like a star, and we will make sure she takes all of her medication and rests when she needs to."

"And she said she wants to go?" Hannah asked.

"She did. At first, she freaked out like you, but she wants to go. Let me give this to her. I'll even bring her back myself. We will pick her up on the bus, drive down there, and I will drive her home and then fly to meet the band. I already talked to Mason, and he's putting everything in order." Abel wasn't sure why he was fighting so hard for this, but he couldn't get the idea out of his head.

"If you do this, I want videos. I want to be able to look back at everything. Do you understand?" she finally said through gritted teeth.

"We will keep a full video diary for you. I swear," he answered.

"Okay, but only because I know it will make her really happy, and all I really want right now is for her to be happy," Hannah agreed.

Abel pulled her into a hug, and she gave him a halfhearted pat on the back. She wasn't really supportive of the idea, but she was giving in to it. "I will talk with the doctor when we go tomorrow. If we need any kind of special accommodation, I will let you know. Not Mason. This is your idea so I will talk to you about it."

"Fair enough. The only time you might have trouble getting me is when I'm working, but I'll call back," he answered.

"Well, try not to call in the middle of the night if you do." Hannah laughed. "Now, you might should go say good-bye so I can get you back to Birmingham. I know you have an early flight."

"I don't want to wake her," he said looking back at the house.

"Wake her. She would be upset if you didn't," Hannah answered and motioned for him to go inside.

Abel knew where the bedroom was, but he hadn't been inside. Softly knocking on the door, he peeked inside and saw just her head peeking out from under a mound of blankets. She looked to be shivering, and he went over to make sure she had enough blankets on her. "Hey, Alanna," he whispered.

"I'm cold," she whispered back as if she wasn't really sure what was going on.

"I can get you another blanket. There's one on the couch," he said and started to get up, but she caught his hand with hers.

"It won't help. I'm just cold. Are you leaving?" she whispered, blinking her eyes open to look up at him.

"I am, but I will see you really soon. We are going to the show together, and you are going to have an amazing time," he answered smiling and leaning down he kissed the top of her head. He really hoped she made it that long. He had no idea how long she had left. It seemed no one really did.

"I'm looking forward to it. Don't let me down," she said smiling when he kissed her.

"Never. Hannah and I are going to work out all the details. I'm going to make sure you have the best time of your life," he said and gave her one more kiss. From the corner of his eye, he saw the small medication bottle on the bedside table. A trimmer ran the length of his spine, but he pushed back against the familiar voice in his head telling him to reach for it. With a deep breath, he got up and went for the door. "Until then, I'll call you and check on you."

"Be safe out there," she said. She didn't get up, but she watched him until he closed the door.

His body was shaking as he made his way back out to where Hannah was waiting by her van. His bag was already loaded up. "Abel, you know the more you do the harder it is going to be. Right?"

He knew. He knew more than he wanted to admit. But he also couldn't seem to stop himself. "You said you wanted your mom to be happy at the end of her life. That's all I'm doing. I want to make her happy."

"You don't have to do any of this, though. You didn't have to even respond to my letter," she said as she pulled onto the road to head back toward the airport.

"I know I didn't, but I want to. I don't really know why, but I do. I want to. So let me," he answered.

A silence fell over the van, but it wasn't as comfortable as it had been earlier with Alanna. Tension lingered in the air between them, but neither of them really knew what to say. He pulled out his phone and looked at some of the pictures he had taken. She wasn't the woman from the photo in his wallet, but she was still something unlike anyone else he had ever met. It wasn't going to be easy, but he also knew he really wanted to give this to her. The words from Hannah's letter played in his mind. She was a beautiful woman with a not so beautiful life. If nothing else, he could give her a beautiful end.

CHAPTER FIVE
ALANNA

Everything was packed, and apparently all of the arrangements had been made. The doctor had sent some extra medicine just in case, but she did say she thought Alanna getting out would be good for her. Abel had called her every day since leaving, even if for only one or two minutes to check on her. It was odd, but she enjoyed the calls either way. Now she was nervous. Hannah and Lacey were there. Lacey was swimming in the pool while Hannah rushed around frantically making sure they had everything.

"Okay, so you have your meds in here. Mason is going to be in charge of them to avoid any issues. Your oxygen is packed here in case you need it. Abel said he got a wheelchair for you, so you don't have to walk around everywhere. I think that is everything," Hannah said, going over her checklist for the millionth time.

"Hannah, I'm going to be fine. Besides, if I forget anything, I'm pretty sure there are stores in Florida. There certainly were last I checked," Alanna answered.

"I'm sorry, I'm just really worried about you," Hannah answered and took a seat next to her mother.

"I get it, but this is going to be good for me. Even the doctor said so. We will take lots of pictures and videos, and I'm just going to have a good time," Alanna said with a smile. She was more excited than she wanted to admit.

A bus came rumbling down the drive, and Alanna couldn't fight the smile that rose up on her lips. She still wasn't sure what the hell was happening. It all seemed crazy, but she was excited either way. Lacey got out of the pool and came over to stand with them as the bus pulled closer before coming to a stop. Alanna's heart was pounding so hard it made her dizzy, but the last thing she needed was to stumble the moment she got up, so she took a second to steady herself. The door of the bus opened and off stepped Abel. Lacey went running toward him and wrapped her soaking wet arms around him.

"Abel!" she screamed, and he knelt down to give her a proper hug.

"You remember me?" he asked, not bothered by getting drenched by the young girl.

"Yes! I saw all the pictures. You take care of my grandma, or I will beat you up," Lacey said then gave him another hug.

"I promise," he answered and kissed her head before standing back up.

Another man got off the bus that Alanna didn't recognize, so she assumed he was Mason. He walked up to them and held out his hand. "I'm Mason, so I am here to get bags and meds. I have a locked cabinet on the bus that no one else has a key to. Abel was pretty adamant about that," Mason said.

"Hi, I'm Hannah. We talked on the phone quite a bit. This should be everything. Her meds are here and for the most part she does well taking them, but with how busy things might be, I was hoping someone else could have backup alarms," Hannah explained.

"Hannah, I'm not a baby!" Alanna protested, finally getting up. "I can take care of myself."

"No, it's okay. I don't mind being a backup. Especially since I'm going to be the one to get everything out. It might be easier for me to know as well," Mason said. "Just let me know what to set them for."

"I put a list in the case, so you should have it," Hannah said next, and Alanna couldn't help but feel absolutely mortified by how much her daughter was treating her like a child.

Abel finished making his way over and gave her a hug, which helped to take away the discomfort. "You ready for this?"

"As ready as I'm ever going to be," she answered.

"You better take care of her, or I swear I will hunt you down and," Hannah began and then remembered Lacey was standing next to them. "Well, just use your imagination. I know you have a pretty good one. Whatever you think of, it will be worse."

"Yes, ma'am," Abel teased by giving a salute and then gave Hannah and Lacey another hug. "I will have her back in one piece on Monday. I swear."

Mason took the bags, and Hannah brought over the medication, waiting at the door of the bus for him to come back and grab it. Once everything was inside, Alanna gave Hannah and Lacey a good-bye hug and kiss before following Abel onto the bus. She had never been on a tour bus or even a nice bus. The only bus she had ridden had been the big yellow one in high school. This was more like an extravagant RV than a bus. The stairs led them into what looked like a skinny living room kitchen combo where several other men were sitting. Some were doing things on their phones while others were playing a game on a rather large TV. She knew they were the rest of the band.

"This is the cabinet that everything is locked in, just so you know," Mason explained, patting the door of a cabinet that looked more like a safe.

"Guys! This is Alanna. She is going to be hanging out with us this weekend, so try not to be too much of a pain in the ass," Abel said making his way through. "Okay, well, here is the tour. This is well, you can see what this is. Through here is a bathroom and then bunks."

Abel didn't seem to care if he got in the way of the game. He just walked through, holding her hand as he did. She could feel the other men watching her, which made her feel self-conscious.

"Okay this is the one I will be sleeping in. If you ever need me, just wake me up. Okay?" He had pointed at one of the bottom bunks but didn't really give her much time to look at it before he led her through a door that opened into a bedroom. "This is my actual room, which you will have access to. There is a private bathroom, and the door does lock if for some reason you feel you need to lock yourself in. I already had all the bedding washed so it should be nice and fresh for you."

"Oh darn, and here I was looking forward to sleeping in your leftover sweat and whatever else. Now how am I supposed to bask in the scent of you," she teased, and he burst out laughing. Part of her had actually hoped the bed would smell like him, and it might still.

"Let me introduce you to everyone," Abel said, taking her hand and leading her back out of the room. "Okay, everyone, listen up. Like I said, this is Alanna. That there is Cage, he is the lead guitarist. Derrik is on drums, Trey is rhythm guitar, and Spencer is bass. There are some other people, but they are on a different bus. You will meet everyone else later, but this is my core group. Well, and you know Mason."

"Nice to meet everyone," she said, her voice shaking. They were all staring at her, and she found herself moving behind Abel a bit.

"You like to play cards?" Derrik asked, holding up a deck? He was handsome, though to be fair, they all were. He was a little slim for her personally but still had a nice face. He was the youngest as well, having just joined the band a few years earlier. His hair was short, and he had two sleeves of tattoos up his muscular arms. Alanna had always been convinced that the drummer of a band got the most workout. This man proved that.

A smile spread over her. "Oh, I can wipe the floor with you when it comes to cards."

"You think so? Well, then, let's see what you got," he answered and motioned for her to sit down with him.

Abel moved in to sit next to her, and Mason sat next to Derrik so they would have a full table, "What are we playing for?" Abel asked.

"Well, doesn't seem fair to play for money, so how about dares," Derrik suggested.

"Sounds risky, but I can get down with that," Alanna answered, feeling very confident.

The bus started to move, and she jumped a bit. Her heart was still pounding with excitement, but it felt nice to be welcomed into the group. Trey came over to stand and watch. He had a mess of curly dark hair that had been gelled or oiled. Alanna couldn't tell. He didn't have as many tattoos as most of the other guys, but he had a couple. He was also a little more built than the others.

Cage and Spencer were both playing a video game, so they didn't move. Cage had really long red hair and pale skin which he had covered with tattoos. Sometimes he was referred to as the Irish Giant because of that. Alanna wondered if he still burned in the sun with all the ink covering him. Spencer had long brown hair, not quite as dark as Abel's and was wearing a hoodie and sweatpants so she couldn't see the ink she knew was under his clothes.

Derrik shuffled the cards and let her cut before dealing them out. They were playing standard poker. "Okay, so since we aren't playing for money, here is how this is going to work. There is no folding. You play the whole round. At the end, everyone shows their hand. Whoever has the best hand gets to dare the person who has the worst hand to do whatever they want. Sound fair?"

"Sounds like we're in high school, but sure," Abel answered. He didn't pick up his cards, just slid them close to him and lifted the edges so he could see what he had.

Alanna picked up her cards and turned a little away from Abel so he couldn't see. Once she saw them, she pressed them to her chest. Everyone took a moment and then started trading out cards. She didn't have the best hand, but it wasn't bad with two pairs. When it came to the flip, Mason got the short end with a seven high. Derrik had three of a kind and took the hand. Abel had one pair.

"Fuck! You rigging the deck?" Mason complained.

"Nope. Alright, you know, I think you need to go eat that pepper we have been saving for a rainy day," Derrik demanded.

Alanna didn't think much of it until Mason pulled out a ghost pepper they had in a jar in the fridge.

Mason turned red the moment he started to eat it, and before long he was guzzling water to make the pain stop. Everyone laughed their asses off, and Mason looked like he might get sick. The game went on like that for hours with everyone taking turns doing stupid high school dares to each other and just acting like idiots.

At one point, Alanna was tasked with drawing a new "tattoo" on Derrik, to which she promptly drew a rainbow with a unicorn right on his chest with permanent marker. After a while, everyone else joined in, and the game got a little more adventurous. However, nothing ever went too far.

Hours seemed to pass before her alarm went off, and it was like a hush fell over the bus. "Umm, excuse me," Alanna said to Abel so he could let her out.

She felt like the entire bus was burning holes in her as they stared while Mason pulled out the bag and she took out bottle after bottle of medication.

"I'll be back," Abel grumbled and left the table to go toward the bedroom. She watched him for a moment before going back to what she was doing.

Once she had everything, she put the bottles back, and Mason locked everything up. She turned to the group who all quickly looked away as if they weren't staring at her. "Damn, you would think I was standing here naked. Have you never seen someone take pills before? Jesus."

"Sorry, just, we know what's going on, and I think... well I know for me, I'm not really sure what to say or do," Derrik said from where he still sat at the table.

The others joined in on his thoughts. Alanna figured that was the case, so she took her pills and answered. "Just treat me like you would treat any other person. That's all you have to do. I'm nothing special."

With a deep breath, she went to find Abel. Her mood was a little spoiled, and she was starting to feel pretty tired. It was going to be a long drive, and she knew she would need some rest. Abel sat on the bed, and she went to sit next to him. "You okay?"

"Yeah, I'm fine. I think part of me doesn't want to see everything you are going through. Does that make me an asshole?" he whispered, turning to look at her.

"Abel Sharp, lots of things make you an asshole, but that isn't one of them. You asked me to be here. You had to know that this was part of it," she answered.

"I did, but I just wasn't really expecting it to hit me like it did. When I hung out with you, you went in your room to take your meds," he answered.

"Then how about we figure out a plan. I don't want you to feel uncomfortable, and I certainly don't want to spoil the mood every time I have to take my meds," she suggested. "Now, I think I need a nap. I have a long weekend ahead of me, and I want to be able to enjoy every moment of it."

"Sure, I'll leave you be. Come get me if you need anything," he answered, getting up and kissing the top of her head.

Once he was gone, she took in and let out a deep breath. She hadn't realized just how tense her body had become until he was gone, and she was able to relax. She didn't bother to change, instead just kicked off her shoes and got between the covers. Despite having been cleaned, she could still smell a scent that was all him, and it made her smile as she drifted off to sleep.

Chapter Six
Alanna

Alanna hadn't meant to sleep as long as she had, but by the time she woke back up, the bus was parked. She knew because she could no longer feel the sensation of the road beneath the wheels. Pushing the blanket off of her, she sat up on the side of the bed and tried to put herself together. Beyond the door, everything seemed quiet, which made her wonder if she was alone.

After a moment for the bathroom, she ran a brush through her hair before opening the door to see what was going on. When she cracked it open, all she heard was the sound of someone writing. Not wanting to interrupt, she slowly made her way down the hallway. It seemed everyone was gone. All the bunks looked empty. As she reached the main area, she saw Abel sitting at the table scribing frantically. He was staring at the paper with such intensity that she didn't want to interrupt. Whatever he was writing, he was in the zone. So, she stood there watching him. Now and then he would mumble a few words in a melodic tone, and she realized he was writing music.

Abel was the main song writer in the band and was known for his intense lyrics and meanings behind his songs. It was breathtaking to watch him work. She just leaned against the wall and let him work until he seemed to get frustrated. He threw the pen across the table before crumpling up the paper and then got up to toss the paper into the trash. Finally he turned and saw her. She gave him a soft smile and watched as his face went from being frustrated to... well, maybe he was just hiding it.

"I didn't hear you get up," he said, walking over to her and looking down as if trying to make sure she was okay.

"I don't make a lot of noise. When I saw you were working, I decided not to bother you," she answered, looking up at him. The bus was dark, and when he stood over her, he cast a shadow over her body. Half of his face was in the light with the other hidden, and she couldn't help but see the interesting juxtaposition like he was some sort of angel and demon hybrid. Maybe it was the artist in her, but it seemed like two sides of him, and she was getting to see both at the same time.

"Well, I was just waiting for you to wake up. I made plans to take you shopping and to get your hair and makeup and everything done. Whatever you want to do," he said, brushing a strand of her brittle hair back.

She hated what had happened to her hair. Some people lost all of their hair, but hers had just gotten really thin and brittle. Alanna had a feeling it would eventually all fall out, but she was still desperately trying to hold on to something. She had always loved her hair.

"I don't know if anyone can help me."

"Well, I searched for the best, so if anyone can, it will be them," he answered, a grin spreading on his face and chasing away the rest of his frustration.

"Alright then." She laughed a bit and shook her head in disbelief. He seemed to be far more optimistic than she could muster.

The sun was bright when they left the bus, and she was surprised to see how many people were moving around. The fans weren't there yet, but the bands were, and everyone was getting ready for a four-day festival full of music and god only knew what else. Abel led her to a car she guessed he had set up. He'd also gotten a driver, likely because he didn't know his way around.

"You know, I didn't ask how you slept," he said, leaning down a bit.

"You still haven't." She giggled. "But I slept okay. Apparently, I needed it."

"Yeah, I guess you did. You looking forward to all of this? It's going to be really busy."

"I imagine it will, but it's going to be amazing. I know it," she answered, leaning her head against his shoulder. She wasn't sure why she felt so comfortable with him, nor was she sure he felt the same, but he never shrugged her off, so she didn't ask.

The driver took them to a shopping area with a lot of designer shops and boutiques, a far cry from the chain stores she was used to. "So, it isn't LA, but it is the best they have here."

He opened the door and leaned in to take her hand and pull her out of the car. The driver let them know he would be waiting for them, and then they walked toward the stores. Alanna had never owned anything as nice as some of the stores they were walking toward. These stores were labeled with designers that she actually knew the names of. He kept his hand wrapped with hers and walked with confidence.

She wished she could share that feeling, but this wasn't her element, especially with the state of her body. They got to a door that he opened and held for her. Once she was inside, he followed her and started to lead her around as if looking for something specific. This wasn't her money or her idea, so she had no idea what she was doing.

Abel pulled out his wallet and went over to a woman who seemed to be one of the salesclerks. Alanna stood back while he talked to her and glanced over everything. She thumbed through a rack of shirts, most of which looked too big for her. Her focus was various black shirts of different styles that when Abel tapped her shoulder, she jumped.

"Come here," he whispered, and she followed up toward where the clerk was going through a few racks.

"So what size are you?" the woman asked, and Alanna looked down at her disappearing body. It wasn't like anything she owned actually fit anymore, and Hannah had gotten her a few belts to help with her pants. She felt like she had stepped back into the late nineties when everyone was obsessed with baggy jeans.

"I honestly don't know, but these are a size two and they are too big," she answered, almost embarrassed to be having that conversation with anyone.

"Okay, let me see what I have in the back, but do these look like something you would like?" the woman asked, holding up a pair of flared low rise leather pants. It was the pants... but more expensive. She had always hated that she ruined those pants when she had worn them in the rain. With a glance over to Abel, she realized he was watching for her reaction.

"I love them," she answered, moving over to feel them. They felt so soft, and she knew they would be comfortable.

"Okay, I think I have some in the back that might fit," the woman answered and walked off.

"I... you remembered?" she asked, looking from him back to the pants.

"Well, I have been planning this for two weeks. I want you to feel alive while you're here," he answered.

The woman came back with a few different pairs of the pants along with some other options and colors. As much as she wanted to protest, she couldn't bring herself to. As they went through all of the clothing options and started a pile of things to buy, she just fell into the joy of it all. However, she refused to stand at the register to see how much he spent. It would have probably killed her to know.

After taking all the bags to the car, he walked with her to a salon. Apparently, they were expecting them because a beautiful woman came over right away to welcome them.

"Alanna, this woman specializes in working with hair fragile because of treatment, and she is going to get you all fixed up," Abel explained. She could hear his voice catch for a slightest moment as if he didn't want to talk about her being sick and going to doctors.

"Hi, I'm Maria, let's see what we have going on. Go on and have a seat," she said and pointed Alanna toward the chair.

Abel and Maria stood back for a second and talked, and she saw him hand the woman something. The woman held it for a second as they whispered before handing it back to him. Then he went to sit down as if he didn't have anything better to do than sit there while she got her hair done. Alanna didn't have a lot of faith that the woman would be able to do much with her hair, but she appreciated the effort either way.

"So, is there anything in particular you want done, or would you just like me to see what I can do?" Maria asked, coming over and looking at her hair and scalp. Alanna had been told that doing anything with her hair might cause more harm than good, but she also really wanted to look nice for her adventurous weekend.

"Abel said you are a specialist?" she asked with a deep sigh.

"I am. I work with people like you every day. Honestly, you seem to have gotten lucky. You don't have too much damage, and you only have thinning, not a lot of bare spots. I could probably thicken it up some. I wouldn't recommend keeping the extensions in long, especially if you are still doing treatment, but I can put some in that you can have removed in a week or so," Maria suggested, still running her fingers through Alanna's hair.

"Well, I will trust you then. To be honest, this is all his idea. I still don't even know how all this is happening," she answered, talking low enough so Abel wouldn't be able to overhear.

"Perfect. Well then you relax and just let me know if I do anything that makes you uncomfortable. If I run into any problems, I will let you know before I go any further," Maria explained.

They were in there for a long time, and Alanna found herself dozing in and out as Maria worked her magic. When she was done and Maria turned her to look at herself, Alanna had no idea who the woman was looking back at her. She hadn't seen her hair look so nice in a very long time. It brought tears to her eyes, and she was shaking.

"What do you think?" Maria asked.

"I think I'd forgotten what this woman looked like," Alanna answered.

Abel came over and stood next to her, looking at her through the mirror.

"You look amazing," he said. "Though you were beautiful before."

Alanna just shook her head. He had a tendency of saying that to her, but she never believed him. He was just being nice to her. "Thank you," she whispered, wiping tears from her eyes.

Abel leaned down and kissed the top of her head before once again going to pay. She felt so guilty, but she knew that arguing with him wouldn't have done any good. Besides, part of her liked being pampered. It wasn't like anyone had ever done that for her before. Since she was a teenager, it had been her against the world. Well, she and Hannah. The idea of anyone taking care of her had always felt like an impossible dream. It might be temporary, but she could give in and let Abel do that for her.

"Well, do we need to do anything else, or do you feel ready for the weekend?" he asked, leading her back toward the car. Abel had offered to have her makeup done as well, but Alanna had let him know she would rather do it herself. She had her own style after all.

"I could use a coffee if you're up for it, but then I need to get back and take my medication," she answered.

"Coffee it is," he said and let the driver know.

After going through a drive-through to get coffee, they headed back to the venue and the bus. In all honesty, their adventure had tired her out again, but she didn't want to go back to bed. There were far too many cool things to do, and she didn't want to miss a moment of it. Once she had taken her medication, she went to sit outside with the band and watch all of the people rushing around to get ready for the next few days of shows. Music played everywhere, and before she knew it, she was singing along. Everyone else seemed so busy that they didn't notice, or maybe she just didn't realize what she was doing until she opened her eyes and saw the entire band staring at her.

"When the fuck did you become a singer?" Trey asked, his eyes a little wide.

"Umm, I think I was born one. When the fuck did you become a musician?" she answered.

The guys burst out laughing, and she joined in.

"No, seriously though. You can sing, like really sing." Trey said after catching his breath.

"You should see her concert," Abel said, the only one not surprised.

"She has a concert?" Derrik asked.

"Yeah, from a festival where she is from. What about a thousand people or so in the crowd," Abel answered.

"Feels like a million years ago," Alanna added.

"Dude, you didn't say she could sing. That seems like pretty important information to share," Cage said next and started to make his way onto the bus. "Mason, did you know about this?"

"Umm yeah," Mason answered and followed.

Everyone else started to pile onto the bus, and Alanna got up the stairs just in time to see Mason pull up Hannah's YouTube channel. Her body froze. It wasn't like she just sang. No, she sang their music. The idea of watching them watch her perform was terrifying. Mason hit play on the concert in question, and Alanna felt the world slow down.

She could remember every detail of that day. The rain had been cold, but the day had been so hot that the water felt good. Even when the rain came in, no one left. They had all been there, waiting to see her band perform. She had gotten her four-hundred-dollar pants, similar to the ones Abel had just bought her, and was dressed to kill. Hannah had been a bit embarrassed but was also proud. Alanna loved how much her daughter had always supported her music.

The video played through one song and into another as the band watched. The first was playful, how she always opened shows. The next was more serious and more difficult to sing. When she hit a rather harsh scream moment, the band erupted in shock and awe, making Alanna blush.

"Damn, that's not karaoke for sure. You should have been a rock star," Derrik said.

"Well, it's a little too late for that now," she answered and then walked through the room. She wasn't sure what had happened, but suddenly, her heart felt broken, and all she wanted was a few moments alone.

CHAPTER SEVEN
ABEL

He saw it. At times something would cross Alanna's mind, and she would hide what she was really feeling. Most of the time, she was all smiles and laughter, but now and then her face would fall, and he would notice the sadness behind her eyes. There was nothing he could do would make it go away. Logically he knew that, but he also couldn't help but try.

After their adventures shopping, she had needed some time. The guys had found out about her singing, and apparently it either embarrassed her or made her sad. Either way, she had run off to be alone. His body ached to go and check on her, but he decided against it. Instead, he stayed with the guys, who didn't seem to notice just how upset Alanna had gotten. Maybe that was for the best.

They watched a few performances before moving on to doing other things. They weren't scheduled to play until the third night, but usually they had other things to do. Interviews as well as meet and greets were scheduled. Abel remembered what Alanna had said about the one time she did a meet and greet. It was all of thirty seconds—something he had easily forgotten but something that had stuck with her. He had never thought about it from the fan point of view.

It wasn't that he didn't like his fans. No, they were the reason he was still going after nearly twenty years in the business. He just hadn't realized how difficult it was to truly connect with them. There was only one him but a million of them.

It was getting late, and Alanna still hadn't left the room. Abel decided it was time to check on her, so he went to the back of the bus and tapped on the door. When he didn't get an answer, he slowly opened the door and peeked inside, hoping he wasn't interrupting her or catching her in an uncomfortable position. Instead, he saw her lying on the bed, hugging his pillow to her chest. She was still fully dressed as if she had fallen asleep by accident.

With slow soft steps he moved into the room. He gathered up the blanket and laid it over her before reaching down and brushing hair from her face. Part of him was checking for warmth in her body, and he shuddered at the thought of finding her gone. It certainly would have ruined the trip, but he had faith that everything would be fine.

For just a moment he stood there and watched her sleep. Then he realized how creepy he was being and turned to leave. It had been a long few days, and he was ready for some sleep. His goal was to have Alanna see every band she wanted and meet as many people as he could manage to introduce her to, regardless of any personal opinions he had of them. Abel wasn't always the most popular guy backstage, but this trip wasn't about him. It was about her.

The day started early for him. Abel wasn't used to sleeping in the bunks, and his back had a bit of a twitch in it when he slid out. Already he could smell coffee, and it helped push him to finish getting up. The bedroom door was cracked open, and when he looked inside, he found it empty. He moved toward the front and saw it, too, was empty.

His heart raced for a moment, not sure where she would have gone. The guys were all still sleeping, so he knew none of them had gone off with her. He breathed a sigh of relief when he stepped off the bus and found her sitting in one of the chairs set up just outside. She had a cup of coffee in her hands, and her eyes were closed as she mouthed the words to whatever song was playing in her ear buds. It was quiet outside still with a bit of damp warmth in the air that was common of mornings in Florida.

He ran his hand through his long hair to get it to lie down better and went over to sit next to her but didn't interrupt her peace. She seemed to know he was there because a soft smile lifted on her lips a moment before she reached over and patted his hand. She didn't look at him or stop her soft singing. All she did was let him know that she sensed him.

Abel leaned back and extended his legs, closing his eyes to take in the peace of the morning. The quiet could be hit and miss for him. Sometimes he found it peaceful, yet other times his brain would race either with song lyrics or darker thoughts. His past still haunted him, no matter how much he tried to pretend otherwise.

After a while, the sounds of other people around the venue started to rumble as everyone started to get up and get to work. In the distance, concert-goers were already making their way in. It would only be a couple of hours before the first bands started. The days were usually lesser-known bands still working to make a name for themselves. Bigger names and headliners were saved for later in the day and night.

"We should probably get some breakfast before things start to really pick up," he whispered, finally breaking the comfortable silence they had built between them.

"I'm not hungry," she answered, looking over to him. "But I'll take another cup of coffee if there is any."

"You sure? It's going to be a long day," he asked, leaning forward.

"I'm sure. I'll let you know if I need anything. I told you that already," she answered. Her voice was soft, holding an almost content tone to it.

"Alright, well I'm going to hold you to that. I don't need you passing out on me while we're out and about," he said getting up.

"Abel?" Alanna said his name more like a question than a statement, and he turned to see what she wanted. "I'm sorry about last night. I don't know, but something about it just hit me wrong. I didn't mean to ruin the evening."

"You didn't ruin anything. Don't think anything of it," he answered and leaned down to kiss the top of her head before going back onto the bus. He wasn't sure how she liked her coffee, so he brought out the pot along with some cream and sugar. Once she had her refill, he went about hunting down real food.

The other guys had all gotten up by then, and Mason was working on getting Alanna's medicine to her before they all got too busy to think about it. Hannah had been right about the alarms. Already they had been late getting with her doses, and the shows hadn't even started. It was another thirty minutes before Alanna got back on the bus so she could go and change.

Everyone exchanged good mornings, but the tone stayed quiet as everyone woke up. There was not enough coffee, and they had to make a second and third pot. Derrik just gave up and went to get an energy drink instead.

When Alanna walked out of the bedroom dressed in the clothes he had bought her, Abel felt his breath catch. She looked like she had stepped straight out of a rock concert. It was like he was looking at some strange combination of Lita Ford, Lzzy Hale, and Nita Strauss. He hadn't expected the hunger that rose in him, and he had to swallow hard not to react like a complete idiot. Stunning. It was the only word he had for it.

"Damn, you look awesome," Spencer said, and the other guys joined in on giving her complements. She looked like a fucking rock star, and they appreciated it just as much as he did. Well hopefully not quite as much.

"Thank you. I feel a little strange. It's been a while, but I think Abel did a good job picking out some clothes," she answered, looking at him with a wicked grin. Did she know she did that? Was she purposely teasing him, or was it just her natural personality?

"Well, I had a bit of an idea what you like. Now, are you ready to start the best fucking weekend of your life?" he asked.

"Lead the way," she answered.

They got her set up in the wheelchair that he had gotten her. He could have gotten one with a motor, but he liked the idea of pushing her around everywhere. They attached the oxygen tank just in case she started having any trouble breathing, and she had a dose of her medication on her just in case they were too busy to go back to the bus for it.

"So, who all do you want to see today?" he asked, handing over a flier with the list of all of the bands and when they would be playing.

"All of them, but that doesn't seem feasible especially since there are two separate stages going at all times," Alanna answered reading over all of the options.

"We will do as much as we can and as much as you can handle. Where to first?" he asked.

She pointed to the name on the flier she wanted to see first. It was Fortune of Regret, a newer band that Abel had worked with a few times.

They couldn't really be out in the crowd much or they wouldn't be able to get anywhere, so instead he weaved her through the various back alleys that had been set up for the artists to get around without being accosted by fans.

Along the way, they would stop and talk to different people. No one treated her like she was sick. They just treated her like the person she was. They took pictures, some gave her shirts or autographed photos, which seemed to make Alanna both happy and shy. When they got to the stage, he found a spot where they could see without being in the way, and he parked the chair. She didn't need the chair all the time, but he had decided to use it to get around and prevent being out when they did need it.

While the band played, Alanna got up and danced around. When she stumbled, he caught her and started dancing with her, not letting the fumble ruin her moment. He wasn't a fan of all the bands they saw, but he didn't care. She wanted to see them, so he watched too. She sang, she screamed, she danced, and she looked happier than he ever thought to see one person. For several hours, they both seemed to forget that she was sick. He was just a man who had taken a beautiful woman to see some amazing live music. It felt so normal. So real.

Midday they took a break so she could get some rest, and he could do some actual work. Mason stayed with her on the bus while Abel went to do interviews and meet fans. He did his best not to be too distracted, but his mind kept wondering if she was okay there without him. Of course she was, but he felt responsible for her.

"So, Abel, you have been seen wheeling a rather pretty woman around the festival. Is there anything you want to share about that?" the current interviewer asked.

He hadn't realized just how much people would notice, but he should have. There was always talk when someone famous was seen out with a new person. Especially one of the opposite sex.

He gave a smile and sat back a bit. "She's just a friend who needed some time to enjoy life. We are having a good time, and she is getting to see all these amazing artists. I'm happy I could bring her and let her have this weekend."

"So, she isn't someone you are seeing?" they continued to ask.

"No, just a friend that I met along the way. She has had some rough stuff happen lately, and I wanted to help make some of that better," he answered. He wasn't going to go into details. It was no one else's business what was going on with Alanna. That was her story to tell, not his, and he certainly hadn't done this for publicity.

"Well, that is pretty cool of you," the interviewer said and then went back to asking him about his music and the tour he was currently on. It only had a couple of weeks left in it, and he was looking forward to the upcoming break.

By the time he got back to Alanna, she was already up and ready to go. She was dancing around the bus with Mason who had a look of both joy and fear. His manager wasn't much of a dancer, but he had given in to the woman anyway.

"Abel!" she exclaimed and went to wrap her arms around him. He gripped around her waist, and they swayed a second as she started to laugh.

"What has gotten into you?" he asked.

"Music! Oh, I'm so ready to get back out there!" she exclaimed. He wasted no time. After grabbing a quick bite to eat, he headed out to take her to see more shows and meet more people.

Alanna seemed high on life, and he was loving every moment of it. They stayed out until the last song was played and the lights went down. By the time they got back to the bus, she was exhausted and ready to get some sleep.

He was pretty tired too, but after she was settled and asleep, he found himself sitting at the table working on music. His mind was racing. A song was in there, itching to come out, but he just couldn't get it to surface. It was frustrating, but something in him told him it was there.

CHAPTER EIGHT
ALANNA

The first two days of the festival had been a dream. Alanna had never been happier, and she knew she was not going to want it to end. It was as if she was living in a bubble. One where she wasn't sick and dying. No, the music was pumping healing energy through her veins and reviving her body, all because of Abel. He had gone above and beyond to ensure the trip was as perfect as possible. She had stacks of photos and T-shirts that she had no idea what she was going to do with. The whole band had taken turns recording videos and snapping pictures throughout so there would be lots of stuff for Hannah to enjoy. If someone could survive on adrenaline alone, this would be eternal life.

However, the third day of the event was the night Abel was playing, so he was a bit busier. She had known he would be, so it didn't bother her at all. Alanna liked watching him work, and she noticed a difference in how he interacted with his fans. He seemed to be taking a few extra moments to really look at them, and she couldn't help but wonder if what she had told him had made the difference.

Now and then he would look over at her and give her a smile. It always made her heart rush when he did that. She knew it was some silly fan girl fantasy, but it was much harder to ignore it with how much time they were spending together. So, she kept reminding herself that he was just being nice, and no way could anything else happen.

Once the current meet and greet was done, he came over and asked her what she wanted to do next. "I want some french fries," she answered, and he cocked his head to the side.

"You're actually going to eat like real food?" he asked, arching a brow at her.

"Yeah, fries with cheese," she answered, and he shook his head.

"How am I supposed to steal some of your fries if you put cheese all over them?" he asked, taking hold of the chair to start pushing her toward the food vendors.

"You aren't. That's the whole point," she answered.

"You are a mean bitch. Aren't you?" He laughed and sped up to a bit of a jog.

Alanna burst out laughing and threw her hands up in the air as if she were riding a roller coaster. He liked to do fun stuff with the chair so she wouldn't feel like she was just being pushed around out of pity. In fact, everything he did was to make her feel more like a normal human. It helped keep the bubble firmly in place. They got to the food truck, and he got them both food before moving over to a table to sit down and eat. The only thing she didn't like was not being able to be out in the crowd. While she loved watching from backstage, she felt like she was missing out on some of the show. Either way, though, it had turned into such an amazing experience that she refused to complain about anything.

"So, while I'm on stage tonight, Mason will be with you in case you need anything. After the show, I will have some post-show stuff to do. I don't know how long I will be, so Mason will take you back to the bus. I'll check in with you, though, when I get back. Sound good?" he asked.

They hadn't gone over the plan for when he was performing, so she was glad he finally brought it up.

"Sounds like a perfect plan," she answered.

He snatched one of her fries that happened to be free of cheese and went to pop it in his mouth. "Hey! Asshole! That is mine!" she protested, trying to catch him before he could eat it.

"Not anymore." He laughed and ate it.

They both burst into near hysterical laughter, catching looks from a lot of the people around them. She didn't care. Things were too perfect for her to care what anyone else had to say about it.

"Alright, I'm just going to be out there. Sorry I can't watch this show with you," he teased before kissing her cheek.

Abel was dressed all in black with his hair damp, slick, and oh so sexy. The humidity in Florida kept making it frizz, so he had been keeping it wet. She was pretty sure sweat would keep it that way through the rest of the show. As she stood next to him, she watched as he got himself in the right head space for his performance. She understood the ritual because she had a very similar one when she used to perform. He took several deep breaths and shook his body to loosen his muscles.

The band went out first, starting to play and getting the crowd hyped with the preview of what the first song would be. Abel gave her one last look, and she wished him luck before he ran out on the stage to start his show. She felt like she was in a dream. It was the only way to describe the rush that flooded her as he started the first song. No matter how many times she had seen him perform, she was always stunned by it, but this one was different. Alanna couldn't put her thoughts into any kind of words, but it was just different.

She sang and screamed every word as if she were out there with him. Her body moved and danced, unable to sit down with the excitement coursing through her veins. No longer able to resist, she began to head bang when he hit a rather harsh vocal, and when she stumbled Mason took hold of her and just held her while she continued to lose her mind.

"Hey, guys! Give me one second," Abel said to the crowd who continued to cheer back in response.

He walked toward her and held his hand out with the evilest grin. She had no idea what he was doing, but as Mason nudged her toward him, she took his hand. Before she knew what was happening, he was walking her out onto the stage. Alanna looked back and saw Mason holding his phone and a camera up.

"What are you doing?" she asked, hoping no one could hear her.

"Sing with me," he said and turned her toward the crowd. There had to be more than twenty thousand people out there. Lights shined like stars from the mass of people, and it stole her breath.

"Everyone, this is my friend Alanna. Now, this isn't a song I usually do live, but it happens to be her favorite song, and I want her to sing it with me. Will you indulge me in something a little different tonight?" he asked the crowd who again erupted in a chorus of cheers of excitement.

While he had been getting her, a stagehand had rolled a piano out onto the stage. He took a seat and patted the spot next to him. He put one of his earpieces in her ear, and then he started to play. A calming hush came over the crowd for a moment as he let the music fill the air. Alanna was shaking, but she wasn't really nervous. Her eyes were locked to him, and as he played, the entire world disappeared. It was just the two of them.

Louder in Silence didn't have a lot of slow songs, but this was one of them, and one she knew was very personal to him. He looked over to her and nodded, and she leaned into the microphone and slowly started the song. The crowd roared in excitement, but she was focused. The words started off soft, but she felt them rise up in her, full of emotion and passion. Toward the end of the first verse, the intensity had grown, and she was belting out. He joined her in the chorus, and they seemed to fall into a perfect harmony. She couldn't count the number of times she had sung that song, but she was sure it had never sounded so perfect.

He took on the second verse and then they went into a split harmony during the bridge. His voice became rougher and more distorted while hers stayed soft and melodic. They both belted out into the night, building the song higher and higher until she was singing out the final note holding it for far longer than needed. Her heart just wouldn't let it go, and when she finally ran out of breath, she heard the thunderous applause of the crowd, and tears stung in her eyes. He had done it. He had made the biggest dream she had ever had come true. For five short minutes, she was a rock star, singing in front of a crowd that most only dreamed of.

He held his hand out and helped her stand before turning her toward the crowd again. "Alanna Grace everyone! Keep showing her love, and I'll be right back."

Once they were off the stage, she turned around and threw her arms around him. The tears were flowing like rivers down her cheeks. "Thank you so much," she whispered, her whole body shaking.

"No, thank you," he answered. "I gotta go. See you later."

He didn't have time to talk to her. The band had already started playing the next song, and he had to rush out to get started with his part.

"You did an amazing job out there," Mason said, coming to stand next to her.

The shock took a while to wear off, but before long she was singing and dancing along again. She didn't want the night to end. She didn't want the weekend to end. After Abel finished the last song and did his bows, he rushed off the stage and gave her a very sweaty hug. She didn't care. Alanna held him probably a little longer than she should have before pulling away to tell the rest of the band how much she had enjoyed the show.

"I have to go, but I'll see you in a few hours on the bus. If you need to go to bed, do so. I won't be upset," Abel said, almost out of breath.

"I'll see you then," she answered.

A wave of exhaustion hit her, and she sat down in her chair, unable to stay on her feet. Mason started to take her back to the bus, and that was when she realized just how much she had overdone things. Her body hurt, her head was spinning, and she was finding it hard to breathe. Before they even made it back, she was having to use the oxygen to fight off the sensation of pressure that was constricting her lungs. Once back at the bus, it took almost all of her energy to climb the stairs, but Mason helped her. While she went to get changed, he got her medication out. He'd learned what all she needed and when.

"So, I have the alarm set, and I'll wake you up for another round when it goes off. Do you need anything else?" Mason asked, giving her the handful of pills and a bottle of water.

"No, I'm good. I'm just going to lay down and get some rest. I think I did too much today," she answered.

"You did, but it looked like you had a good time," he said.

"The best time," she answered.

She took the pills and closed the door. Alanna stripped to a band shirt and panties before climbing under the covers. In an attempt to ward off the chill sinking into her, she wrapped herself up as much as she could. As the high of the concert wore off, she found herself getting cold. They had to keep the air conditioner for the bus on because of the terrible Florida heat, but that didn't mean she enjoyed it. She already had multiple blankets, but she curled in on herself to see if she could get warm. Before she did, the medication kicked in, and she passed out.

CHAPTER NINE
ABEL

Abel was tired by the time he got back to the bus and cleaned up. He had peeked in on Alanna, but she had been very asleep, and he refused to wake her up. Some of the guys had gone off to parties, but he had gone back to the bus to try and work on the song that had been haunting him. It was another couple of hours when the guys came back.

"Dude, Derrik has lost his damn mind," Cage said sitting down at the table.

"What did you do?" Abel asked, looking toward his drummer.

Derrik pointed to the fresh tattoo he had on his calf. It was the same drawing Alanna had done on Derrik's chest during their poker game. "I needed something to remember this crazy idea you had. Alanna's a cool chick, so I figured she deserved to be immortalized."

Abel laughed and shook his head. "Yeah, but really. A rainbow with a unicorn?"

"It's what she drew. I like it, though. It has character." He laughed.

They all joked around and played games for another hour before going to bed. Sometimes being tired didn't mean much. It could take hours to calm down from being on the stage. It was why most musicians lived a night life. A hush fell over the bus, and before long, Abel drifted off to sleep, content and happy with how the night had turned out.

He wasn't sure how long he had been asleep before he felt a soft hand tapping his shoulder. The sensation caused him to jump out of his sleep, and he nearly hit his head before he realized Alanna was trying to wake him.

"Hey, what's wrong?" he whispered.

"I'm cold," she answered.

"Oh, okay, well let me find you another blanket," he answered and slipped out of the bunk.

He walked with her to the bedroom and shut the door so their noise wouldn't wake up anyone else. She slid back into the bed, but he could see her shaking. She was wearing one of his band's T-shirts and he assumed panties, though he hadn't been able to see under the shirt to know for sure. His heart pounded for a moment, thinking of the fact she was half naked in his bed. They had shared such a beautiful moment on stage that he hadn't been able to shake it. Why did they have to meet in such a horrible situation? It wasn't fair.

"I think I have one more blanket in my closet. It isn't much, but maybe it will help. Sorry, I can't turn off the AC. It will kill the band, and I kinda need them," he joked, pulling out the only other blanket he had. He laid it over the other two that were already piled on top of her and then sat down next to her waiting to see if it helped at all.

"I get it. It isn't your fault. Sometimes the cold just gets into me, and I can't shake it," she answered, her voice soft and quivering.

"Feeling any better?" he asked after a couple of minutes.

"No not really, but I guess I will be alright," she answered.

Without a second thought, he stood up and pulled off his shirt. "Scoot over."

"What are you doing?" she asked, moving further back on the bed.

"Body heat. I'm warming you up," he answered, sliding in next to her and pulling her to lie against him. He wrapped his arms around her and curled them up until he was covering as much of her as he could. She continued to tremble, and he rubbed his hands up and down her arms, trying his best to help and attempting to ignore how good it felt to have her so close to him.

"Abel?" Alanna whispered.

"Yeah?" he asked.

"Thank you," she said, looking up at him. She was so beautiful. Even fragile and broken, he was captivated by just how stunning she was.

"You don't have to thank me," he said, leaning down and kissing her forehead.

"Yes, I do. You didn't have to do any of this, and you gave me the most amazing weekend of my life," she answered. "It may sound cheap to say, knowing what's coming, but I am going to remember and cherish this for the rest of my life."

It was his turn to shiver. That small reminder of reality had crept in, and he wanted it to go away again. "You are an amazing woman. It was the least I could do, and honestly it has been one of the best weekends of my life, too."

She looked up at him again and the softest smile was resting on her lips. His body shook, and he was barely able to breathe. There was no fighting his desire anymore. He leaned down and softly pressed his lips to hers. With a deep inhale, he savored the scent of her strawberry shampoo and the sensation of her soft lips on his. Slowly he started to move his lips against hers, but she turned away.

"Abel..." she whispered.

"I'm sorry," he sighed, even though he wasn't. He was far from sorry, and the kiss was nowhere close to what he really wanted to do.

"This is crazy," she said next but hadn't turned back to look at him.

"I know," he moaned and reached over to turn her toward him. He began to kiss her again and groaned when she kissed him back.

They kissed, soft and sweet, for several seconds before she turned away again. "Abel. This is stupid. You know this doesn't end well."

"Yes, I know," he answered and then started to kiss her again. She wrapped her arms around him, and he shifted so he was lying over her.

They were both shaking as the kiss grew more heated. He ran his hand up her thigh, lifting the shirt enough to confirm the panties that had been hidden beneath. He wanted her more than he had ever wanted any woman in his entire life, so much it made his head spin until all sense of reason had fled. Moving the kisses down her neck, he continued to lift the shirt higher, his fingers tracing her soft skin.

"Abel... We... I..." Apparently her rational head was still awake but barely.

"Shut up," he whispered before kissing her again. He didn't mean it in a bad way, just in a he didn't want to be smart in that moment way. No, he wanted to feel her.

She moaned into his kiss, and it fueled him on. His knee pushed her legs open, so she was on either side of his hips, and he pushed more firmly against her. Her breath caught and electricity shot down his spine.

"Abel," she gasped between the kisses she was giving him.

Taking a deep breath, he forced himself to stop and look down at her. "Am I going to hurt you if we do this?" It was a justifiable question, so he let himself ask it.

"I don't know. I haven't since... well, it's been a long time," she answered, her eyes wide and her breath coming heavily. Her hips lifted against him, sending heat down his spine, and he wondered if she even knew she had done it.

"Okay, then, if you really want me to stop, say so now. If I hurt you, tell me. Otherwise, shut the fuck up and let me make love to you," he said. He gave her two seconds to respond, and when she lifted up and kissed him, he took it for the answer it obviously was.

A savage hunger took them both as he kissed her hard and deep, feeding from her mouth with an almost violent need for her. She kissed him back with just as much intensity as her hands worked to untie his pajama pants. She slid them down, using her legs to get them as far down as she could. He wasn't about to get up and interrupt the building desperation between them. Fuck it, he would do this with them both still half clothed. He didn't care.

With a firm grip, he ripped her panties off and tossed the fabric away before shifting her enough that he could feel himself pressed against her opening. He had no idea what had gotten into him. It had been a very long time since he had lost control like that, and as he claimed her, he found himself taking her with hard fast strokes.

They kissed full and deep as they moved together. Her nails dug into his back, sending an electrifying sensation of pain and pleasure through him. They were savage, primal, fucking like they were facing the end of the world—in a way they were.

At some point they'd thrown the pile of blankets off of them, and he had managed to finish kicking off his pants, though he wasn't sure when or how. He took her harder and faster, building them both higher and higher toward that peek he needed from her. She gave as much as she got, and her head had fallen back as she gasped for air with every thrust. The sweet sounds she gave him started to raise in intensity, and he could feel her body tighten around him.

She was close. He knew it, and a moment before she started to scream out for him, he covered her mouth with his hand and joined her in the most explosive release he had ever had. His lip was nearly bleeding with how hard he had bitten down on it to keep from making too much noise and letting the whole bus know what they were doing. When the last shiver left his body, he all but collapsed on top of her and then shifted just enough so he wasn't crushing her under his weight.

"Oh fuck," she panted, her body still partly arched as she tried to catch her breath.

"Yeah," he answered, still trying to find his own composure.

"What the hell did we just do?" she asked, her body slowly relaxing.

He couldn't help but chuckle as he reached over and turned her so he could kiss her. "You still cold?"

"No," she answered and giggled a bit. They were both desperately trying to stay quiet, but it wasn't easy.

The way her body shook next to him made him want more, but he figured that might be pushing it. "Did I hurt you?" he asked, wanting to make sure he hadn't made things worse for her.

"Oh no, not at all," she answered before she started kissing him. "Let's do it again."

It was as if she had read his mind. She moved so she was on top of him and finally removed her shirt. They had gotten so caught up in the moment that he hadn't been able to get it off, and he hadn't even cared. He sat up so he could kiss her as she lifted her body to impale herself on him.

His hands roamed all over her as she rolled her hips and began to take from him everything she needed. She took him just as passionately as he had her, but this time, they weren't so desperate and were able to enjoy it more. He ran his lips over her neck, down her chest, and to her nipples. She was sweaty, and the salty taste mixed with the sweetness of her skin making him crave more.

Before long, his hands gripped firm on her hips, helping her move with him as they started to build up toward another powerful release.

He could spend the rest of his life in that moment and be the happiest man in the world. Her talents were certainly more than just singing. She knew how to move. He remembered how she could roll her body and dance, and it explained everything. Damn, this woman was more than any one man should be able to hold.

"Alanna, I got your meds..." Mason said from the door. "Oh shit!"

"Mason get the fuck out of here!" Abel yelled, tossing something at him. He wasn't really sure what it was, but the man left the room without another word.

However, Alanna started laughing, and her head fell forward to rest on his shoulder.

"What the fuck are you laughing about?" he groaned. Part of him wanted to join her, but he was too deep into her body to do that.

"I just feel like a teenager getting caught," she answered.

He just growled and started kissing her again, and a moment later, it was like the interruption had never happened. He could feel it coming. Tingles ran the length of his spine, and he was fighting to hold on for her. He knew she was close. Her body was so tight on him he could barely breathe. Her breaths had taken on a more tense cadence, and he could feel her shake a moment before her head flung back.

Once again, he covered her mouth, and he bit down on the curve of her neck as he came hard and deep inside of her. His other arm gripped tightly around her back, and he savored every shiver of his body as she spasmed against him. The first orgasm had been good, but it was nothing compared to this one.

It took them several more breaths to come down from it, and his head was spinning. Softly he kissed her again—not to start things again but just because he needed his lips on hers. She kissed him back for a second and then slowly slid away from him.

"I need, to, ummm," she started to say but couldn't seem to catch her breath enough to talk.

"Yeah, I know," he answered.

She couldn't do more. Her body couldn't handle all of the exertion, and apparently it was past time for her medicine. Abel fell back on the bed and took several deep breaths, trying to get his brain to function again.

"What the hell are we doing?" she asked, but he heard a bit of laughter in her voice.

He sat back up, swinging his legs to the side of the bed so he could look for his pants. Alanna found them first and tossed them to him so he could put them back on.

"I have no idea. I really don't. Look, I'm going to give you a minute, but I'll be out there. I know you need to come get your meds and such, and I need food."

Abel leaned down and kissed her one more time then left the room to give her privacy for whatever she might need to do. In the living room area, he saw Mason sitting at the table with a concerned look.

"What the fuck, man?"

"I don't know," Abel said, putting his hands to his face and leaning against the fridge.

"This doesn't end well. You know that. What the fuck do you think you're doing?" Mason continued as if trying to berate some sense into him.

"I really don't know. She was cold, so I went to get her a blanket, and then it wasn't working so I got in the bed to help warm her up, and the next thing I knew I was inside of her. I can't explain it. I know it's stupid, but I really..." He couldn't bring himself to say it because saying it would make it real. Neither he nor Alanna could afford for it to be real.

"This is stupid. Very stupid and you know that. Nothing good is going to come from it. Look I'm fucking tired. Do you think you can handle this one time?" Mason said frustrated as he pointed to Alanna's case of medication on the table.

"Yeah, I got it. Go get some sleep. I'm sorry," he answered.

Mason was right. A relationship with Alanna was stupid, but he hadn't been able to stop himself. He wanted her more than he could explain even to himself.

With a sigh, he took a seat at the table and continued to try and catch his breath to bring back any semblance of sanity. No matter how much he wanted to pretend otherwise, Alanna was dying. There was no future with her. A shiver raked down him, and he did his best to brush it off. Instead he turned his focus to the collection of medication bottles on the table. Most of the bottles had names of medications he had never seen before. Most of them. Then he saw one, and it was like twenty years of his life disappeared in a flash. Morphine. His hand shook as he reached out to take the bottle.

"Come on, baby. Try it one time. Do it with me," a voice from his past whispered through his mind. *"You will love it."*

CHAPTER TEN
ALANNA

S he walked into the living room area from the back to see him sitting at the table with her medication set out in front of him. He was trembling as he held one of the bottles in his hand, staring at it like it was a ghost. His breath was hard and heavy, but he didn't move, frozen by whatever demon had risen up in his mind. She didn't need to read the label to know what it was. His history was no mystery, and she was well aware of what was in her case that would cause that kind of reaction.

Careful not to startle him, she took a few more steps into the room. Alanna couldn't imagine what was going on in his mind at that moment, and she just wanted to help make it go away. "Abel, look at me."

"Twenty years. It's been twenty fucking years and still, I can feel it, screaming at me," he whispered, but he didn't look away from the bottle. It was almost like he was speaking to the room and not to her.

When she got to the table, she slid in next to him as best she could but didn't make any move to take the bottle from him. For some reason, she felt like he needed to make that decision.

"Abel, look at me, baby," she whispered again, hoping to break him from the trance he was in.

A shiver ran the length of his body, and his fingers tightened on the bottle. She could see his chest rising and falling, and each exhale carried with it a trimmer. Drug addiction was something she had never faced, but she knew people who had. It could tear a person apart, and she was aware of what it had done to his past. Abel was lucky to have come out the other side and found so much success. Most weren't.

"Just one time," he whispered, and again she didn't think he was talking to her. "Just try it one time."

Alanna placed her hand on his cheek and turned his face to her. "Abel, look at me," she said again.

It took a moment for his eyes to refocus on her. There was such a deep haunting fear behind them that it made her heart sink. "Baby, that's poison. You don't want that. Hell, I don't want it. Nothing good can come from it. Please, don't let me be the reason you lose it."

He turned his attention to the bottle and then back to her a moment before his hand opened, and he let the bottle fall to the table. It rolled a bit before stopping against another bottle. His head fell forward toward her, and he rested his forehead against hers as he tried to find himself once more.

Alanna reached out and grabbed the bottle, tucking it back into the case and out of view as she continued to hold him. "It's just poison. I've got you. I have you."

"Thank you," he whispered even though he was still shaking against her. This wasn't the tremors of post passion; this was the shivers of a desire and fear she would never understand. So, she just held him until he felt strong enough to let her go.

"I didn't do anything," she finally said.

"You did," he answered.

Alanna went about gathering the rest of the medication and going to the counter so she could take what she needed without him watching. She hadn't realized how difficult it would be for him. Maybe he hadn't either.

"No, I didn't. Abel, I weigh less than a hundred pounds and have no body strength left in me. If you wanted, you could have taken it back from me. You chose to let go. You did that, not me."

She heard him give a halfhearted chuckle as she finished what she was doing. Once the cabinet was locked, she went to the bunk she knew to be Mason's and tossed the key inside. She heard a bit of a grumble but nothing else. Abel seemed more put together by the time she turned back to him.

"Tell me about it."

He looked up at her, his face still tense. "You want to hear about my drug addiction?"

"You know all my dark secrets, or well, most of them. It's only fair you tell me yours," she answered, going to sit next to him. She rested her head on his shoulder and took his hand.

"You listen to my music. There isn't much more to tell," he answered.

"Yeah, I've heard your songs, but that isn't the same. Talk to me. Tell me the things no one else knows," she said again, rubbing her thumb against his.

He took a deep breath and turned to kiss the top of her head before he began to speak. "You know how they say everyone remembers the first time they have sex?" he asked, and she nodded, letting him talk. "Well, I honestly barely remember mine, but I remember every fucking detail of the first time I shot up. I'd already been drinking and doing pills, but... well, I was at a party, and there was a girl there. She was so hot, and I just wanted to get my hands on her. We ended up in a room together, and she started pulling this stuff out of her purse. I was drunk out of my mind and kept like leaning over and kissing her."

He stopped for a second, taking another deep breath and licking his lips as he tried to find the right words. She let him take his time. They weren't in any rush. "Maya was her name. She had long black hair and wore too much makeup. She looked at me and asked me to do it with her. She said I would like it and just to try it one time. Just one time, that was all it was supposed to be. So, I did it with her. She showed me what to do and helped me out that first time. I don't even think I can put into words what that first time felt like. I remember the high more than the rest of the night. Fuck, it was the best feeling I had ever had, and I spent years trying to find it again. Nothing ever felt like that first time."

He licked his lips and looked at her.

"I can imagine. So what happened?"

"A few months later I found out she died. I hadn't even seen her again, but it hit me hard. It sent me into a spiral. My dad was a drunk, my mom was an addict and my sister too. It was like we were all meant to live in that pit. They didn't even notice how far gone I had gotten. I was seventeen the first time I overdosed. Wish I could say it was the only time, but it wasn't. I was a fucking mess. The second time was after my sister killed herself. I was trying to do something with my music, but I was so fucked up all the time that we couldn't really accomplish anything. I was getting into fights all of the time, and they were escalating. I swear I fought so I could feel something because the drugs left me numb most of the time. It was like a vicious cycle that I just couldn't escape."

"That's awful. Sounds lonely," she whispered, moving in closer to him.

"It was," he answered. "I got into so much trouble that I was in and out of jail, too. But then I broke one of my probations, and the judge had enough of me. So, he locked me up for real. Fuck I thought I was just going to die in prison. It's actually easier to get drugs there than outside, strangely enough. Last time I ODed was in there, and then I was put into detox and rehab. I stayed clean for a long time in there and wrote a bunch of music. When I got out, I thought I was just going to jump back into things, but it was hard to find a band when you're known for being such a problem. So, I went back to it. I kept following that cycle. To be honest, I am surprised I'm alive. But then I got Briar's mom pregnant, and the last thing I wanted was to abandon my kid. I got my shit together, and I did it all for her. Then music started to take off, and well, here I am. And even after all that time, I can still hear it, screaming in my head. One more taste. One more hit. Just give in. I really thought I would be okay. I knew what kind of meds you were on, but when it was right there in front of me, I couldn't do it."

"But you did do it," Alanna whispered. "You let go, and I'm so proud of you. You're stronger than you think."

"Thanks, now, your turn. Tell me something you never talk about," he said, letting out one last shaky breath.

She felt his body relax, and she was thankful for it. He was right, though. He had opened up to her, so she might as well do the same.

"I don't know what to say. I guess the biggest thing I have never talked about is what happened between me and John. The last guy I was with before I got sick," she sighed.

"He's the one who hit you," Abel said, not bothering to make it a question.

"It didn't start out that way. We met at a club. I was singing there, just trying to make some extra money and well, because I love singing so much. We hit it off really well and started hanging out more. He had a band and invited me to join in on some practice sessions. God the sex was so good in the beginning, I think my head couldn't reason with all the dopamine."

"Don't need to hear about the sex." Abel chuckled.

"Why? Jealous?" she asked, giving him a wicked look.

"Not at all," he answered and leaned down to kiss her. It was just a quick kiss so she could get back to her story.

"Well, after a while I was singing lead. We mostly did covers of your music, as you know. Now and then we would throw in a song or two by some female-led bands to give me more to do. Everyone loved having me, but I think the more the guys warmed up to me the more jealous John got. The first time we got into a fight was after the first show we did together. The crowd had really taken to me. John would do the rough stuff that I just wasn't willing to do, but he had been the lead singer before I came along. So, by the time we got back to my place, we were screaming at each other. The fight transformed into every grievance we ever had. It was no longer about the show, even though that was how it started. I tried to slam the door in his face, but he kicked it open. One thing about John, he was pretty good at hitting me in places that I could easily cover up. Don't get me wrong. I fought back, but I'm not exactly a large woman," she explained and then had to take her own deep breath.

"I'm going to kill him," Abel grumbled next to her.

"No, you aren't," she said and then continued. "We would fight and then we would make up. It was like the passion between us fell into two extremes with no in between. I don't know why I stayed. After a while he started threatening to hurt Hannah, and I became too afraid to leave. I think she knew it was going on but didn't know what to say either. I mean, it's not a kid's place to have to defend their parents. John and I were together for years. We would go months or even years without getting into a fight, but then something would trigger it, and we would fall back into the cycle. That concert, the one you saw the picture of with the bruise, we had gotten into such a bad fight the night before that I thought I was going to die. I couldn't breathe when I woke up the next day, and we had a show to do."

"Yep, I'm fucking killing him," Abel said again, and she just shook her head.

"There is no point. When he found out I was sick, he decided I wasn't worth dealing with anymore. Just like Hannah's dad, when things got hard, he left. Seems I have a type. The men in my life liked it when I was fun, but when real life got in the way, they didn't want anything to do with me," she said.

"Hannah was right," Abel whispered next, and she turned to face him.

"What do you mean?" she asked, not sure what he was talking about.

"In the letter she wrote me. She said you are a beautiful woman who lived a not so beautiful life. Every time I hear something new about you, that's what I think of," he said and then leaned in to kiss her.

Deep down, Alanna knew that kissing him was just asking for pain. Them being together was a horrible idea. She had an expiration date that was quickly approaching, but when he kissed her, it stole away all the reason in her mind. She wanted to kiss him. She wanted to feel him. Her arms wrapped around him and the kiss deepened. They got caught up in it, and she found herself moving onto his lap, needing to feel more of him. She could live in the bubble a little longer. The fantasy could last for a couple more days before she had to return to the tragedy that was her life.

"We should go to bed," Abel groaned between kisses.

"I'm not tired," she answered as his kisses moved down her neck.

"I didn't say sleep," he said and then managed to get them both out from the table without setting her down. He carried her all the way back to the bedroom, kissing her the entire way and making sure to lock the door. They didn't go to sleep for hours, and she loved every moment of it.

CHAPTER ELEVEN
ALANNA

S he woke to him making love to her from behind. One hand cupped her breast, and the other was running up and down her neck. It was the best way to wake up. When her release hit, he once again covered her mouth to keep her from being too loud. He buried his face into the pillow by her head as he shook from his own climax. Alanna had no idea what time it was, nor did she care. She could spend the last of her life in that bed with him, and it would be the happiest way she could think of to leave the world.

Slowly turning toward him, she gave him a soft kiss before laying her head on his chest. She loved the sound of his frantic heartbeat. It reminded her of drums and made her smile.

"Do you really think they don't know what we've been doing in here?" she asked, and he laughed.

"Oh, I'm sure they do know, but we don't have to give them any more ammunition," he answered.

Alanna hadn't thought about the fact she was on a bus with nothing but men. Suddenly the idea of going out there to face them was no longer appealing. Abel probably wouldn't get it, but she did not want to hear the teasing that might very well occur once they escaped the room. "Oh god, I have to go out there."

Abel gave her a questioning look. "Yeah, why?"

"You don't get it. You're a guy. It's not the same for us girls. I'm going to go out there and, oh god, I'm so embarrassed." She buried her face against his chest in total mortification.

"They won't say anything." He laughed.

"Oh, they won't have to," she said and then climbed up on his lap. A growl escaped him, and he pulled her down to kiss him.

He helped her forget once more before pain started to set in. She needed her medicine. It was hours past time for her to take it, and the pain was starting to rise. So they got dressed, and she fought through her anxiety to make her way out of the room.

No one said anything, but she swore they were looking at her. She knew she had to look like a total mess. That fresh-fucked look had to be all over her face. Not sure what else to do, she just threw her hands up in the air. "Fuck, just let me get some coffee and my meds."

That did it. Everyone burst out laughing. It had been her own fault, but she needed it to happen. Something about just letting it out made it feel less awkward. She got her meds and took them down with a hot cup of coffee before sitting at the table.

Derrik came over and put his leg up so she could see it. "Hey, look what I got."

Alanna looked at his calf to see a very fresh tattoo. It was the drawing she had put on his chest during the poker game, and it made her smile. "Why did you do that?"

"I mean, you won the game. Besides, I think you're pretty cool," he answered and sat down next to her.

"My granddaughter, Lacey, that is what she draws all the time. She would love to see it," Alanna said.

"It's crazy to think that you have a granddaughter," Derrik said next.

"Well, that's what happens when you are stupid and get pregnant in high school, but I wouldn't change it for the world," she answered.

"Well, I'll get Mason to take a picture of it and I'll sign it for Lacey then," Derrik said then kissed her cheek. "If she's your granddaughter, she must be pretty fucking cool."

"For a five-year-old, I think so," she answered.

"Okay, last day. We don't have any work today, so I am all yours. What do you want to do?" Abel asked, leaning against the counter and eating some breakfast.

She gave him a wicked smile, and the room burst out laughing again. But when it calmed down, she answered. "You know what I want to do. I want to do everything. It's my last day before I have to go back to reality. Let's make the most of it."

"Then that is exactly what we will do," he said.

One thing about being sick was that no matter how much you tried to pretend you weren't, it always won. Abel had taken her to as many shows as he possibly could. They ate junk food, or more, he ate, and she nibbled. They were living off of coffee and adrenaline, but as the night wore on, she could feel that monster coming for her. They were at the last show. It was another of her favorite bands. The female-led Storm Siren that she adored. Her whole body was shaking. Even in the heat, she was freezing. Mason had run to get her a hoodie, but it wasn't helping much.

"You sure you want to stay," Abel asked, kneeling down next to her.

"Yes. I have been looking forward to this show all weekend. I love them. She is so fucking hot. I would totally marry her," Alanna answered with a tremble in her voice.

"Oh, am I getting replaced?" he playfully asked, and she couldn't help but laugh.

"Maybe," she answered, and he leaned in and kissed her.

"I'm totally going to remind you later why I'm not being replaced," he said and then stood up. "Get up."

She gave him a curious look, but when he motioned again for her to get up, she carefully did so. He reached out to help her, and then he sat down in her chair before pulling her down to sit in his lap. He kicked his leg up on one of the large cases and pulled her in close, resting his chin on the top of her head. When he held her, she wasn't as cold. Alanna watched the show from the circle of his arms. At times it was almost impossible to keep herself from dozing in and out. They had certainly overdone things, and her body was starting to protest her ignoring it.

The show went on like a haze, in and out of dreams. Abel didn't make a move to take her back to the bus, even though she was sure he wanted to. Instead, he held her and let her enjoy the show when she was awake enough to do so. At some point, she felt him shifting and moving, and she turned to look at him. He had pulled out his phone and was attempting to text with one hand.

"What's going on?" she asked, having fallen asleep again at some point.

"I'm just asking Mason to come here. Go back to enjoying the show," he answered. He didn't even tell her to go back to sleep. No, he respected the fact that even though she was not really paying attention, the show was where she wanted to be.

When she was awake enough to pay attention, she would softly sing along, even though most of the songs were much harder. As much as she wanted to get up and dance and party to the music, she couldn't bring herself to do it. So, she settled for singing along. Now and then, Abel would join her. Alanna loved when he sang with her. It was one of the things she knew she would cherish most when all of this was over.

At some point she completely fell asleep and woke up when the music stopped. A gasp left her as she started to sit up, but Abel pulled her back down into his arms. "Don't worry. Everything's fine. Just relax. The band is about to leave the stage, so let's just stay out of the way."

"Okay," she whispered and settled back down. He had given her the best weekend of her life, and she would forever be grateful for it.

"Abel Sharp, I had heard you had a guest at the event," a woman's voice said, and Alanna cracked open her eyes enough to see Leia Rice, the front woman of Storm Siren standing there. "Guess you aren't as much of an asshole as everyone says you are."

"Oh, I am, just not this weekend," he answered.

"She is even prettier close up," Alanna said, not realizing the words had left her lips.

Leia laughed and knelt down. "So, what's her story?"

"Maybe I will tell you one day, but right now, she's just a friend who deserved to have the best weekend of her life," Abel answered.

"Fair enough," Leia answered. "Hey, why don't you bring her by my bus before you head out tomorrow and I'll sign some stuff for her?"

"Yeah, I can do that," he answered.

"She smells good too," Alanna whispered. She was delusional, and a wave of nausea hit, making her bury her face in Abel's chest.

"I think she is trying to replace me," Abel joked.

Leia laughed and then got up and walked away.

"I'm going to be sick," Alanna said as her skin got warm, and she felt a sensation of saliva filling her mouth.

"Hold on," Abel said, lifting her and carrying her to the bathroom backstage. They passed Mason on the way, and he called out to his friend, "Get her chair. I'll be there in a few minutes."

He managed to get her into the bathroom before she got sick. They collapsed to the floor and everything she had inside of her came back. Abel didn't say anything. He just held her hair back until she was done and then sat down on the floor with her and held her while she shook and cried in pure embarrassment.

The trip had gone so well. She hadn't gotten sick or felt weak the whole time. Why did it have to end so badly? Alanna didn't just cry. It was that ugly cry of someone who felt defeated, which was exactly how she felt in that moment.

"I've got you," he whispered over and over as he petted her hair and held her on the floor of the bathroom. Surely that couldn't be where he wanted to be. He deserved better.

Once he knew she was better, he picked her up and carried her toward the bus. "Move!" he called out anytime someone got in his way. He wasn't nice about it. Even when he got to the bus, he roared out at his band mates to get out of his way as he carried her to the bedroom.

She was so dizzy and cold that she felt like the world was spinning. Mason came in with her medicine, but she didn't think she could take it. "Just set it on the table," Abel demanded and turned back to her.

"Hey, look at me. You are going to be okay. I promise. Just breathe," he said, cupping her face in his hands.

Him holding her steadied her for a moment, but the pain spiked and sent another wave of nausea through her. She rushed into the bathroom, falling to the floor before lifting herself up to be sick again.

"Dude, does she have anything in that bag of hers for nausea!" Abel called out.

"I don't fucking know! I'm calling Hannah!" Mason called back.

"I got you. You're going to be fine," Abel kept saying as he held back her hair and rubbed her back. There was really nothing for her to get rid of, but the sensation would not settle.

Mason rushed into the room with her bag, and she could hear him rummaging through it. "She has some shots in here, but I don't fucking know how to do that."

"Just give it here," Abel yelled and snatched the bag from him. "What's it called?"

Mason answered as Alanna fell from the toilet into Abel's lap. He pulled her up to rest her back against his chest. Her head wouldn't stop spinning, and she felt another attack start to rise up in her.

"Stick the needle in here," Abel explained as he held up the vial and used his teeth to work the syringe. "Okay, make it go to the line of whatever number the bottle says."

Mason did as Abel asked as he took hold of her arm. She could feel him breathing hard as he wrapped a leg around her to help hold her up.

"Abel, let me go," she said, feeling like she would be sick.

"No," was all he said as Mason handed over the needle. "Okay, rub the alcohol right here."

Mason did as Abel instructed and then a moment later, she felt the rush of the medicine as it entered her blood stream. She gasped out as a wave of dizziness hit her, and she fell backward against Abel. His whole body was shaking as he dropped the needle to the floor and held her to him. They didn't move, just sat there on the floor as the medicine took effect.

"I'm sorry. I'm sorry. I'm sorry," Alanna chanted in a whisper.

"It's fine," Abel answered and continued to hold her to him. "Mason, can you take care of that please?"

"Yeah, I got it," Mason answered.

"Can one of you bring me some towels and cold washcloths?" Abel called out. A few minutes later, Derrik was there with the requested items.

Alanna didn't want them to see her like that, but she didn't really have much of a choice.

"Is she going to be okay?" Derrik asked.

Abel didn't answer. Alanna figured he didn't know the answer and wasn't about to lie. Instead, he rubbed the cool cloth over her face. "It's okay. I got you. Don't worry. I got you."

There was a strange transition as the medication took effect, and she was no longer sick He picked her up and carried her to the bed and laid her down.

"Can you get me like some sort of large bowl or something with some hot water and some soap?" Abel asked Derrik, and he went to do as requested.

"This is not how I wanted to end my day," she whispered. The nausea medication took away some of the pain, but it was still there. Everything hurt, and she really needed her other medication, but she was afraid to try and swallow it.

"Me either, but we take what we can get. Now, let me just take care of you," he answered. "I hope I did that right."

She didn't have it in her to say more, but she smiled. Of course he had done it right. He knew exactly what he was doing, even after twenty years. She wondered if he had ever done that before, given someone else a shot. Had he sat with lovers on the floors of bathrooms when they were sick? Had he held them as the high took them? She didn't have it in her to ask.

Derrik came back with the water and soap, and Abel took his time cleaning her up. By the time he was done, she felt well enough to take her other medicine. Abel stayed with her until the pain faded, and she fell asleep. Faintly she felt him get up and leave, but she was too weak to ask him to stay.

CHAPTER TWELVE
ABEL

He had to get out of there. He had to get away from everything, or he was going to hurt someone. His whole body was on fire, and he knew if he stayed it would get bad real fast. Once Alanna had fallen asleep, Abel left the room and went straight for the door.

"I'll be back."

He heard someone come up behind him and Derrik called out to him. "Hey, you okay?"

"No!" he yelled back and then took off in a run.

The energy running through him was unstoppable. He ran and ran. Then he ran more. He found himself near some dumpsters, and there he let out all the fury he felt building inside of him, smashing bottles and throwing crates. He destroyed anything he could get his hands on, not caring that someone would have to clean it up later. A roar of rage ripped out of him until he finally just collapsed to the ground. His anger still high, he started to just punch the pavement below him until his knuckles were bleeding.

There was no saving her. As perfect as the weekend had been, the truth would not be held back. It reared its ugly head in fantastical fashion. This wasn't fair. Nothing about this was fair. Why did he have to meet her like this? The world just liked to torture him. Of course, it had been his decision to go meet her. It was his choice to invite her to the festival. It wasn't like he didn't know how sick she was. They could pretend all they wanted that she was normal, but death didn't care. It was still pulling at her and would take her sooner rather than later.

Another scream tore from him before he collapsed against a dumpster and just cried. Yet, despite it all, he wouldn't change any of the decisions he had made. Abel wouldn't regret meeting her or bringing her to the show, nor was he going to stop seeing her or talking to her. As stupid as it was, he had let this woman get to him, and he would be damned if he did to her what everyone else in her life had done.

"You going to be okay?" Derrik asked, taking a seat next to him against the dumpster. His friend bent his knees up and rested his arms on them.

"No," he answered. As much as he wanted to say he would be, deep down he knew nothing about this was okay.

"You aren't going to spiral on us. Are you?" the drummer asked next.

Abel hadn't even thought about the needle like that. His head had been focused on helping Alanna, not what that meant for him. "No, I'm not going to spiral. She needed me, and I knew what to do."

"Okay, I just wanted to check. A lot went on in there, and I needed to know what was actually happening," Derrik said. They sat there silently for a moment, and Abel could feel himself starting to calm down.

"I'm such a fucking idiot," Abel groaned, tossing another bottle to smash against the dumpster across from them.

"No, you aren't. For once in your life, you wanted to do something nice for someone, and you just got caught up in it. There's nothing wrong with that, but what are you going to do now?" Derrik asked, turning to look at him.

"I don't know. None of this was supposed to happen," Abel answered. "I feel like I'm losing my fucking mind."

"Yeah, well, you need to figure your shit out. Alanna is awesome and all, but you know how this ends. The band has to keep going after that," Derrik said next.

"I'm well aware. Look, I just needed to get this out of my system. Things happened so fast tonight that I just needed to get it out," Abel explained.

"Yeah, I get it. I'm going to head back and get a shower since, well, we are sitting in trash and god knows what else. I'll see you in a while," Derrik said, getting up and walking away.

Abel took a few more deep breaths, leaning back against the dumpster. He was already filthy, so staying there a few more minutes wasn't going to hurt anything. In the distance he could hear people partying and having a good time. All he wanted to do was scream or cry or kill something. Or find another way to escape the pain.

A shiver ran down his spine before he heard Alanna in his head whispering, "*Baby, it's poison.*" His whole body shook, but he fought it, desperate to calm down. Alanna needed him.

Finally pulling himself up from the ground, he walked back to the bus. He was exhausted and in desperate need of a shower.

No one said anything to him as he walked in and went back to his bedroom. He stood at the door for a few seconds before he braved going to the bed to check on Alanna. Terror filled him as he slowly reached out to touch her forehead. Warmth. She was warm. Letting out a sign of relief, he went to the bathroom and stripped down to shower. He smelled like stale alcohol and garbage and was covered in stuff he didn't want to think about.

Abel got lost in the ritual of washing his body and hair, letting the hot water soak into his skin. As the filth left his body, so did the intense emotions that had flooded him earlier. He just stood under the water, breathing and relaxing.

He jumped when he felt a tiny hand touch his shoulder and turned to see Alanna standing there. She was just outside of the shower, dressed in the pajamas he had managed to get her in before he had run off.

Her face was creased in a strange look that resembled something between pain and sleepiness. Unable to stop himself, he reached out and pulled her into the water with him. He could smell mint on her breath and knew she had taken time to clean up before reaching out to him. Water soaked her through as he kissed her with everything in him. He didn't want to talk. The last thing he wanted was to rehash the events from earlier. No, he just wanted to kiss her and hold her and have her in any way her body would allow.

He stripped off her clothes, and they fell to the floor of the shower with resounding plops until she was naked with him. Then he lifted her to wrap around him. Her whole body was still shaking, and he knew he was pushing her. But she wrapped her legs around him, and he simply couldn't bring himself to stop. Pressing her to the wall, he kissed her harder and deeper, fully taking in the taste of her. That was it. He wanted to taste her. He wasn't sure if her body was capable of making love to him, but they didn't have to do that.

With one hand, he turned off the shower and then carried her soaking wet to the bed and tossed her down. He threw her legs over his shoulders and leaned in to kiss the valley between her thighs as passionately as the full lips on her face. His hands roamed her body as he devoured her, drinking her in like she was the drug he craved most. That was it. She was a drug—a new drug he was falling victim to, and he was all too willing to submit himself to her.

He brought her to orgasm over and over with his mouth and tongue until she was pushing him away. Then he kissed his way up her body until he was kissing her lips once more. As much as he wanted to take her further, he knew they couldn't. So, he settled in next to her and pulled her into him.

For the first time, he saw the scars on her body. His fingers traced over them, and he realized he truly was blind to the reality. The first time he had seen her in person, he had seen the sickness, but through the course of that day, it had faded. When he looked at Alanna, he saw a woman he had never actually met. He saw the woman from the photo in his wallet.

"What is this," he asked, running his finger over a raised circular area on her chest.

"It's basically an IV port for treatment and medication," she answered.

"Oh, probably should have known about that sooner," he said, leaning down and kissing it.

"What are these from?" he asked. His fingers moved over the scars along her abdomen, and he watched her look down.

"They tried to cut out some of the cancer. They even took my ovaries which got a good chunk of it. It helped, but it had spread so much that they couldn't get it all," she answered. Alanna had explained to him before that the type of cancer she had was ovarian cancer, but even during that conversation he had not wanted to stay on the subject. It made the situation all too real, and he preferred it when they pretended she was healthy.

His hand trembled as he traced over those scars, letting himself actually think about the truth staring back at him. "I can find better doctors. I can get anyone in the world," he whispered, unable to look up at her.

"Abel," she breathed.

"You know, I don't see this when I look at you. I don't see the cancer," he said, his voice cracking with pain. "I can pay the best doctors in the world to make what I see real."

"I know, but the best doctors in the world can't work miracles," she whispered, and he finally turned to look up at her. "I waited too long. I didn't listen to my body and let it happen. There is no changing it now. Hell, I only agreed to do treatment for Hannah. I've known from the start what was coming."

"No, I refuse to accept this!" Abel yelled, sitting up and leaning over the edge of the bed to rest his head in his hands. "There has to be something I can fucking do."

"You did," she said, moving in behind him. It was apparently her turn to comfort him. "You have given me the best memories, the best experiences of my life. You made my biggest dream come true. You have no idea how much that has meant to me, and how much all of this is going to mean to Hannah and Lacey. You did this." Abel turned to look at her over his shoulder. "You made me happier than I have ever been, and there is nothing that I can ever do to thank you enough."

"This isn't fair," he whispered and pulled her closer so he could kiss her.

"Life has never been fair," she answered. "We can't change that. Now, can we try not to let this ruin what little time we have left in this weekend? I've had too good of a time to ruin it now."

He pulled her into him and kissed her hard and deep.

When he broke the kiss, he got up and went to a small box he kept in his cabinet. It held some of the jewelry he often wore on stage or just in general. Abel rummaged through the box for a moment, and then pulled out one of the rings before he went back to bed and held it out to her.

"Take this," he said. He knew it would be way too big for her, but he wanted her to have it.

"What is this?" she asked, taking it and looking it over. It was a black ring with engravings of silver skulls and crosses alternating around the band. Back when he first started touring, he would wear it during shows to boost his confidence. That was when he still questioned his strength after leaving prison. "I can't take this."

"You can, and you will," he said. "It is just something that used to make me feel strong, and then one day I didn't need it anymore. Now, it can give you strength."

He got back up and found an old chain. Once it was slid through the ring, he put the necklace on her before kissing her softly once more. The night was getting away from them, so he lay her back on the bed and curled up with her. They kissed as he held on to her. His heart ached, and he knew it was the result of all the mistakes he had made. He should have never answered that letter. He should have never invited her to the festival. He would never regret a moment of it.

CHAPTER THIRTEEN

ALANNA

They were in the car on the way home. When they'd woken up the next morning, she'd felt an ache in the pit of her stomach that she couldn't stand. The weekend was over, and it was time to return to reality. She didn't want to return to reality. Nothing good ever happened there. Before they left, she got to actually meet Leia Rice. She'd given Alanna some signed prints, and they took pictures together before they all had to get ready to leave.

As promised, Derrik had gotten Mason to print off the photo he took with his new tattoo and signed it just for Lacey. Alanna smiled seeing the young drummer crouched down and turned to the side to show off his leg. He had his hands up with his horns in the air and a silly almost screaming look on his face. It was a very rock star pose that she was sure Lacey would get a kick out of.

Before she left, she gave all the band members hugs, sad that she would probably never see them again. It had been a wonderful weekend, but she had known it wouldn't last. Before long the extensions would come out, the makeup would come off, and she would once again be just a dying woman living in a small house in Alabama. The last few weeks had felt like a dream, between meeting Abel and spending an exciting and far more sexual weekend together than she had ever imagined. She couldn't help but smile at the memory of it all as she leaned back against her seat.

Neither of them had brought up the incident from the night before. It had been a moment outside of the bubble that neither of them seemed ready to pop just yet. Music played from the radio as Abel sped along the road in the rented car. He had gotten something sensible to be less conspicuous, which meant it was also pretty comfortable. Alanna did tease him about it at first, though. They were about two hours into their trip before she finally braved talking about anything other than the fun time they had.

"Abel, we should really talk about what happened," she said, still looking out of the window.

He didn't say anything at first but finally answered, "What about it?"

"Look, I don't really know what happened, but I can't bear the thought of going home thinking I was just some sort of groupie," she finally said. It made her feel dirty just thinking about it.

"Alanna, you are not a groupie, and that is not what happened. I'm not really sure what happened either or how it happened, but it wasn't that," he answered, and she turned to look at him. "I wanted to be with you. No, I want to be with you. As stupid as it sounds, as fucked up as it is, I want you. When I was holding you, it was all I could think about. Not because you were just some warm body in my bed. No. It was because it was you."

"You know how this ends, though. I mean, why would you do that?" she asked and felt another ache pierce through her.

"Maybe I'm crazy. I don't know. What I do know is this weekend wasn't a mistake, and when I call you tomorrow and the next day and every day after until I see you again, those also are not mistakes. I'm not going to regret this. As much as the finality of it might say otherwise, there is a reason we are together right now, and I can't let it go," he said and reached over to take her hand.

"I don't want to hurt you," she whispered but lifted his hand to her lips and breathed him in. His knuckles were scraped up and scabbed. She wondered what happened, but she didn't ask.

This whole thing between them was insane and broke her heart a bit. The last thing she wanted was to make his life worse or be the reason he spiraled out of control. He had already shown her how difficult it was just to be around her medication. What happened when things progressed, and that medication became more necessary?

It didn't really matter. She was sure that once he went back on tour, he would slowly let go. Surely, he was smart enough to realize that continuing whatever this was would only lead to pain.

"You won't hurt me. You can't hurt me," he said and gave her the most beautiful smile. "Fuck I don't want this weekend to end."

She didn't either. While the edges of the bubble were growing weaker with every mile that passed, they were still there. Her heart started to pound in desperation to keep them in the bubble forever or at least a little while longer.

"Pull over."

"What? What's wrong?" he asked, a concerned look coming to his face.

"Well, last I checked it is pretty dangerous to climb on someone's lap when they're driving, so pull over," she answered, taking off her seatbelt and sliding out of her pants. She leaned over to kiss along his neck, not giving him much time to react.

"Fuck," he whispered but turned off the road and down some random dirt path to hide them from any oncoming traffic.

The moment the car was in park she crawled on top of him. He pushed the seat back as far as it would go as they began to kiss, hard and deep. Everything happened in a flurry, but she knew she had to have him. Even if it was the last time.

For the first time, they were truly alone, and neither of them held back. When she grew close, he all but growled in her ear for her to scream for him, and she did. Over and over as every wave of pleasure rippled over her body. No one had ever made her feel the way he did. Every nerve of her body was tingling, and she never wanted the moment to end.

"That was the most beautiful fucking sound I have ever heard," he whispered as he kissed her.

They were coming down from another high, and as much as she wanted to keep it going, she knew they couldn't.

He held her to him for several moments, just letting the two of them breathe, before she finally slid off of his lap and back into the passenger seat. For a second, she thought she heard him whisper something, but she didn't ask as they pulled themselves back together so they could get back on the road.

Once they were back to driving, he took her hand again and brought it to his lips to kiss it before lowering it, but he never let it go.

At some point she had fallen asleep, but when she woke, she recognized where she was. They were less than thirty minutes from her house, and all she wanted was for them to go back. Abel reached down to pick up his phone long enough to dial Hannah's number. He apparently hadn't realized yet that she was awake.

"Hey! How's the trip going?" Hannah asked as the call answered through the car speakers.

"It's going pretty smooth. We are about an hour or so away. Where are you at?" he answered, and Alanna couldn't help but wonder why he lied. The GPS had the time displayed. There was no way he didn't know how far away they were.

"Oh okay, well I am having to do something at Lacey's school, so I won't be there for a couple of hours. Are you still going to be there when I come by?" she asked.

"Yeah, I should be. I'm actually not sure if I'm going to leave today or wait and leave in the morning. I don't have a show until the day after tomorrow, so it isn't a big rush. The weekend was pretty busy so I'm pretty tired," he answered.

"Okay, well if you want to stay at Mom's, I can set you up when I get there. If not, I can point you to some nice hotels in the area. Just let me know when I come over, but right now I have to go," Hannah said.

"Sounds like a plan. See you later," Abel responded and then hung up the phone.

Alanna waited a moment before she spoke up, "You lied to her."

"What do you mean?" he asked, but she could see his wicked grin.

"We are like ten minutes from my house. Not an hour. Why did you tell her that?" she asked, shifting a bit to sit up better.

"Because I didn't want her to be there when we got there," he answered, and the look he gave her was not playful. It was full of lust that made her body start to burn.

"You're being rather presumptuous," she teased, trying to keep herself in check at least until they could get to the house.

"The weekend isn't over yet," he answered.

As soon as they were at her house and parked, he was around the car, pulling her out and picking her up. He kissed her all the way into the house and through each room, never letting her go. They hadn't bothered to get her stuff out of the car, but he didn't seem to have time for that. Not that she cared. They were keeping the bubble up and going, and no way was she going to stop him for something as trivial as getting her things out of the car.

She knew reality was waiting on the precipice just outside of their reach. It was beating at the bubble ready to break it open, but for a couple more hours, they kept it at bay. Alanna knew she was going to miss him, so she savored every touch and every kiss. Part of her wished she knew what he was thinking and feeling, but another part didn't. They lived in the moment which seemed like the best idea.

However, there came a time when they could no longer keep going. Her body was weak and tired. So, while she took her medicine, he went through the house and gathered their clothes so there was no evidence for Hannah to find when she came in.

"I'm going to stay the night if that's okay," he said as he put his pants on. Hannah would be there soon, and they had agreed that whatever had happened between them was staying that way.

"Okay, but I'm not making you dinner," she answered and laughed.

"Damn, I guess I will just have to find something else to eat," he teased and leaned in to kiss her.

She couldn't help but laugh and playfully swatted at him. "You're incorrigible."

"You love it," he answered.

A moment later they could hear Hannah calling from the other side of the house. Abel tossed on his shirt and ran his fingers through his hair. "Do I look okay?"

Alanna giggled and nodded. "Yeah, you look fine. Lucky for you, your hair is easy. You don't hold on to that fresh-fucked look."

He laughed a bit more and then slid out of the room as if he were trying to be quiet. From the other side of the door, Alanna could hear him talking to Hannah.

"Hey, she is going to take a nap. It has been quite a long weekend."

"Okay, well, I can come back later and check on her. I know yesterday wasn't an easy day," Hannah said.

"We got through it. She's doing much better today. It was just a long drive," he answered. "Speaking of. I think I am going to stay tonight, but I don't need you to do anything. There's a blanket on the couch. I can figure it out."

"Well, if you're sure," Hannah said, but she heard a hint of a question in her voice.

"I'm sure. Believe it or not, I have slept on a few couches in my day," Abel joked, and Alanna had to fight not to join him.

"Okay, okay, I get it. Well, if you need anything, let me know. I'm going to let Mom get some rest, and I'll check in with her later to hear all about the trip. Oh, and Abel, thanks for doing this for her. I know she had an amazing time," Hannah said.

A few more moments passed before Abel came back into the room. Alanna could hear Hannah's van driving away as Abel stripped down and slid into the bed next to her. He gathered her in his arms, kissed the top of her head, and they fell right to sleep.

Chapter Fourteen

Alanna

"So, one of the guys in the band, Derrik, he got this tattoo and then took a picture just for you," Alanna said to Lacey as she handed the photo over to her granddaughter. She had already put it in a frame so it wouldn't get messed up.

"He wrote on it," Lacey said as a huge smile spread over her lips.

"Yes, he did. He signed it for you. It says '*To Lacey, I bet you are one bad ass kid. Stay a rebel,*' and then he signed his name," Alanna said.

"He has my drawing," Lacey said next as she pointed at the tattoo.

"Yep, he sure does. He was a really cool guy," Alanna answered.

Hannah was helping go through all of the T-shirts and memorabilia Alanna had gotten at the festival. There was so much that they had to put a lot of the shirts into a trash bag to get them home. "What are we going to do with all of this?"

"I figure we can box most of it for Lacey for when she gets older," Alanna answered, pulling out a couple of the shirts she wanted the most.

"Yeah, I guess we can do that. You certainly can't hang them all up. You would end up just wallpapering the whole house." Hannah laughed.

"Very true, but we can hang up some of the photos I got," Alanna said, going through everything. Most of them would end up in an album of some sort, but she wanted to hang up and enjoy a few.

It had been a few of days since she got back, and true to his word, Abel called her every day. Most of the time he would call after his show, and they would talk for hours until she fell asleep. They still hadn't really put any kind of label on whatever was going on between them, but she could feel it building in her heart. It was dangerous, and she knew it. The last thing she wanted was for him to be hurt, but he was determined to keep up their relationship. And with death so close, she was selfish enough to hold on to it.

"Tomorrow we have your appointment, so try to get some good rest tonight," Hannah reminded her. Alanna didn't like going to the doctor anymore. She knew there was really nothing that could be done, but she went because it helped Hannah, and that mattered to her.

"While we are in Birmingham, I need to find someone to take these extensions out of my hair," Alanna said.

The hair was still holding up, but she knew the longer they stayed in, the more damage they were going to do. As much as she enjoyed having them, they weren't worth the effort now that she wasn't trying to look like a normal person.

The festival had been an amazing weekend pretending she had no worries in the world, but she was no longer in the bubble. Abel had made her feel beautiful and alive. For those few short days, it was like she had been transported back in time to a woman who was long gone. Alanna got so lost in her thoughts that she didn't realize Hannah was talking to her.

"You know, Mason called me," Hannah said when Alanna finally heard her.

"What do you mean?" Alanna asked, not sure what Hannah was talking about.

"When Abel took you on stage, Mason called me so I could watch it. I didn't realize how much I missed watching you sing. I was crying like a baby because you were incredible. My whole life, I've always seen you sing these songs, so full of passion and grit. It was like you could feel every word in your soul. Watching you sing with Abel on stage, it was hard not to wonder what kind of life you would have had if I hadn't come along and you'd had the chance to chase that dream," Hannah said.

Alanna reached over and cupped Hannah's cheek. "Baby, I wouldn't change anything. You were the best thing to ever happen to me. Yes, that was magical. For what, five minutes I got to be a rock star and sing in front of more people than I ever dreamed of, but if having that life meant giving you up, I wouldn't have made any other choice. You and Lacey are everything to me."

"I know, but I still always wonder. When you are on stage and when you sing, you're just a different person. I'm glad I have so many videos of you doing it because I want Lacey to be able to look back and see just how amazing her grandmother was," Hannah said then leaned over and wrapped her arms around Alanna. They hugged for a while before leaning back.

Feeling left out, Lacey rushed over and wrapped her arms around Alanna too. "Can I have one of the shirts?"

"Yes, pick out any one that you want. You can wear it as a night-gown," Alanna answered, and Lacey started going through the pile until she found the one she liked the most. It was for a band Alanna had enjoyed, Fortune of Regret.

"I swear she is a carbon copy of you." Hannah laughed.

"Nothing wrong with that, but it does mean you will have your hands full in a few years." Alanna laughed.

"Don't I know it," Hannah said.

"Well, you are certainly looking good. I think the trip did you some good," Dr. Carter said when she came into the room.

"You have no idea," Alanna answered.

Hannah had taken Lacey to the bathroom, so Alanna had a moment alone with the doctor, which she appreciated since she wanted to ask a personal question that she didn't want Hannah around for. "I need to ask you something before Hannah gets in here."

"Okay," Dr. Carter said before closing the door and standing near it to make sure it didn't just swing open. "What's up?"

"So, with everything going on with my body, is it dangerous for me to, ummm, you know, have sex?" Alanna asked. She hadn't noticed anything wrong, but it had been nagging at her brain and figured it was best to ask the expert.

"Oh, you had a really good time at the concert." Dr. Carter laughed a bit, and Alanna felt herself start to blush. "So long as it doesn't hurt or make you feel bad, enjoy your life. That is the best advice I have for you. So, go for it."

"Thank you," Alanna said and pulled out her phone. "So, this is Abel Sharp, the guy who took me to the festival.

"Wow, that is a lot of ink, but he is also very handsome. Good for you, girl," the doctor said. Alanna flipped through a few of the pictures, and Dr. Carter seemed to enjoy getting to see them. But soon enough it was time for them to get to the reason for the appointment. "Okay, I want you to come back in a couple of days and do some scans and follow up tests. I just want to get a better idea of where we are with everything. How are you feeling overall?"

"Most of the time I'm just really tired, which is probably because of the meds and all that," Alanna answered.

"Yeah, the medication you are on is bound to make you tired. It's a good thing that you aren't having too many other issues. It's another reason for the scan. Maybe things have slowed down," Dr. Carter added, writing notes in Alanna's chart.

One thing she liked about Dr. Carter was the fact she was very honest with her. Some doctors would try to feed fake hope, but that wasn't what Alanna wanted. She wanted the truth regardless of how much it hurt.

"Since you aren't seeming to be getting worse, let's keep the medication as it is. Once we have the scans back, we can talk about if we need to do any more rounds of treatment or what direction we want to go in from there. For now, like I said, if it doesn't seem to bother you, and it makes you happy, enjoy it. There is no point being miserable," Dr. Carter explained.

"Thank you," Alanna answered.

"Of course, oh and, yeah, I would have enjoyed a weekend with that guy too. Good for you," Dr. Carter added.

Alanna was laughing as the doctor left. Hannah walked in with Lacey, and she shot Alanna a confused look.

"Did I miss something?" Hannah asked.

"No, not really. She is setting me up with some scans and stuff, but for now everything is good. Ready to get out of here?" Alanna said, sliding off of the table.

"Sorry I wasn't in here during the appointment," Hannah answered, taking Alanna's arm to help keep her steady.

"You do realize I'm a grown ass woman. I don't need a babysitter to sit with me while I'm in the doctor's office," Alanna answered.

They laughed as they made their way to Hannah's van. Alanna had set up a hair appointment to have the extensions removed, and then they were going to go shopping. As the hair was removed, they realized it had caused more damage than they had hoped. It left Alanna's head patchy, which disheartened her. Tears streamed down her face as she watched clump after clump fall from her scalp and to the floor. It wasn't enough that she was dying. No, fate had to take everything from her along the way.

"Hey, I know a place that sells these beautiful head scarves for people in your situation. They aren't far from here, and I'm sure you can find some nice stuff. A lot of my clients find they like the scarves more because of how hot it is here. Wigs can get too hot and itchy," the stylist said as she continued to work.

"That would be nice," Alanna answered, trying not to feel brokenhearted at the loss of her once gorgeous hair. Abel certainly wouldn't see her as beautiful now that she was going bald.

They drove to the store the stylist suggested, and true to her word, the lady who owned the shop had created some beautiful headpieces. Alanna got several, and the owner took time with her to show her how to put them on and wear them. Though she missed her hair, the scarves did help her feel pretty.

"I love the purple one," Lacey said, holding the thin fabric in her hands.

"I like it too. I like all of them," Alanna answered. They bought some in several different colors, and she left wearing a lovely red and gold one.

With the shopping out of the way, they detoured to the park for lunch and so Lacey could get some of her energy out. While she sat at a table and watched Hannah and Lacey play, Alanna decided to take a picture of herself. There was good lighting and the backdrop of the tree behind her gave a good setting. After snapping a few photos, she sent one to Abel in a text.

> Got some new head pieces today. Not as pretty as my hair, but I like them.

It took a few minutes before she got a response, but when her phone beeped, she checked it to find a picture of Abel without a shirt on and his hair wet.

> You are the most beautiful woman in the world. I love the wrap. You will have to tell me all about it when I call after the show. For now, I'm on my way to be a thirst trap to all these women who came to see me. Think I can pull it off?

His words explained the sexy photo and made her laugh so loud that Hannah came over to see what was going on. Alanna let her see the phone, and her daughter rolled her eyes and laughed before going back to the playground.

> Yes, you are one sexy man. Go knock 'em dead. I'll talk to you tonight.

His only response was an emoji of a kiss, but it was enough. He had a way of making her feel special and beautiful even when she felt the most defeated. As she continued to watch Hannah and Lacey play, Alanna realized that, despite how much she knew it would hurt the people she cared about when this all came to an end, she was having the best time of her life.

Her mind thought about what Abel had said. They had met for a reason. There was a reason they had come together no matter how much it seemed like a bad idea. She knew that meeting him meant more than a pity visit and random excursion to a festival. The fact he continued to talk to her after leaving was proof of that.

Before long, both Lacey and she were tired, and it was time for them to head home. The car ride was quiet, and she spent a lot of it sleeping. Apparently, Lacey had as well. When she got home, all she wanted to do was sit in her music room and listen to songs until Abel called. Oh, how she looked forward to those calls every night.

CHAPTER FIFTEEN
ABEL

The remainder of the tour was not nearly as eventful as the festival. He only had a few weeks left, and by the time it was over, he was ready for a break. It had been more than a month since he had gone home to see his daughter, and he was missing her terribly. Summer was in full swing, and being off of the East Coast was a blessing. However, a part of him thought of taking a detour to visit Alanna.

They talked every day, most of the time doing video calls. He would stay on the phone with her until she fell asleep and sometimes, he would even just sit there and watch her sleep for a bit before ending the call. She had become an obsession for him, but he didn't really talk to anyone about it. Alanna kept trying to push him away a bit. It wasn't that she didn't want to talk to him or see him. He knew it was her way of trying to protect him. Not that it mattered. There had never been a time in his life when he didn't know what the fuck he wanted, and that certainly wasn't going to start now.

As he walked toward baggage claim, he saw his daughter waiting for him, and a huge smile spread over his lips. She looked a lot like him—tall, black hair, just a hint of a tan. Sometimes he had to fight back the urge to slap a chastity belt on her. The idea of her being older now and dating always turned his stomach. He remembered being her age, and he was very sure guys hadn't changed since then.

"Dad!" she exclaimed and threw her arms around him. He hugged her close for several moments, glad to have her there.

"Damn, you have got to stop getting prettier. I'm not allowed to own a gun to shoot the boys after you," he said and kissed her cheek before going to grab his bags.

"You do realize I'm an adult now. Right?" Briar said laughing.

"Doesn't mean I have to like it," he answered and walked with her out to the car.

Once they were settled, and he was driving out of the airport toward home, Briar brought up the question he didn't really want to talk to her about, "So what's up with the girl?"

"What girl?" he asked, hoping to avoid having a very uncomfortable conversation with his far too curious daughter.

"The girl you took to the festival in Florida. Come on, Dad, it's been all over the media," she answered, putting her phone in view so he could see the article.

"*Mystery Girl Spends Weekend with Abel Sharp.*" There was a picture of them together, and it made his chest hurt. It was the last show when he was holding her in the chair. Alanna was so tired and really needed to go back to bed, but she wanted to finish the show, so he'd stayed there with her. That night had turned bad, but he very much remembered that specific moment. It had all felt perfect and beautiful in all of its tragedy.

"Remember how I went to see that fan instead of coming home?" he asked, figuring if anyone deserved the truth, it was her.

"Yeah, I figured that was her," Briar answered.

"It is. I don't know. We clicked really well, and she just deserved to have something really special. You have no idea just how amazing this woman is, and she doesn't have a lot of time left," Abel explained.

For all the songs he had written in his life and all the hardship he had endured, he could not seem to put to words the relationship he was building with Alanna.

"Well, that was pretty cool of you," Briar answered, but he could hear the question in her voice. She knew it was more than him showing a sick woman a good time. "So, what are you going to do?"

"I have no idea. I really like this woman, and I like spending time with her," he answered.

"Yeah, Derrik was telling me that you call her all the time," Briar answered, and he realized she knew more than she was leading on.

"Since when do you talk to Derrik?" he asked, trying to change the subject.

"He's in your band. That's a stupid question," Briar answered. "So, tell me about her."

Abel took a deep breath and then proceeded to tell her about Alanna. He told her about her singing and performing and how her life had been hard. She listened as he went into the details he knew about her getting sick and then the letter Hannah had sent him. While he left out how far he had taken their relationship, he did tell his daughter just how much he was starting to feel for the woman. It was difficult to reconcile his emotions because he knew the end was coming, and pain would win.

"Do you think it's a good idea for you to be continuing this with her? I mean, things are new with the two of you. You could still walk away," Briar said. She was being rational, and nothing about him had been rational since he got that letter.

"I can't do that. You don't understand. I just can't," he answered. Every man in her life had walked away from her. The last thing he would do was be like them.

"You really are an all in kinda guy," she laughed. "So, when are you going to see her again?"

He hadn't honestly thought about it. His first thought was to get home to Briar. Alanna had told him not to stop living his life, and being there for his daughter was too important for him to push to the back burner, regardless of the situation. "I'm home to see you for a while."

"Dad, I'm a big girl and don't need you all the time. I'm still going to be here, but if you really care for this woman, it might be a good idea to go spend time with her while you can. Now, I'm not saying I fully approve of this, because I don't like the idea of you being sad, but I know you. Once you have your heart set on something you do it," Briar said.

"Are you sure?" he asked. Briar was home for the summer. He had taken off as well so they could spend time together. It had been his whole plan up until a month or so ago.

"I'm very sure," she answered.

He gave his daughter a smile, and then reached over and pulled her into a half side hug, which was the best he could do while driving. "When did you get so smart."

"I don't know, but I am in college now, so that probably has something to do with it," she answered.

"Hey, can you pick me up from the airport tomorrow?" Abel asked Hannah when she answered the phone.

"What are you talking about?" she asked, and he could hear her shuffling around. In the distance he could hear Alanna singing with who he could only assume was Lacey given the tone of childishness that accompanied it.

"I'm coming out to see Alanna and wanted to know if you could pick me up at the airport. I can rent a car, but that is a pain in the ass since I would need to return it once I got there," he said, packing up his suitcase with fresh clothes.

He hadn't even been home long enough to fully unpack. Instead, he dumped everything out and started on a fresh batch.

"I don't think that is a good idea," Hannah said. "Look, what you did for my mom was wonderful. It has made her so happy, and I think it has made what is coming a lot easier for her to face. But you getting more involved is not smart. Do you really understand what you are getting into?"

"Yes, I'm fully aware of what I'm doing," he answered.

He heard a door close and could no longer hear the singing in the background.

"No, I really don't think you do. Abel, she is dying. It could be months, it could be weeks, it could be days for all we know, but either way she is dying. There is no changing that, and you getting more involved is just going to hurt you in the end. I can't not be a part of this. I'm her daughter, and she is part of my world. You just came into it. Walk away. It's the best thing for you."

Like everyone else, Hannah was trying to protect him with facts and reason. None of that mattered. He wasn't thinking with his head. "I'm coming to visit. Now, will you pick me up? Or do I need to rent a car? Either way, it's happening, and nothing you can say will change my mind."

"Ugh, fine," Hannah huffed. "Send me your details, and I will pick you up. But I'm serious here. You are just heading down a bad path."

"I know," he answered and then hung up.

Once Mason had all of the flight details, Abel forwarded them to Hannah, who responded with a thumbs up. He tripped over some of the clothes he had thrown on the floor and cursed as he fell onto the bed.

"Hey, Dad, is Alanna's daughter's name Hannah?" Briar asked, coming into the room with her phone in her hands sideways.

"Yeah, why?" he asked.

"She apparently has a YouTube. Look at this," Briar said and passed the phone over.

He had watched several of Hannah's videos, and she was still posting them, keeping her viewers abreast of the situation going on with her mom.

"Hey, guys! So, as I told you, my mom went to a big music festival in Florida. I wasn't really a fan of the idea of her going, but she really wanted to go, and I knew she would be well taken care of. For those of you have been following me for a while, you know just how much she adores Abel Sharp and Louder in Silence. You also know I wrote him a letter to tell him about her. Well, he is the one that took her to the show, and he did the most amazing thing for her. I swear to all of you, I sat here crying while his manager or whoever the guy is video called me. So, it's been a while, but here is my mom, Alanna Grace, performing once more," Hannah said into the camera before it cut to the video Mason had taken of them singing on stage together.

While he had been sitting right next to her, they had both been so caught up in singing together that he hadn't been able to really appreciate it. She had given her all. Sick, tired, and falling apart, she sang each word with such deep passion that he had to fight the tears forming in his eyes. She was beautiful and magical, a rare treasure.

Once the video was over, he looked through some of the comments and smiled reading some of the support people were showing. Hannah didn't have a big channel. It certainly wouldn't have come up on his radar had she not written to him, but this video had gotten a lot of views, and he was sure her channel had grown from it. What would the viewers do when there were no more videos of Alanna to post? It was just one more thing for him to pile on the hill of topics he wasn't ready to talk about.

"She was really good," Briar said when he handed the phone back.

"She really is. I'm going to have to do more singing with her while I'm visiting," he answered and kissed his daughter on the cheek. "You sure you're okay with me doing this?"

"Yes, I'm one hundred percent okay with this. In fact, if you don't, I will be mad at you because you will just be wallowing around here like a miserable asshole. Besides I'm just going to throw wild parties here while you're gone," she said.

He knew she was joking, but he gave her the "I dare you to try" look before pulling her in and ruffling up her hair. "You know, you are too much like me for your own good."

"Hopefully I only got all the good parts." She laughed.

"I don't know, your mouth certainly is spicy," he said, getting up to zip up his bags.

"Well, I don't consider that bad," she continued. "So, I'll drive you to the airport in the morning. Do you need me to do anything while you're gone?"

"Yeah, don't throw wild parties at my house. If you are going to do that, throw them at your mom's house," he called after her as she walked out.

"Nope! She's home!" she yelled from down the hall.

CHAPTER SIXTEEN
ABEL

Hannah had picked him up against her better judgment. They didn't say a lot on the ride to Alanna's house, and honestly, he was thankful for it. He was so focused on getting to Alanna and figuring out whatever he was doing with her while he was there. If things were different, maybe he would have been able to do more. Of course, if things were different, they would have never met.

When he got out of the van, he didn't hear the music playing throughout the place like he had the first time he had come to visit. Instead, he heard the piano coming from Alanna's music room. Warmth filled him as he followed the sound of her voice until he was standing in the doorway watching her. She belted out a song as if it was bleeding from her very soul. He had heard it in passing but never enough to say he knew it. She did, though. The sound of her voice echoed through the room as she sang. It was heartbreaking and powerful and made him wish he knew the words so he could sing it with her.

Alanna's eyes were closed, and her fingers danced over the keys of the piano with expert skill. She had told him it was the only instrument she had managed to learn, but it was a difficult one. She made it look easy. He leaned against the doorjamb and just watched her, entranced by her song. Abel hadn't told her he was coming, having wanted it to be a surprise, but it turned out he was the one surprised.

Hannah came up behind him and lightly touched his shoulder. "She has been doing this since getting back from her trip with you. I thought she was losing her voice, but with you she found it again. Look, I don't really approve of all of this because I know you are going to get hurt in the end, but I know you are making her life better, so I can't be angry about that."

They talked so quietly, and Alanna sang so loudly that she didn't notice they were talking at all until she finished the song. She was panting as if running a marathon and sat there shaking for several moments before looking up. Apparently, that was when she noticed the change in the lighting and air pressure and turned toward the door. A huge smile spread over her lips when she saw him.

"Hey, baby," she said, and just the tone of her voice sent a shiver down his spine.

Her smile made her whole body light up. She had wrapped a green and yellow scarf around her head and the tail hung over her shoulder as if it were a ponytail. She was dressed in a pair of yoga pants and one of the concert shirts she had gotten in Florida, and all he could think was that she was the most beautiful thing he had ever laid eyes on.

Abel grinned at her as he moved closer. "Hey, baby," he answered before kissing her cheek.

Hannah was there, so they had to keep things a little more PG. Last he knew, they weren't telling her daughter just how far things had gone between them.

"You just like surprising me. Don't you?" she said and got up so they could hug. He could swear she had lost more weight, but he didn't want to think about it.

"Well, it's a good surprise. Isn't it?" he answered.

"A very good surprise. How long are you here for?" she asked, her hand cupping his cheek. Damn he wanted to kiss her, and it was taking everything in him not to.

"I don't know. Until I feel like going home. Briar kicked me out. She said she's going to throw a rager while I'm gone," he answered, and she broke out in laughter. "Yeah funny, she is going to die if I come home to a trashed house."

"You would do no such thing." Alanna giggled.

"Hey, Mom, we still have Lacey's thing tonight. Do you feel up to going?" Hannah asked from the door.

"Yeah, I feel wonderful. Abel, do you mind going to see Lacey sing at school. Her class is doing one last performance before they let out for summer," Alanna said.

"What do I need to wear?" he responded, and they walked out of the building so he could get his stuff and take it into the house.

"Most of the parents and grandparents are going to be in like Sunday clothes, but since I didn't have a chance to say anything, I think just you being there will be good enough," Alanna answered.

"I can come up with something," he answered. He didn't have a lot of "Sunday clothes," considering he wasn't one to go to church, but he did know how to clean himself up when he needed to.

"Well, I need to get Lacey ready for tonight. Abel, my mom has a car. She just isn't allowed to drive with the medicine she's on, but you are welcome to use it while you're here. I can text you the address to the school, and you guys can meet us there. It starts at five thirty," Hannah explained.

"Sounds perfect," Abel answered, getting the last of his stuff out of the car and carrying it in the house.

As soon as they were inside, and Hannah was gone, he swept Alanna up in his arms and kissed the hell out of her. Unable to stop himself, he lifted her up and set her on the kitchen counter so he didn't have to lean down so much. His hunger for her had brought him to insanity. He wasn't sure if they had time for what he wanted to do. Hell, he didn't even know if she was feeling well enough to do what he wanted, but he planned to take his time kissing her, touching her, and hopefully making love to her. She tasted like heaven. No, she tasted like the only drug he had let himself indulge in for nearly twenty years.

"God, I missed you," Alanna said when he finally pulled away to let her breathe. Her hands were fisted in his shirt, and her whole body was shaking.

"I've missed you, too," he added. "I went home. I had planned to spend time there for a bit before coming back to see you, but my daughter said she would rather me be here with you."

"So, you told her?" Alanna asked.

"Yeah, I told her," he answered and then started kissing her again. Maybe if he tried hard enough, he could just kiss the sickness out of her. It was stupid, but part of him wanted to believe he could do it. "I need you."

"Yes," she whispered and took hold of his shirt, pulling it over his head and tossing it to the ground. He did the same to her and then picked her up again to carry her farther into the house. Her legs wrapped around his waist, but he held under her ass to support her.

Once in the living room, he set her down just so they could finish stripping down. What was it about this woman that made him lose all control of himself? He couldn't keep his hands off of her... or lips, for that matter. His hunger only grew more and more the longer he was in her presence, and as soon as they were naked, he pulled her down on top of him on the couch. Her legs fell to either side of him as she rubbed herself against him.

One of his hands slid up her spine and gripped behind her neck while the other rocked her hips against him, making him want more. "Fuck, baby, don't just tease me. I need you."

She chuckled a bit and then shifted, lifting herself enough to let him slide inside her. He growled at the sensation, and his head fell back, shivering when she cried out as well. She braced herself on him, and they found a rhythm with each other. Those skillful rolls of her tummy let her stomach constrict, which had her tightening on him. Abel loved just how hot and tight his woman was, and he couldn't get enough of her.

The intensity of his need for her had him craving more. He wrapped his arms around her and flipped them until he was on top of her and could take control of their love-making. He lifted her legs up higher, tossing them over his shoulder so she was angled in such a way that he could push deeper. Her back arched beautifully, and he leaned in to lick and suck on her nipples, alternating between them. Her chants and cries of pleasure sent electric shockwaves down his spine.

"I need you to... I need to come so bad," he panted, kissing her and swallowing down her moans of passion. "Fuck, please."

She gasped his name and made him ravenous. He lost his control, thrusting harder and faster into her, building them until he felt her start to spasm and she screamed out. The sound echoed through the room as her nails scraped down his back. He roared out as his body tensed and pulsed, his release flowing deep into her body and hers milked up every drop of ecstasy inside of him.

Spent he rolled to the side and pulled her into him so they wouldn't fall off of the couch. They lay there panting and catching their breath for several minutes, his lips brushing over her temples and softly caressing her lips from time to time. "I know we need to get ready to go out, but fuck I had to have you. I have thought of nothing else since the last time I saw you," Abel said, his voice still heavy.

"I'm not complaining, not at all, but we should get a shower," she suggested.

"Only if we take it together," he teased, kissing her more passionately again. He was certainly going to have her again in the shower and as many times as possible while he could.

CHAPTER SEVENTEEN

ABEL

B irmingham was a big enough city that he didn't look completely out of place. Sure, he still had more tattoos than most of the people there. To be fair, he had more than most people period, but at least in Birmingham it wasn't completely out of the norm to have them.

However, the little town that Alanna and her family lived in was outside of Birmingham. When he stepped out of the car at Lacey's school, he could instantly feel all eyes on him. It was too hot for him to wear a jacket, so he'd put on black jeans and a black button-up. His hair was brushed nice and slick, damp from the shower but still loose. In all honesty, he'd dressed for Alanna, not small-minded town folk.

Abel opened the door for Alanna and held out his hand to help her out of the car. She was wearing a green and yellow summer dress that matched her scarf. She had fastened a belt around her waist to give it some shape since it was much too big for her after all the weight she had lost. They looked like quite an odd couple as he held her hand and walked with her to the doors of Lacey's small elementary school.

"Sir, do you have a student here?" a woman that he assumed was a teacher said at the door.

"Yes, my granddaughter goes here," he said without missing a beat. It was a lie, but he really didn't want to argue.

"We are Lacey Reading's grandparents," Alanna said next to him.

"Oh, Alanna. I didn't recognize you, and I didn't know you were married," the woman at the door said.

"Well, it has been a while since I came to the school," Alanna answered.

"It has. How are you feeling?" the woman asked, that tone of pity filling her voice.

"Like I want to go in and watch my granddaughter sing," Alanna answered, and she pulled on his arm to lead him past the woman.

They had only made it a little further before another woman who was much younger, maybe early twenties, stopped them. "Alanna! Oh, you look so nice! We are missing Hannah so much. I hope things are starting to get better," she said, giving Alanna a hug.

Hannah had worked at the school before Alanna got sick. Since then, she has been on leave.

"Hey, Missy, things are going. That is all I can really say," Alanna answered.

"Well, it is still good to see you," the woman said before turning toward him. She gave him a curious look and then said, "Has anyone ever told you that you look exactly like Abel Sharp. He's the lead singer of this band I like."

He had to fight laughing and then leaned down and whispered in her ear, "That's because I am Abel Sharp."

The girl gasped, and he chuckled as they made their way toward the cafeteria, which was being used as the auditorium for the show. A small stage had been decorated with giant fake flowers, clouds, and a big sun with sunglasses on it. On one side, there was even a cardboard surfboard, sand dune, and little fake waves blew in the wind of a small fan that was just off to the side. On the other side were a couple of overly large butterflies and bumblebees. It reminded him of when Briar was little, and he went to her school functions.

"You know, you probably gave Missy a heart attack back there," Alanna whispered to him as they found Hannah and went to take a seat next to her.

Abel assumed the man with her was her husband.

"Yeah, but it was fun," he answered.

"Abel, this is my husband Brandon," Hannah said, and the two men shook hands.

"I've heard a lot about you, both before and since you and Alanna started spending time together," Brandon said.

"Well, don't believe everything you hear. Most of it is worse than they tell you," he answered, and the other man laughed. If only he knew the truth. Most of the crap he got into never made it to the news or social media. Mason was good at cleaning up his messes.

"Lacey has a solo, and she is so proud of it," Hannah said, handing over a small program that was little more than a piece of paper folded in half. The front had a pretty spring picture with the name of their little show on it. Inside was the order of the songs along with the list of all the kids who would be in it. When he saw Lacey's name, he smiled, though he wasn't really sure why.

The room filled up quickly, and he continued to get questioning looks, but no one else dared say anything to him. What bothered him more were the looks that Alanna got. Everyone knew what was going on with her, and they all had a look of pity and even shame. They felt sorry for her, but she didn't seem to notice. If she did, she certainly didn't let on that she did. Her head was resting against his shoulder, and he slouched down a bit so she would be a little more comfortable.

The lights dimmed and the show began. It was everything you would expect from a kindergarten class. They sang badly and fumbled around trying to do their dances. Some of the kids were obviously only there because they were forced to be. Others were showoffs, wanting to be seen and heard over all the other kids. Lacey was a bit in the middle. The only time she really stood out was when she stepped out in front for her solo.

Even with how young she was, Abel was impressed. When he watched her sing, he saw Alanna. It was like she was a five-year-old carbon copy of the woman at his side. Lacey knew tone and how to hold her notes. She projected on point. The girl was a talent in the works, and his mind raced with how he would love to help nurture that into something more. Briar was talented too, but she didn't love music like he did. His daughter sang with him because she liked singing with him, not because she wanted to be a singer.

When the show was over, they all stood up and applauded. His heart was filled with pride as if he really was there to see his granddaughter. Briar certainly shouldn't be having kids any time soon, but he could live vicariously through Alanna's family. When the lights came back on, the kids all ran out into the crowd. Lacey raced for her mom and dad first but then turned toward him and Alanna.

"Abel! You came! Did you see me sing!" the small girl asked.

"I did, and you were amazing. Your dad filmed it, and I'm going to get a copy and show my daughter," he said, squatting down so he could talk to her on her own level.

"Thank you! Are you coming to get ice cream with us?" she asked next.

He looked over at Alanna, who shrugged, and then he turned back to the girl. "I don't usually eat ice cream, but I will come along and see what I can find. How does that sound?"

"You don't have to if you don't want to," Hannah said.

"I don't mind at all. Come on, kid, let's go get ice cream. What's your favorite flavor?" he asked, taking Lacey's hand and walking with her out of the cafeteria.

A boy came over to Lacey and gave her a hug. "Have a good summer!"

"You too! This is Abel. He has drawings on him that don't come off," Lacey said.

He shook his head. She really was stuck on that.

"Wow!" the boy said and held his hand out. Abel shook the little boy's hand until his parents dragged him away, shooting him a dirty look.

"Lacey, I don't think the people here understand my tattoos. How about we just go get some ice cream?" he suggested.

He helped her into the van and then took Alanna to the car. Hannah had given him the location, and he put it in the GPS. Alanna was pretty alert, but he didn't want to depend on her to tell him how to get places when he could just use the GPS.

"You lied to the principal back there," Alanna said, and he wasn't sure what she meant.

"Lied about what?" he asked, confused.

"You told her you were Lacey's grandfather," she said, and her voice caught a bit. He had honestly forgotten about it until she mentioned it.

"Yeah, I figured it was a bit easier than trying to explain the whole story, and I seemed to make a lot of people uncomfortable," he answered.

"Fuck 'em. They don't know what they're missing." Alanna laughed.

It didn't take long to get to the ice cream parlor. It was on what looked like the town square and resembled the old soda shops from the fifties. Once again, he helped Alanna out of the car and walked with her into the shop. Lacey had her face pressed to the glass where all the ice cream was stored. It didn't take him long to realize there was nothing there he could have, but he didn't care.

"You want an ice cream?" he asked Alanna quietly.

"No, not really, but I'll get one so Lacey doesn't feel bad," she answered.

"Okay," he answered and walked up to the glass.

Alanna picked out her one scoop, and he just got himself a soda. He would certainly be hungry later, but he could sit through a little family time first.

"Why didn't you get any ice cream?" Lacey asked when they sat down.

"Well, I don't eat ice cream," he answered.

"Why? It's good," Lacey asked next.

"Because I'm vegan. So, I don't eat meat or anything that comes from animals," he explained.

"Ice cream doesn't come from animals. It comes for the grocery store," Lacey said as if that made all the sense in the world.

"I'll explain it to you later." Hannah laughed. "Thank you guys for coming."

"Wouldn't have missed it for the world. Hey, Lacey, you should come hang out, and we can play music together," Abel suggested.

"Can I, Mommy?" Lacey asked.

"How about tomorrow?" Hannah answered.

"Tomorrow is perfect," Abel responded.

Everyone finished their ice cream, except Alanna, who just let hers melt into soup. He could tell she was getting tired and was ready for some quiet. On the drive home, she softly sang along with whatever song played on the radio, but she didn't say much. His head was racing with questions, but he let it so she could have her moment of peace after an afternoon with loud children and rude adults.

Chapter Eighteen

Alanna

She woke to the sound of music playing, not over her speakers but from outside. Pulling on her robe, she made her way through the house and out onto the porch. She could see the door of her music room open, and the sound of the piano echoed from inside. Then she heard him start to sing. Warmth spread through her body, and a smile softly lifted on her lips.

It had only been a couple of hours since they had gotten back from Lacey's show, but the nap had been a necessity. Everyone always looked at her with such sadness and pity-filled expressions. Most of the time the only people who didn't look at her like that were Lacey and Abel. Even Hannah had a tendency of wearing a face of sorrow when she was around her. The last thing she wanted was for people to feel sorry for her. Life was life, and she had just gotten a short one.

Padding around the pool, she went into her music room and sat down next to Abel while he played. He didn't stop singing, just kept going though he did look over at her and gave her a small smile. She knew the song. She could have sung along, but she didn't want to. She wanted to hear him sing it for her. She heard so much pain in his voice, and at certain points it cracked into a distorted mix of singing and screaming that sent chills down her spine. His talent was beyond what any mortal man should be capable of.

When he finished the song, he leaned over and kissed the top of her head. "I'm starving," he said, and she giggled a bit.

"Yeah, I don't have much to eat here," she answered. "We will need to go to the store to get you some food for while you are here. I'm not exactly a vegan friendly house."

"Do you feel up to going to the store? If not, I can order something," he said, reaching over and taking her hand.

"A lot of places don't deliver out here. I can't even get a pizza. We either go to the store or you starve to death," she answered.

He laughed and kissed her. "Then to the store we go. This should be fun."

They got up and she went to change. He had put his casual clothes back on but grabbed a hat and a hoodie. "You know you won't be able to wear that. You will melt."

"I don't know how you stand it living in this swamp," he groaned, tossing the hoodie on the chair.

"You get used to it," she answered.

"I will never get used to this," he answered and then came over to help her fasten her scarf. Once she was finished, he took a moment to run a finger over her cheek. "I like the scarves and the short hair. It's very hippie."

"You don't miss the long hair from the festival?" she asked, looking down and feeling ashamed that more of the things she felt made her pretty were fading away.

"No, you are beautiful no matter what. That is never going to change," he answered and gave her the first real kiss since she woke up. They stood there in the middle of her living room, kissing and forgetting that they had plans for several moments before he pulled away. "Yeah, I'm still starving. We will have to come back to this later."

Once inside the car, he pulled up the GPS so he could input the directions for the store. "Is there one that might be a bit easier for me to go to without causing any kind of scene?"

"The one that would cause less of a scene won't have enough food for you. Sorry, but you are going to have to go all the way into town to Walmart."

He groaned and gave her the most uncomfortable look. "You don't have anything like Whole Foods or World Market or anything?"

"You know, for a bad ass rock star, you sure are a baby about your food. Come on. I thought you said you were hungry. Walmart will work just fine," she answered but couldn't stop laughing.

The store was nearly twenty minutes from her house, and before they got there, he swung through a drive-through to get himself something to eat. She just grabbed some French fries and nibbled on them a bit. Most of the time she wasn't hungry and would just supplement with nutritional shakes. Her doctor had said it was pretty normal for the stage she was in. Abel certainly made up for it as he ate with one hand and drove with the other.

When they got to the store, he parked and then told her to stay in the car. She wasn't sure why until he came back with one of the wheelchair carts they offered for customers. It made her smile that he thought of things like that without having to wait to see if she was tired. She didn't think she would need it, but she got into the chair anyway. Once she was settled, he pulled his long hair back and put the hat on his head. It didn't really disguise him much. He stood out like a black bean in rice.

It was an odd experience being out with him in her small town. She could never figure out if people were giving her strange looks or him. It was probably a little bit of both, but it still made her uncomfortable.

Abel didn't seem bothered by it as he went about putting various things in the cart. "Hey, do you like mango?"

"I do," she answered, and watched as he put a package in the cart without another word.

From the other side of the produce stand, Alanna could hear a couple of girls whispering about them. "There is no way that is him."

"Who else would have tattoos like that, and the hair. No, it has to be him," the other girl answered.

Reaching out, she got Abel's attention and had him lean down so she could talk to him. "I think some girls over there recognize you."

"Where?" he asked, his eyes darting around.

"Well, if you are so sure, go talk to him," one of the girls said and he grinned.

Standing back up, he went back to shopping but kept an eye out for the girls. Apparently one of them finally got the nerve to say something to him. "Umm, excuse me, but you're Abel Sharp. Aren't you?"

The girl couldn't have been more than fourteen years old. Maybe sixteen if she was there without her parents. She had her hair pulled up in a ponytail and was wearing shorts and a tank top—the staple clothing for summer in Alabama.

"I am," he answered and held his hand out. "You are?"

"Amanda, I'm such a big fan of yours. My parents hate it," she answered, and he laughed a bit.

"Do you want a picture?" Alanna asked, holding her hand out for the girl's phone.

"Regan, it is!" Amanda said, and her friend came over to shake Abel's hand too. Amanda handed over her phone, and the three of them got ready to take the picture.

"Take your hat off, Abel. Give the girls a good picture," Alanna said then a moment later took a couple of pictures. She handed the phone back, and the teens raced off in pure excitement.

"You know, I don't usually do that when I'm out," he said, squatting down and putting his hat back on.

"Well, it isn't like you get around here much, and most of the people here don't even know who you are. Taking a second to make a couple of teenagers' day doesn't hurt," Alanna said, and he shook his head before taking hold of the chair and leading her further into the store.

When they got to the baking aisle, Alanna saw vegan marshmallows and chocolate and got an idea. "Baby, get those," she said pointing to the bag of marshmallows.

He gave her a curious look before putting the bag in the cart. She was able to reach the chocolate from where she was and tossed a couple of bars into the cart as well. "What are you up to?"

"When was the last time you had smores?" she asked, and he smiled.

"I'll have to see if I can find the cookies. This store doesn't have a lot to work with, but I'm finding some stuff," he answered. The cart was nearly full, so she wasn't sure what he was complaining about. He was probably just being difficult for the sake of being difficult.

"Still better than the other grocery store," she answered.

Overall, they were there an hour as he loaded up on groceries for his stay. It was so much food, which made her wonder just how long he was planning to stay with her, but she didn't ask. Part of her just wanted to live in the moment and not question everything. It was easier. They only had one other run-in with a fan, and he again took pictures before going back to the shopping.

Once everything was brought in and put away, Alanna grabbed the ingredients for the smores and went to turn on her small fire pit. Abel put on the music and then joined her. She had long metal sticks to roast with, and reclining chairs were set near it just off to the side of the pool.

"So, I get to see you eat something real for a change," Abel said as he roasted his marshmallow. She was burning hers, exactly how she liked it.

"You see me eat. I had fries earlier," she answered.

"You had exactly five fries," he said before sliding his marshmallow between the chocolate and crackers. He helped her finish hers, and then they went over to one of the reclining chairs. Instead of sitting in his own, he sat down and then pulled her down to sit against him.

Her first bite of the smore did not go well. It made her stomach turn a bit, but she took a few breaths and focused on how she enjoyed the taste. She used to make smores with Hannah a lot when she was younger and had started doing it with Lacey on occasion as well. It was more about the experience than the food, but she liked it either way.

"This isn't bad," he said as he ate his sweet sandwich from behind her.

"Better when you use normal marshmallows, but you get a pass since the way you take care of yourself makes you so hot," she teased.

He burst out laughing and then kissed the side of her cheek. "Glad to know that is how you see it."

"Well, a woman would have to be blind not to see it," she added, taking another bite of her treat.

Silence fell between them after that as they lay there, listening to the music and eating their snack. She wasn't sure how long they stayed that way, but several songs played before either of them spoke again.

"I want to show you something," Alanna said, and got up from the chair.

"Okay, do I need to get up?" he asked, following her with his eyes.

"No, just stay there," she answered.

Torches were set up around the backyard to keep it lit. Brandon had wired them up the same time he did the speakers. However, they were all connected to one main circuit. Going to the box, Alanna flipped it, and the yard fell into complete darkness. She knew her way well enough that she was able to get back to Abel without any issues.

She moved to sit back between his legs and pointed up to the sky. "Part of the reason I wanted to live out here was so I could look up and see the stars. Sometimes I come and lie out here just to look up there and watch them twinkle and dance. It's calming and just... amazing."

"Wow, I have to admit, LA does not have skies like this," he whispered, wrapping his arms around her.

"I've always loved it, but the last few months I have learned to appreciate it more than I did before," she whispered and nuzzled closer to him. Him holding her made her feel safe and cherished. He didn't have to do anything he was doing, but he was, and she treasured it.

"The only time I get to see anything like this is when I go out to the desert. You know, there is a long stretch of it between LA and Vegas. Sometimes I will drive out there and take in the peace of it," he whispered. "Though, I do it less and less these days. Maybe one day I can show you."

Her breath caught, and the sting of tears filled her eyes before a couple fell to her cheeks. "Abel..."

"Don't," he said next.

So, she didn't. They just sat there, letting the night carry on while enjoying each moment as the stars and moon shown above them like the lights of the fans at a concert. She smiled, remembering that one song she got to sing with him on stage. It had been a dream come true for her.

Finding his hand, she laced their fingers and just let the memories take her and the tears fall. There was not enough time, and she wasn't ready.

CHAPTER NINETEEN
ALANNA

"Okay, I have the camera," Hannah said, taking a seat in one of the chairs by the pool. Lacey was on the stairs of the pool with her floating swimsuit on, and Alanna had finally gotten a suit that fit for the most part. She and Abel were in the pool, getting ready to put on a show for Hannah and Brandon.

For the last couple of weeks, they had been secretly teaching Lacey some of Abel's songs. The little girl loved it, and anytime they got to a curse word, Alanna would tell her she had a grandma pass. Since they didn't have the band, Abel had loaded up his track that he used for practice and during recording at times. As the music started playing, Lacey began to head bang a bit and splash around in the water.

"Seriously, Mom! She is five!" Hannah called out.

"Sing songs that mean something!" Alanna called out but refused to apologize.

Abel burst out laughing, but then it was time for the singing to start. Lacey began to belt out the words, her little mouth moving fast during parts that had a bit of rap feel to them. When the chorus hit, Alanna joined in, singing hard, dancing, and head banging right along with her granddaughter. Abel at times came behind her to help hold her, but the water did most of the work of keeping her standing.

Lacey knew every word and sang like she also knew what they meant even though she was far too young to understand them. When it got to the really rough parts, Abel would take over, but Lacey would still scream out as loud as she could. For several songs the three of them sang together, not caring about anything. The last song was so hard that neither Lacey nor Alanna could really sing it, but Abel wanted to do it as it was part of the storyline of the album.

"Okay, remember what I told you. Plant your feet so you don't fall," Abel explained standing on the edge of the pool with Lacey.

The drums and guitar in the song went crazy, and they started doing a propeller sort of head banging that Alanna loved most. He did the same thing in the music video, and it was always one of her favorite parts. Lacey still screamed as many of the words as she knew while Abel performed the harsh distortion, and when they were done, Hannah and Brandon stood up and cheered. Lacey took a bow and then both she and Abel jumped back into the pool.

"Mom, I can't believe you taught my child to cuss." Hannah laughed.

"She gave me a grandma exception," Lacey called out. "But only for the songs."

"Good because if you say those words at school, you will get in trouble," Hannah said, moving to sit on the edge of the pool.

Abel went over to talk to her, but Alanna couldn't hear what they said. Instead, she continued to play with her granddaughter. The pool made everything easier. She could swing the girl around and not actually have to use much strength. Of course, the small concert they had just done took a lot out of her, Alanna was having more and more trouble giving in to being weak. She wanted to be strong. She wanted to live every moment she could as each one ticked her closer to the end.

However, she got to the point where she had to rest. Getting out of the pool, she went to sit on one of the reclining chairs and covered up with a towel. Abel stayed in the pool with Lacey, tossing her around and playing with her like she was his own daughter, or granddaughter. It was strange to think that either of them was old enough to be grandparents. She was just over forty, and he wasn't much older than her.

"Lacey will love having this to look back on," Hannah said, showing Alanna the camera before sitting down next to her.

"That was part of the point of it all. I hate I won't be able to teach her more," Alanna said. Though the thoughts were sad, she didn't say them that way. "But I have a feeling she's going to be just fine."

"I don't think any of us are going to be just fine, but we will make it," Hannah said.

It had always been just them. Even when she got married, Hannah had continued to lean on their relationship more than her relationship with her husband. Alanna knew they were having trouble, especially with Alanna's sickness taking more and more of Hannah's time, but her daughter never talked about it. Alanna figured she didn't want to make her feel like a burden or as if it were her fault.

"I've been trying to film as much as I can, but I feel like I'm never going to have enough," Hannah whispered as she watched Lacey and Abel playing in the pool. "You ready for the doctor tomorrow?"

"I'm not going to the doctor tomorrow," Alanna answered.

She had been thinking about it all day. The truth was, she didn't want to know what the doctor had to say. She could feel it inside of her.

"You have to go to the doctor tomorrow. They got the scans back. We need to know what's going on," Hannah said.

"I'm not going, and that's final," Alanna said again and got up to walk into the house.

She couldn't explain the anger that started to course through her. It didn't make sense. For months she had known what was coming. The only reason she did any treatment was in hopes of living a little longer for Hannah and Lacey. Had they not been a factor she wouldn't have even bothered, but she knew that it wasn't doing anything other than making her feel sick. Instead of going to a doctor to hear what she already knew, she just wanted to spend time with her family, with Abel, and enjoy what little time she had left.

"Hey, what is this about a doctor appointment tomorrow?" Abel asked, walking into the house. He was drying off but still dripped all over the floor.

"It's nothing. I'm not going," Alanna said and walked away toward her room.

"Like hell you aren't going. If you have an appointment, you are fucking going," Abel demanded.

They had never gotten in a fight. Their relationship had held this sort of bubble-like perfection through most of it. Now and then there were little breaks when she was sick or something went wrong but never a fight.

"No, I'm not."

Her skin sizzled and she started to bite the inside of her cheek. Part of her wanted the fight. It burned in her, made her feel alive in a different way from the passion they usually shared. She was daring him to push her, and he walked right into it.

"You are fucking going to damn doctor if I have to toss you over my shoulder and carry you there myself."

"No, I'm not. I don't want to go. I don't need to go. I'm staying here. I'm tired of it. You don't get it. You weren't there; you haven't been here!" she yelled and watched as his face set hard. "You have no idea what I have been through. You waltz in here and think you can save the fucking day. Well, news to you, you can't!"

He started to take a step toward her but froze. "Don't be such a fucking bitch. You are going, I'm taking you, and there is nothing you can do about it. Remember, you are just a tiny woman."

"Oh, yeah, I remember, a tiny fucking woman. I dare you to fucking make me do anything," she growled. She wasn't afraid to get in his face, so she moved into him until they were so close together that she could feel his breath on her skin. "What are you really going to fucking do?"

He froze. His body was so tense that she could see the veins in his arms and the shaking just under his skin. His breath came in a slow hard pace, and finally he closed his eyes. The energy between them continued to sizzle and grow until she could barely breathe, but she wasn't backing down. Finally, he started to speak, this time barely over a whisper. "You may not want to know, but the rest of us need to know."

With that he turned and stormed out of the house. Alanna could hear him scream his frustration outside, and she started to cry. She wasn't even sure why she was crying, only that she was. Overwhelmed, she went to her room and slammed the door. Her legs gave out, and she slid down against the door with her knees pulled up and sobbed.

He was right. It was selfish of her to just ignore the appointment, but he had no idea how difficult it would be for her to face it. Knowing in her mind and hearing the words come out of someone else's mouth were two different things. Even though the doctor had said she looked better the last time she was there, it didn't mean she was getting better. A weekend in Florida was bound to make most people look better.

As the high of the trip had worn off, Alanna had started to notice more and more problems. She slept less, ate less. Her dependency on her medication was growing. Breathing was difficult, and she grew more and more unsteady. As much as she tried to hide it from everyone else, she knew it was there. She could feel it.

One night before Abel came to see her, she thought of just ending it and taking away the lingering horror of the slow death. She was sure it would have actually been easier on everyone else, but then she thought better of it. There were still a few things she needed to do. Her only hope was that she would have time to do them.

CHAPTER TWENTY
ABEL

Hannah was in the house cooking dinner, but Alanna had yet to come out of her room. He sat outside on the porch stairs spiraling with his loss of control. He had yelled at her. She was a dying woman, and he had yelled at her like a fucking animal. What the fuck was wrong with him? The truth was, he wanted to know what the doctor had to say. He needed to know how much time he had. No matter what they said, though, it wouldn't be enough.

"Are you mad at my grandma?" Lacey asked, coming to sit next to him. He had really grown to love the little girl, and spending time with her made him remember when his daughter was small.

"No, I'm not mad at her," he answered. "Lacey, do you know what is going on with her?" It wasn't his place to talk to the child about it, but he was curious what she did know.

"Mommy said that one day soon Grandma is going to go to sleep, and then she will go away," Lacey explained. "She said it will be sad."

"Yeah, it will," he answered, leaning down a little further so they could talk without being overheard. "Well, I care a lot about your grandma and seeing her not feeling well bothers me sometimes. I'm trying to be strong and just happy, but sometimes it's hard."

"Like when I colored on the walls. Mommy said she loves me, but she was not happy with me," Lacey said.

"Yeah, like that," Abel answered. "Your grandma... she, well, she is someone very special, and I don't like that she won't be here very long."

"I don't either. She won't be able to teach me to play piano," Lacey said next. "She was going to teach me before she got sick."

"I'll teach you," he said without hesitation. "I'll teach you to play whatever you want, and if for some reason I don't know how to play it, I will find someone who can teach you."

Lacey turned to look at him with the biggest smile. "Really?"

"Yes, really," he answered. Looking left and right and all around, he made sure it was still just the two of them. "Can you keep a secret?"

Lacey nodded and held up her pinky finger. He locked his with hers before continuing. "I'm claiming you as my granddaughter now. You can't tell your mom or anyone yet, though, okay. It stays between you and me, but just remember that, okay. I'll always be here for you."

The girl squealed and then threw her arms around him. He hugged her close, realizing just how much he missed his daughter being small. As much as he tried to be there for her, he had also missed a lot. It came with the job, but it didn't mean it hadn't bothered him.

"I love you, Abel." Lacey said softly.

"I love you too," he answered. "Hey, do you have some markers?"

Lacey nodded and went to get an art bag out of her mother's van. Bringing it to him, he pulled out several and started drawing on her arm. He made a pretty design of a heart with wings and a drop of blood dripping from the bottom. Taking his time, he colored it in. While he wasn't the best artist, he did the best he could. Then he took a picture of it.

"I have a tattoo now too!" Lacey exclaimed.

"Well, yours will still wash off, but yeah you do," he answered. "Do you mind if I hold on to these for a couple of days?"

"You can have them," she answered and then went inside to show her mother her arm.

Abel got up and followed her in just in time to get a glare from Hannah. "You drew on my daughter?"

"Yeah, so she can't get in trouble. It's all my fault," he answered, then gave Lacey a wink. She winked back, and he knew that she was locked in on their little secret.

"Dinner is about ready. I think I got the hang of this vegan thing. I swear, you have no idea how it is here in Alabama." Hannah laughed.

"Mommy, can I be a vegan?" Lacey asked.

"When you are older and can actually understand what that means, if you still want to, I don't care. But until then you eat what I cook you. Now go wash your hands for dinner," Hannah said.

Brandon whispered something to his wife and then left, and Abel got the feeling something was going on that he wasn't aware of. He thought about asking but decided against it. If Hannah wanted him to know, she would tell him. Otherwise, it was none of his business. They had just all sat down to dinner when Alanna walked out of her room.

She went to sit down at the table with them, and he could tell she had been crying. They never talked about the bad things. They never discussed her illness or the fact she was dying. It hung over them like a guillotine ready to cut off their heads, but they always pretended it wasn't there. Moments like that one made it difficult to ignore.

"Do you want some pasta, Mom?" Hannah asked, holding the pot out toward her.

Alanna didn't answer, instead she just shook her head and reached to take a drink of her water. After a couple of deep breaths, she looked over at Lacey.

"I like your tattoo," she whispered. Her voice sounded harsh and weak.

"Thank you. Abel drew it for me. He said it will still wash off, though," she answered.

"Well, maybe one day you will get a real one," Alanna said.

"Do you have one?" Lacey asked.

"No, I never got one, though I thought about it a few times. I decided it was better for me to get nice things for you and your mom instead," she answered.

"Maybe you should," Lacey said, and for the first time since coming out of the room Alanna smiled.

She looked over at him, and in the softest voice whispered, "Hey, baby." And those words let him know that everything was okay between them.

"Hey," he answered. "I'm sorry."

"Me too," she responded and then leaned her head against his shoulder.

It made it difficult to eat but he didn't care.

"I'll go."

Later that night, when Hannah and Lacey had left and Alanna had gone to sleep, Abel went back into the living room and sat down at the small coffee table with Lacey's markers and one of the few T-shirts he had that wasn't black. It was gray, but the markers should still show up. Taking his time, he etched out the letters, making sure they lined up right and looked decent. Once the outlines were done, he started to fill them in.

From there he made some other little drawings until the shirt looked like something Lacey would wear, but he liked it. Leaving it to dry for a few minutes, he sat back and looked around the room. Hannah had made a print of the picture of them from the concert. It was the one that had apparently been printed in the news as well. Briar had shown him.

It hung on the wall across from him, and he smiled seeing it. He had taken her seat and was holding her close. He could still remember how she smelled like a mix of strawberry, sweat, and smoke, and still he loved it. She was shivering in his arms and kept falling in and out of sleep, but she wanted to hear Leia Rice, so he stayed there.

What happened after that was probably due to the fact that he didn't make her go back to the bus sooner, but he still didn't regret it. Seeing that photo reminded him of just how worth it the whole weekend had been. His heart ached, and he knew he was the reason it was being destroyed. Everyone had told him that getting involved was stupid. Everyone had warned him about how exactly it would end. Even Alanna had tried to tell him, but he hadn't listened.

Alone in that room, he knew the truth deep down. He had fallen for her the moment he met her. As much as it was going to hurt, he would see this to the end and beyond. What he had told Lacey was the truth. They were family now.

His eyes closed, he let out a deep breath then pulled out his phone to call Briar, needing not to feel so alone in that moment.

She picked up after three rings, and he could swear he heard someone else in the background. "Hey, Dad? How is the trip going?"

"Had a rough day today. Actually, had a very mixed day. It started out great but then got rough," he answered. "You got company?"

"Yeah, I had a friend come over. I know, not the epic party I told you I would throw, but still," she answered.

"Who is your friend?" he asked, feeling that protective urge rise in him.

"A friend," she answered without actually answering. "So, what happened? Why was today hard?"

"I'm going to lose her," he said, and realized it was the most real thing he had said in a very long time. They loved to pretend, but the truth was he was going to lose her, and nothing could stop that.

"I know," Briar whispered. "Are you going to be okay?"

"I shouldn't be burdening you with this. You're just a kid and should be out enjoying life," he sighed, trying not to wallow to his daughter on the phone.

"You aren't burdening me with anything. Now, are you going to be okay?" Briar said.

He loved his daughter. She had grown to be such a compassionate person, but he had no idea how. She didn't get it from him, and then he looked around and realized that maybe she did.

"No, I'm not going to be okay, but I also can't change it. I'm sorry I'm not there right now," he answered.

"Don't be sorry. I'm a big girl, remember," she said and laughed a bit.

It made him smile and eased some of the pain he was feeling.

"I'm so proud of you. I know you are falling in love with that woman. I see it when you send me pictures and videos. I've never seen you like that with anyone, and there have been lots of someones. This woman is special, and even if it is short, it's special."

"That it is," he answered. "Well, we have to be up early. She has a doctor appointment tomorrow. She doesn't even want to go, which does not make me feel good. She knows something she isn't telling anyone."

"We all know our own bodies better than anyone else," Briar said.

"When did you get so smart?" he asked. He had a tendency to ask that fairly often.

"Well, you did send me to college. It was bound to happen," she answered. "Why don't you get off the phone and go be with your woman? You can tell me all about it when you call me tomorrow."

"Yeah, I'll go do that," he said. "I love you, kid."

"I love you too, Dad," she answered.

The T-shirt was dry, so he picked it up and took it to put with his stuff which was in the guest room. While he was fairly sure Hannah knew that her mom and he had developed some sort of relationship, Alanna still wanted to keep it from her as much as she could. He didn't understand, but he also didn't question it. Exhausted, he got cleaned up and ready for bed, he then walked back to Alanna's room.

Alanna was lying in the bed with a mountain of blankets on her. He had gotten her a heated one the other day, and she seemed to like it. It made things hard for him when he slept with her, and they often woke with him completely out of the covers and her under all of them. But if it made her feel better, he didn't care. For a moment he sat on the bed and watched her sleep. She looked so small and so fragile in that moment, and he had to fight not to lose it.

His eyes fell to the bedside table, he saw that all of her medication had been left there. Most of the time, she kept it where he couldn't see it. He knew it was there, and he knew what it was, but it wasn't in his face. So he opened the drawer and carefully put each bottle inside. His hand lingered on the bottle of morphine for just a moment, but then he heard her voice whisper in his mind, "Baby, that's poison. You don't want that." And he put it in the drawer before closing it and getting into bed with Alanna.

He wrapped his arms around her and pulled her into him, inhaling deeply to take in the scent of her. Home. It was the only description he had for when he held her in bed. It was peaceful and relaxing, and just felt like a home he had never had before, and he was going to lose it.

With a deep breath, he leaned in closer. She was very asleep and hadn't even woken up when he got in bed. His breath caught, and for a second, he thought better of it. Then, in the softest voice, he whispered, "I love you."

CHAPTER TWENTY-ONE

ALANNA

She had heard him. While she hadn't moved or spoken when he came to bed, she was awake. She just didn't feel like talking. The day had been a roller coaster, and she wanted it to be over with. As she lay there, she listened as he put the medication in the drawer before sliding in with her. When he held her, she felt safe in a way no other man had ever made her feel. Even after their small fight, she knew he would never do anything to hurt her.

Then he said it. He hadn't known she could hear him, and his whole body shook when he did. His arms tightened around her for a moment, and for a split second she thought about saying something back but didn't. The moment needed to happen exactly as it had, and talking would have ruined it. Instead, she just lay there and let the warmth of his arms lull her back to sleep.

The next morning, they got up early, showered and dressed. He was eating breakfast when she came out of the bedroom tying one of the scarves around her head. Instead of his usual black, he was wearing a gray T-shirt with the words *Emotional Support Rock Star* written on it. Around it, in a style that looked like something out of the late eighties or early nineties were various instruments and music notes. It was cheesy but made her smile. "Nice shirt."

"Oh, this old thing? Yeah, well, I need to do laundry," he answered and then walked over to her and kissed her.

She could feel it. His words poured out in his actions, and it made her heart skip a beat. He didn't have to say them for her to know they were true. She had been trying to pretend not to notice. The last thing she wanted to do was hurt him.

"I'm so sorry about yelling at you yesterday."

"Don't worry about it. Honestly, I kinda liked it," she answered with a grin.

"Oh, you did. Did you? I will have to yell at you more then," he teased, pressing her up against the counter. The next kiss was not loving. It was passionate and full of desire.

The bubble was about to burst. She knew it with everything in her, but she was going to savor their last few hours in it. He lifted her up and continued to kiss her as he set her down on the counter. They didn't have time to do what they both actually wanted to do, but they gave in to the kissing for a while, letting it wash away whatever still lingered from the day before.

"As much as I just want to make love to you all day, we need to go," he whispered against her lips before kissing her hard and deep again.

She still didn't want to go, and she wrapped her legs around him to hold him to her. Maybe she could convince him not to take her. He growled and gripped her hips, pulling her closer to him. Her hand sank into his hair, and she started to roll her body against him. Yes, distract him with sex. Then they wouldn't have to go.

"Fuck," he whispered against her lips, sending his own down her neck and tracing his fingers up until they played at the edge of her shirt. "You really know how to distract me."

"Is it working?" she asked, knowing that if he was still able to talk like that, it wasn't.

"Almost, but we have to go," he whispered. He kissed her hard and deep one more time before pulling away with a groan of agony.

"We will pick this up later," he said and then helped her down.

They rocked out together as they drove to the hospital in Birmingham. It helped distract her from the inevitable news they were going to get. Yes, the bubble. Stay in the bubble. Abel drove like a mad man, and she loved it. He made her little sedan weave in and out of traffic like it was a sports car, which had her heart racing.

When they got to the hospital, he held her hand as they made their way up to the oncology department. Unlike her small town, more people recognized him, and he stopped for each of them to sign autographs and take pictures. True to his shirt, he was being a support, even to the strangers waiting to find out their own fate. Even a woman who had to be in her seventies was ecstatic to meet him. She was apparently a big fan, which made Alanna giggle. If she had lived to that age, she would have been just like that woman.

Before long, the nurse called her name, and they made their way to the back. She stopped just outside of the room and almost turned to run away, but he took her hand and walked with her inside. She was panting and dizzy, and everything was starting to lose focus. Before long, Dr. Carter walked in with her clipboard and file. Then the woman stopped and smiled seeing Abel there instead of Hannah.

"Oh, who do we have here, today?"

"Abel Sharp," he answered, reaching over and shaking her hand.

"Girl, better in person," Dr. Carter said with a wink, making her blush and helping pull her out of her panic. "So, Alanna, how are you feeling?"

"I've been doing pretty good. We have been having fun spending time with my granddaughter and singing and such," Alanna answered.

"Well, that is good. So, before we go over anything, I want to make sure it is okay for me to go over your personal medical information with Abel in the room. If not, we will ask him to step out."

She looked over to Abel and then back to the doctor, "It's fine. He knows everything already."

"Okay," she answered before taking a seat and wheeling over closer to Alanna.

Abel had leaned against the counter on the other side of the room, trying to stay out of the way, but she could tell he was listening to every word and taking everything seriously. Alanna wasn't ready. She didn't want to do this. Everything in her was screaming at her to run. Closer and closer the pin drew. Reality was about to come crashing down on them, and there was no stopping it.

"I got the results of your test and scans," Dr. Carter said, opening the file so she could look it over as if she hadn't already done so. "As you know, things were already very advanced. I haven't beat around the bush as far as that goes. I know we did the surgery and that got out a lot, and the treatment did slow things down some, but we aren't really seeing a lot of progress. Alanna, I think it is time for you to really start thinking about how you want this to go from here."

She stopped breathing, and in that moment the bubble burst. Her whirlwind affair. Her summer of joy. All of it was gone. "How long? That is what they want to know," Alanna said, though she barely remembered doing so.

"It's hard to say. You have had some really good things going for you lately, and I think it is helping your body push through some of this, but not long," Dr. Carter answered.

"How long?" Abel asked, and Alanna looked over at him. Her eyes were already so full of tears that she could barely see him through them.

"Couple of weeks to a couple of months. It really is hard to tell," Dr. Carter answered.

"What about more treatment? Are there other doctors? There has to be something." Abel's tone became frantic, and Alanna could hear him starting to break.

Her heart shattered, but she sat there taking in breaths one and after another, trying to keep a hold on herself.

"Abel, I'm sorry. I don't think more treatment will help. We can certainly try, but in my professional opinion, I think it is time to start looking at quality of life over quantity of life," the doctor said. "I'll give you a minute."

The moment she was out of the room Alanna screamed. It was the sort of bone-chilling shattering scream that could break glass in movies. It didn't, but it still tore from her as if it would break her. Abel rushed over to her and pulled her into his arms. They fell to the floor, and he wrapped as much of himself around her as he rocked her.

"I've got you. I've got you, baby."

"I told you! I told you I didn't want to come. Why did you make me come!" she screamed, and another piercing shriek tore through her. Part of her knew she was disturbing other people in the hospital, but she didn't care. Her clock was running out, and she had no idea what to do. "I told you. I told you."

"Baby, look at me," he said, and she turned her tear-covered face up to him. "Do you want to go to California?"

"What?" the question threw her so off guard that it broke her out of her hysterics.

"Do you want to go to my house in California? We can visit all the cool places, and you can see everything. We will do it all, anything you want. And you can meet Briar, my daughter. I know she would love to meet you," he said, brushing the tears from her cheeks.

"You heard her. I can't go to California," she answered.

"I did hear her, and that is why I'm asking if you want to go to California," he said again.

She took a moment to think about it. Hannah would be furious, but it wasn't about her anymore. Alanna's countdown was reaching the end, and it was time for her to do the things she wanted for herself. "Okay."

"Okay, then we're going to go to California. Let me go talk to the doctor really quick. You going to be okay?" he asked, picking her up and putting her back in the chair.

"Yeah," she answered. She wasn't, but she would try.

He stepped out of the room, and a few moments later returned with Dr. Carter. "So, California, huh. That sounds exciting."

"Yeah, I've never been," Alanna answered.

"Well, I have some associates who work out in LA, so I'm going to get your files together so you can take them with you in case you need anyone. Abel, I also have some contacts for nurses. I think it would be best if we got someone full time, just in case. There will still be good days. Shoot, there might still be a lot of good days, but it is better to be prepared. Alanna has a Mediport, which is basically like a permanent IV. We used it during her treatment. So we will make sure the nurse is aware. I think she should be getting fluids daily, and it will also be a safer and less painful way to start giving her some of the stronger medications I'm going to prescribe."

Abel listened and nodded along. Alanna just sat there as if she had been sent into some sort of hellscape dream. "So, we are talking about pain medication given with needles?"

"He can't be around that," Alanna spoke up.

"I'll be fine," he interrupted, but she could see the goose bumps on his arms.

"It is common to start giving medication this way at this stage. Look, when all of this started, Alanna asked me to tell her when to transition into this. I'm not trying to push anything, but this is truly what I think should be done," Dr. Carter said.

"You're right. I wasn't going to accept any more treatment. I had already made up my mind," Alanna answered.

"Why didn't you say anything?" Abel asked.

"Because I loved just being in our bubble, but I guess we can't live there anymore," she answered, and a few more tears fell down her cheeks.

"Get everything in order and let me know what you need from me. I'll get stuff going on my end," Abel said, turning back to the doctor.

He added the emergency line into his phone as well, and they waited for all of the paperwork and prescriptions.

They sat there, waiting, neither of them speaking. He held her hand, and she realized he was shaking just as hard as she was. A few minutes later a nurse came in with a stack of paperwork organized into different folders. She went over everything with them and then let them know they could go. They sat there a couple more minutes.

"I still have things I need to do," Alanna whispered, almost more to herself than anything else.

Abel leaned over and kissed the top of her head. "What things? I'll help."

She gave him a weak smile, more and an acknowledgment that she had heard him than anything else. "It's just things I need to do. Are you sure you want to do this, Abel? It isn't like some bottles hidden in a drawer. This is a lot, and I don't blame you if you want to leave," she said, not daring to look at him.

He reached over and turned her to face him. She could see the pain in his eyes staring back at her. "I'm not going anywhere. I love you."

Time stood still. He said it. The words he had whispered the night before he said straight to her face. Those same words got stuck in her throat. Her hand reached up, and she cupped his cheek, letting her thumb rub against him. All she could manage to say was "I know."

CHAPTER TWENTY-TWO

ABEL

B riar was waiting for them when they got off the plane in LA. Alanna had insisted on walking, so he just held her hand as they made their way through the crowd until they got to his daughter. In typical LA fashion, people took pictures, and he knew he would have people asking him about the strange woman with him. He didn't care. This was all about her and giving her the best rest of her life she could possibly have.

"Alanna, this is my daughter Briar. Briar, this is Alanna," he introduced.

Briar wrapped her arms around Alanna. She was a bit taller than Alanna, so it looked odd, but it made him happy to see her do it.

"My dad has told me so much about you. I'm happy to meet you," she said. "You excited?"

"I am. I've never been to the West Coast, so this is certainly all going to be new to me," she answered.

"Well, let's get out of here. The longer we stand here the more trouble we have," Briar said, helping with the bags.

He and Hannah had gotten into a pretty big argument when he told her about his plan to take Alanna to California. She had not wanted her mother to leave, and he understood her position on it. But he also didn't care. Instead, he made a promise that if things got bad, he would bring her home or have Hannah flown out. Either way, he would do everything he could to make sure she was there for the end.

The end.

As much as he kept trying to push the thought out of his head, it haunted him. They hadn't had enough time, and there never would be enough time. He wanted to do so many things with her. He wanted to show her things he never would be able to, but he was going to use this time to do as much as he could and as much as her body would let her.

So far, he hadn't seen a lot of changes in her. Had they not gone to the doctor, he wouldn't have known what was really going on, but he knew Alanna knew. She had admitted it to him, and part of him had gotten angry. While he understood her wanting to just live in the moment, knowing that she could feel herself slipping further away and doing so in silence and loneliness hurt him.

He had told her that he loved her, and it was the truth. He did. She hadn't said it back, and he wasn't sure why. Deep down, he knew she loved him. He could feel it when they touched, kissed, made love. The energy between them was unlike anything he had ever experienced. She just never said the words.

It had taken them a couple of days to get things set up. Mason had helped him hire nurses, and a room had been converted just for that purpose. The doctor had instructed them to keep her in fluids, and if she had days she wasn't eating much to also supplement. The packet of information was nearly an inch thick, but he had read the whole thing. He was thankful to have the nurses to take care of all the medication and treatment. It would make the visit easier on him since he wouldn't have to be around the drugs.

"So, the guys are going to come over tomorrow and hang out. We are also going to work on some music, but I thought after the trip you might want a day to relax," Abel explained as he drove toward his house.

He lived up on a hill away from a lot of the chaos that was LA proper. Like most celebrities his house was big and secluded. Once upon a time, he saw it as a symbol of how far he had come, but now it just felt empty.

"My dad says you like to sing too, and that you sing with your granddaughter. To be honest, you don't look old enough to have a granddaughter," Briar said from the back seat.

"I love to sing. It was one of the things that made me happiest in life," Alanna answered, turning back to look at Briar. "And I was younger than you when I had my daughter, so it is a little easier for me to be a grandmother at my age. But thank you for the compliment. I bet you hear this all the time, but you look so much like your dad."

"I do hear it a lot," she answered.

"Well, you are beautiful," Alanna said.

"Thank you. I guess that means my dad is too," Briar teased.

"Yes, I'm gorgeous and don't you forget it," Abel announced with a teasing voice.

"So, I see why you hate it at my house. I can certainly see the appeal of the drier air here," Alanna said next. "Though, I'm not sure how I feel about all the earthquakes and fires."

"I'll take earthquakes and fires over breathing water any day," Abel answered.

He reached over and took her hand before lifting it to kiss it. Briar giggled from the back, and he shook his head.

Before long, they were at his house, and he was showing her around. She followed along, taking everything in. Three of her houses could fit in his, but hers always felt warmer. Most of the time, he was the only one in his house. Briar came and went, going back and forth between his house, her mom's house, and now school. The realization of just how lonely his life had become struck him differently, and he found himself pulling Alanna in closer. She was in his house, and while she was, it would feel fuller and less lonely.

"You really have something here," Alanna said.

They had just gotten back downstairs from seeing the bedrooms and bathroom and found themselves in a more formal room. In the center of the room was a grand piano. A few couches sat in the room as well with art on the walls, but the focus was the piano. The back stairs led them into that room, and it was easy for someone to sit on the stairs and see into it.

"That is beautiful," she whispered..

"Yeah, I can have taste when I want to," he answered before leading her to the back den and kitchen area. Beyond that was the pool. Like hers, it was surrounded with seating and tables for entertaining. He spent a majority of his time in this back part of the house. The rest was for show. This was for comfort.

Alanna walked over to the sliding glass doors and gazed outside. His pool overlooked the hills and sparse trees that surrounded LA. The view was beautiful, and she seemed to be taking it all in. Neither of them had said much, but he was enjoying watching her.

"It's been a long day. Do you want to go rest?" Abel finally asked, but she didn't turn to look at him. Instead, she opened the door and stepped outside.

He followed her as she made her way to the far wall, which overlooked the world around them. Her hands pressed down on the wall as she leaned there, her head held back just a bit. When he got closer, he saw she was smiling, and her eyes were closed. The scarf she wore blew behind her, and he couldn't help but take a picture of her. She looked like an angel ready to take flight. Maybe she was.

"Can we rest out here?" she finally asked.

"Of course we can," he answered and went about getting one of the chairs ready for them. She finally came over to him, and they curled up on it together as he just held her. She seemed to be soaking in her surroundings, processing it and savoring it. It had been a long time since he had appreciated the place, but seeing how she was taking everything in made him appreciate it once more.

CHAPTER TWENTY-THREE

ALANNA

S he woke up shivering. The scent of salt still lingered heavily in the air, and she smiled, remembering that they had decided to rest out by the pool. It had only been a few hours since they got to California, and she couldn't get over how beautiful it was. Sure, she had seen pictures, but nothing compared to the real thing, especially since Abel lived in the hills out of the thick of the city.

Abel's arms were wrapped around her, but she could feel the steady rhythm of his breathing, which told her he was asleep. It still amazed her that he was with her. He had put his life on hold and gone out of his way to make every day for her special. They were falling hard, and the heartbreaking part was knowing that, in the end, she would be leaving him in pain.

Like a cat, she rubbed her face against his chest and breathed in the scent of his fancy expensive cologne. She had no idea what it was, but she loved it. There was a bit of a chill in the evening air, but she felt warm. No, not warm, hot. Her temperature rising along with her desire.

With a twist, she shifted in the lounge chair and turned to face him. Up on her knees, she leaned in and kissed him softly as if trying to wake Sleeping Beauty. However, she didn't stop with a simple kiss.

Her hands began to run up and down his body as she kissed along his neck, and she smiled when she heard his breathing change.

"Baby, what are you doing?" he asked, but already his hands were at the base of her spine, slowly sliding up under her shirt.

"I woke up happy and excited," she answered between kisses, "and all I could think about was having you."

"Oh no, what's a man to do when a beautiful woman wakes up wanting him?" he teased and then lifted her face so he could kiss her, hard and deep. His hands pulling her closer to him, he lifted her a bit to shift their position.

When he sat forward, she lifted off his shirt, her hands running over his chest and feeling how the muscles moved. Damn this man was sex on a stick, and she did not deserve him. But she could certainly appreciate it. He pulled off her shirt as well, tossing it to the ground as he started to taste and kiss along her neck and down her chest. She ran her fingers through his silky black hair while he took his time ravishing every inch of her body. He adjusted her to the side and stood her up, his lips still working over her skin as he pushed down her pants. His mouth continued its path down her body, and he lifted her leg up so he could kiss between her folds.

Her body started to arch, and he braced his arm against her back as he deepened his attention, licking and sucking and building a mix of pleasure and tension in her body. It stole her breath and had her shaking.

"I thought I was ravishing you," she said between strained breaths and moans.

He just chuckled but didn't stop, kissing deeper and licking faster as he built her body higher and higher. Before long, her moans turned to cries, her body tensed more, and he hit that spot that sparked electricity over her body and sent her over the edge. His mouth worked her through her orgasm, licking and sucking until she fell forward against him.

Abel was not done with her as he dragged her down onto his lap. He held her up with one hand and used his other to open his pants. As they shifted back onto the lounge chair, he let his pants slide down before settling her on top of him. In one rolling motion, he pushed inside of her and their lips crashed together in a ravenous hunger as his hands gripped tightly to her hips. She loved when he let his passion take over and he wasn't so cautious with her. If she needed softer, she would tell him, but in that moment she didn't want soft.

Her hips rolled against him, her stomach contracting with each pass. It wasn't a slow gentle love-making. No, it was a frantic taking, her desperation for him fueling her to ride him harder and faster. He growled into their kiss as if demanding more from her.

"Fuck, baby," he whispered, nipping at her lips.

Alanna took a couple of deep breaths, each one ending with a strangled cry. Her body was tensing and building, coiling tightly in anticipation. She was still sensitive; Abel's expert mouth had made her so. It wouldn't take long. She knew it, and she had no desire to hold on. They had time, but she needed release. She needed the flood of endorphins his body would feed to her when she let go.

"I'm... I'm so close," Alanna groaned through gritted teeth as Abel sucked hard on her collarbone, sending shock waves of electricity through her body.

"Good. I want to feel you. I need it, baby, fuck," he whispered against her lips, lightly kissing her between words.

His wicked words telling her that he needed her made her body heat to a boil before exploding. She screamed out into the night, her head thrown back as burst after burst of ecstasy raked its way through her. Abel took hold of her hips and began to slam harder and faster up into her body, only increasing the intensity of her release until he cried out his own. His arms tightened around her as he roared out, shaking and writhing along with her.

She collapsed forward, holding him to her as he lay back on the lounger so they could catch their breath and bask in the euphoric bliss that spread through their veins. Alanna didn't want to move. She lay there, a smile spreading over her lips as she listened to the heavy beating of his heart. She wished she could tell him with words just how much she felt for him. He had changed her life, even though it was all ending. He had given her the life she had always wanted. It was unbelievable. And there was no way she could ever thank him for it.

"We probably should have gone inside," Alanna whispered, her fingers tracing over his chest.

"Yeah, probably, but I don't fucking care. You wanted me, and you get what you want when you want it," he answered, turning her face up so he could kiss her lightly. "Now, I'm more than happy to take you inside and go for another round or two."

Alanna giggled and kissed him again. "You are a wicked man."

"Yes, yes, I am, and you love it," he answered.

Abel shifted them and found his shirt, pulling it over her so that she was covered without having to find all of her clothes. When he got up, he grabbed everything else and then held her hand to take her into the house.

"I could also run you a bath and just pamper you before I ravish you again. This is your trip and your time. Anything you want to do, anywhere you want to go, that's what we do."

He led her into the house and grabbed a snack and drink from the fridge before taking her up the stairs. Music was playing from down the hall where she assumed Briar was hiding away. Alanna blushed, hoping she hadn't traumatized his daughter by instigating their outdoor play, but she would never ask.

Abel's room looked like a fairytale with a balcony and lots of floor space. The furniture was deep woods, and he had a mix of art and musical items throughout. Never letting go of her hand, he led her into the bathroom and sat her down before starting the bath.

"You are really going to pamper me. Aren't you?" she said, giggling as he checked the temperature and then lowered the lights.

"To be fair, I'm only doing it so I can trick you into being savagely fucked later," he teased, and she burst out laughing.

"I don't need to be tricked. I'm pretty sure I'm the one who woke you up out there," she said between laughter.

"Yeah, but now I'm awake and I'm hungry," he answered.

Despite his words, he did pamper her, beyond anything she expected. He washed every inch of her body, taking care with her hair, which was mostly gone. It didn't matter how much her body had broken down. Abel never looked at her like she was sick. He never saw that ghost of a person she was slowly transforming into. No, he treated her like she was still the most beautiful person in the world to him.

Once she was clean, he slid in behind her, held her to him, and worked her body with his fingers as he kissed and caressed her. His attention was softer, but the pleasure was no less intense. They stayed in the water together until it started to grow cold. It was a magical love-making that was a complete change from their time by the pool.

"I love you, Alanna," Abel whispered later that night, after she had taken her medicine, and he had made love to her one last time. He had slid from her body and pulled her into him so he could hold her close.

"I know," she whispered, her heart aching because she knew she didn't have the strength to say the words back to him.

Chapter Twenty-Four

Abel

What was meant to be a recording session had turned more into a backyard party when the band showed up the next afternoon. He and Alanna had a magical night, and when they woke up the next morning, they were both pretty refreshed and energized. When the guys got there, they worked on music for a little over an hour before everyone got distracted and decided to just hang out and have fun by the pool.

They had ordered a ton of food and made virgin frozen drinks. Alanna was sitting in one of the chairs by the pool with her drink, and he had noticed her actually enjoying it. He had a huge smile as he watched her laughing and carrying on with the guys.

Music blared and now and then someone or everyone would start singing and dancing around. Taking a seat next to Alanna, he ran his fingers through his hair to get it out of his face before leaning over and kissing her cheek.

"Well, this is not how I thought today would go, but are you having fun?"

"Yes, this is great." She laughed and gave him a soft kiss, then turned back to watching everyone play around the pool.

"You know she likes him. Don't you?" Alanna said, nodding toward Briar, who was talking to Derrik.

"No, that's stupid. He's too old for her," Abel said but watched as they talked and laughed.

"I don't think she cares," Alanna said. "Besides, he isn't really that much older than her. What seven years or so?"

He sat there watching the two interact playful and familiar, and that protective side of him started to flare. That was his baby, and he would be damned if anyone touched her. "I'm going to fucking kill him."

Alanna swatted at him playfully and laughed. "No, you aren't."

"I can find another drummer. I'm going to fucking kill him," he said again, and part of him really meant it.

"You wouldn't find one as good. Now leave it alone. She is a grown woman," Alanna said. She leaned over and pulled his attention away from Briar and Derrik so he'd instead focus on her. "Let it go."

"Can I at least punch him really hard?" he asked next, and she just burst out laughing. "That isn't a no. I'm taking that as permission."

He started to get up, though he was being playful as well, and she grabbed his hand and pulled him back down to her. They kissed and laughed, and he did his best to forget about the fact that his drummer and his daughter might be having a relationship behind his back. For all he knew it was just a crush. Derrik had a lot of girls crushing for him.

Unlike at her house, Alanna didn't get in the pool. When he asked her why, she said she was worried about how crazy everyone was being. He made a note to take her into the pool when everyone was gone. She loved being in the water, and he wanted her to enjoy it. At some point everyone took a break for food, and he picked her up and took her into the water, holding her as she floated around in his arms. She didn't float well, so he kept her supported.

"I love it here," she said, stretching back and gazing up as the sun started to set.

"I love you being here," he answered.

"You guys didn't get very much done today," she whispered as she ran her hands over the top of the water as if she were slowly swimming, but he was holding her.

He loved watching her just enjoy and appreciate life. Abel wasn't sure he had ever sat back to see and feel life the way she did.

"No, we didn't, but maybe we can get some done tonight. You can come sit in there while we play. I can bring out a blanket and a more comfortable chair for you," he said. She had been in the studio earlier when they tried to play, but she hadn't looked comfortable.

"Honestly, I need to go upstairs for a little while, but if you are still playing when I get done up there, I will come and listen in. I know how to carry a blanket with me."

He hated more than anything when they had to be realistic about her life. Most of the time, they both did everything they could to just pretend the inevitable wasn't about to happen, but now and then they had to face it. It always felt like someone had put a spear through his heart. "Are you hurting?"

"No, but it is probably best if I don't let it get to that point. I also haven't eaten anything. They have all my supplements and fluids. You know, the fun stuff," she answered and smiled up at him.

Abel faked a smiled and leaned down, softly kissing her and taking deep breaths to calm himself. It hurt, everything about their relationship hurt, and it was quickly coming to a breaking point. "Well then, let me get you upstairs. I'll come check on you after a little while. Okay?"

"You don't have to do that. Your band needs you. I'm just going to see the nurses and then go lay down for a while. I will be fine." Her hand came to his cheek and lightly rubbed.

He shifted her so she was no longer lying back in his arms. His lips brushed against hers, and he took his time kissing her, soft and full of the love that was overwhelming his heart.

"I know they need me. You need me too. I'll come check on you. Now, let's get you upstairs."

Abel wrapped her in a towel and then walked with her up to the room they had set up for the nurses. He kissed her once more before letting her go. That room was more difficult for him to go into, not just because seeing her like that made him want to scream, but there were far too many memories of a life he had long let go of. Alanna needed the medications, but seeing the needles made his skin crawl and body shake. Twenty years, and he still could hear the demons calling for him to give in.

Downstairs, he grabbed himself some dinner, scarfing it down before herding the band into the studio. They were trying to flesh out the music for several songs, and Abel wasn't sure why writing music lately had been more difficult than usual for him. Maybe it had something to do with the fact his emotions were out of control. Most of his songs were written when his emotions were more stable, so he could reflect. Currently everything worth singing about was happening in real time, and it was hard to focus on anything.

"You going to be able to do this?" Trey asked, leaning against the stool where he was working.

"Yeah, I can do this. It's just a little more difficult than it usually is, but I can't let what's going on with her stop us from our work," Abel answered, even though he knew it was a lie. He wasn't sure he would fully be able to work until... no, he couldn't think about that.

"We could take time off," Derrik suggested.

"No, we have contracts. I'll take time when I need to, but we work when we can work."

Not much was done, but they finished one song. It wasn't perfect, and it would need to be tweaked, but it was the closest they could get. Abel let them know he would think on it overnight. Everyone left, and Abel went upstairs to check on Alanna.

He found her sitting in the chair near the balcony. She was asleep with a blanket wrapped around her. As he often did when he walked in on her asleep, he went over to touch her skin. Warm. A wave of relief flooded his veins as he bent down, picked her up, and carried her to bed.

"Please don't let me find her like that," he whispered to a god he didn't really believe in. "If you are going to take her from me, please let me be there. Let me say I love her. Let me say good-bye."

CHAPTER TWENTY-FIVE

ALANNA

S he felt like she was in a dream. California was the fantasy world she always imagined it would be, and true to his word, Abel did everything he could to make it as wonderful as possible. They made love so much that she thought that might be how it all ended. He didn't hesitate to say how he felt to her and never got upset when she didn't say it back.

They went to fancy restaurants and all of the tourist sites. Most of the time he had to wear something to keep him as disguised as possible, but they still had fans or sometimes people who were not fans come up to them. Sometimes she knew he wanted to tell them all to fuck off, but she would encourage him to be nice. She remembered what it felt like to want those few seconds from him.

They had just gone to one of the nicer restaurants, not that she ate much, but she loved going anyway. He had gotten her some fancy dresses to wear, and they made her feel pretty. They could hear music coming from the back room, and they followed it to find Briar and Derrik very much making out on the couch. She tried to hold him back, but there was no stopping him. Abel marched over to them, snatched Derrik off of the couch, and punched the shit out of him.

"Dad! Stop it!" Briar screamed.

Alanna watched Abel's entire body tense, but he didn't go for another punch.

"Fuck, man!" Derrik yelled from the floor, his hand at his eye.

"Really, Briar? This guy?" Abel asked, turning toward his daughter.

Alanna just stood there watching. She wondered if he would have defended Hannah that way. Would he defend Lacey that way? Her mind drifted with her thoughts as she watched the scene unfold before her.

"What's wrong with *this* guy? Isn't he like one of your best friends? Are you saying you are friends with people you think I shouldn't be around?" Briar demanded, and Alanna saw the same fire in her that Abel possessed. It was the same fire Lacey had. The same one she had inside of her once upon a time.

"I'm saying that he's... fuck!" Abel didn't have an answer because there wasn't one. "He's too fucking old for you."

"He's twenty-five. I'm nineteen. That isn't too old," Briar defended.

"Man, look..." Derrik started to say as he pulled himself up from the floor.

"Not now. I really don't want to have to replace my drummer," Abel said, not turning to look at his friend.

Alanna walked forward and put her hand on his shoulder. "I'm tired."

Those words seemed to snap him out of his anger, and he nearly crawled over the couch to get to her. "Okay, then let's go upstairs."

He put his arm around her waist to guide her out of the room, and she turned and gave Briar a quick wink. The girl blushed a bit and then went to hug Derrik and check out his swollen eye.

"I probably deserved that," Derrik said as they left.

Abel tensed for a second but didn't turn back. When they got to the room, Alanna walked through and pressed the button to turn on the radio. She shifted it until it played slow soft music and then opened up the doors that led to the balcony. A gentle wind wafted through, carrying with it the scent of salt from the sea. She held her hand out, and Abel walked toward her. She lifted the hand he had used to punch Derrik and kissed his knuckles.

"You defended her honor so well. Now leave them alone."

He chuckled and pulled her into him. They swayed back and forth to the song, and she pressed her cheek tight to his chest so the echo of his heartbeat filled her and pulsed through her body. Though they were no longer living in a bubble, and the reality of the world was crashing down around them, she loved the moments when it was just the two of them.

"If I could just pause time and live in this moment, everything would be okay," he whispered and leaned down to kiss the top of her head.

"Yeah, it would," she answered.

"I love you," he said, and a shiver ran down his body. It always did as if the words cut him as much as she knew they would her.

"I know," she answered. It was how she always answered him. She didn't have it in her to say the words. Not to him. She couldn't look in his eyes and say those words, knowing she was leaving him far too soon. "I feel like a princess tonight. This room, this dress."

"I don't think I will ever feel like a prince." A wicked smile spread over his lips before he leaned down and whispered against her ear. "But I can certainly be a beast."

She gasped before he took her lips with his. The soft sweet moment quickly escalated as the kiss deepened, and their sways moved across the room toward the bed. Clothes fell every step of the way so by the time they got there, they were both naked. He sat down and then pulled her to him. Most of the time when they made love, she was on top, mostly because he had grown afraid of hurting her. That wasn't what she wanted, though.

"Take me like a beast then," she whispered next to his ear, and he gripped her closer.

"Baby, I don't want to hurt you," he growled, his mouth moving over her neck and chest, tasting every inch of her.

"I don't care," she answered, and it was as if his hold on his control shattered.

He twisted them until she was on the bed, and he moved between her legs as he delivered savage kisses. It reminded her of the first time they were together, when they were so frantic for each other that they didn't even take time to strip.

He gripped her wrist and held her down as he bit and licked every inch of her he could reach. She was small, so that was a lot of her. Her body rolled and moved with every touch, and she craved him more and more.

Their lips crashed together in a bruising kiss, feeding from each other's mouths with desperate hunger. "You sure?" he groaned between kisses.

"Shut up," she teased just as he had told her that first time, and he knew exactly what she was saying.

He slammed his body into her hard and fast, forcing screams of pleasure from her almost instantly. He used one hand to hold her arms above her head while the other lifted her hips, so he was angled just right to hit that spot inside of her that made her body explode with every thrust. For all the times they had been together he had always held on to a part of himself to keep from hurting her. This time she begged him to give his all to her.

Harder and faster, they moved until it was bruising, but she didn't care. She wanted more and never wanted it to stop. The sensation of his teeth, the tickling of his lips, everything set fire to her. Those moments, with him, like that, made her feel alive. Truly alive. As if death was behind a barrier and couldn't touch her.

"Fuck, baby," he growled, taking her lips again.

Sweat dripped down his body as heat built higher between them. Then between one powerful trust and the next a forceful wave crashed through her. She felt his body stiffen and lose cadence as he roared out his own release. Her legs gripped around him, holding him to her as they both writhed in the sensation.

When he finally fell, he landed next to her, still diligent not to crush her. He ran his hand over her body as if inspecting it. "Are you okay?"

Honestly, the moment she started to come down from the high, the pain took over, but she didn't dare tell him that.

"Yeah, baby, I'm very good," she answered and leaned up to kiss him.

He cupped her cheek as they continued to kiss, and then he pulled away and just rested his forehead against hers. "That was incredible."

"Yeah, it really was," she answered and kissed him again, trying to push back the growing pain she felt. She wrapped herself around him, wanting the warmth of him against her tender body. Trimmers began, and she tried to will herself to make them go away.

"Alanna?" he asked, pulling away. It apparently was written all over her face because he instantly got up from the bed and started to throw on clothes. "Why didn't you tell me to stop?"

"I didn't want you to stop," she answered, unable to catch her breath.

He sat her up and pulled a nightgown over her before picking her up and taking her to the room he had set up for the nurses. She didn't want to go there. She wanted to be in bed, holding him, kissing him, making love to him, but she couldn't really fight back either.

While the nurse worked to get her medication and fluids, he sat on the ground, resting his head in her lap. She petted his hair, loving the feel of the silky strands running through her fingers.

Everything felt like more. She sensed them more, appreciated them more than anything she had ever experienced in her life. As she came to the end, she learned to see the little things for the miracles they were, and it filled her with so much joy that despite the pain, she couldn't help but smile.

"You should have told me to stop," he whispered, pulling her out of her trance.

"No, because I didn't want you to. Now, just sit there and let me play with your hair. Maybe sing me a song," she answered.

He shifted so she could get more of his hair. Softly he started to sing for her. All of his songs were filled with pain and anger, the emotions of a man who had a hard life and had to fight for every ounce of respect no one wanted to give him. When he sang, he felt every word. She felt every word, and they sank into her.

Would he write songs about her when she was gone? Was she just going to be another tragedy in his life that fueled his art? She couldn't catch her breath, so as he sang, she combed through his hair and mouthed the words along with him. She loved him. She couldn't say the words, but she did, with all of her broken heart and shattered soul. She loved him, and he deserved so much more than the shell of a life she had to give.

CHAPTER TWENTY-SIX

ABEL

"Dad! Dad! Wake up!" Briar said, shaking him awake. He pulled at the sheet to cover his very naked body and looked around the room.

Alanna wasn't there and the sun was shining outside. Panic hit him hard, and he sat straight up.

"What's wrong? What happened?" he asked, grabbing a pair of pajama pants from the floor and throwing them on.

"Nothing's wrong, but you need to come downstairs now," she said. He wasn't awake enough to understand the words and how they didn't match the rushing tone.

"Fuck, Briar, I was naked," he groaned, getting up.

"Okay, I wasn't looking. Anyway, come quick," she said and took his hand, dragging him down the hall.

He could hear the piano before he even made it to the stairs. As much as everyone loved that piano, no one really ever used it. He kept it in tune, but they usually used the one in the studio if they were going to work on music. Slowly he made his way down the stairs with Briar by his side. Halfway down he heard her. She belted out a song with such power that part of his heart hoped some sort of miracle had happened in the night.

Able made his way to the bottom of the stairs, and there he saw her. She had on a nightgown and a thin robe, which fell behind her like a cape. Her hair was wrapped in a scarf, and her hands were moving over the keys as she sang with every ounce of passion in her body. It was a love song, something he had heard in passing before but never really paid attention to. But as she sang it, he did. It was about love and loss, and the mix of pain and emotion sent him to the floor. He sat there on the stairs, watching the woman he loved sing and feeling his heart breaking with every note.

He wasn't sure he had ever heard her sing so powerfully. Not in person at least. Even at the festival, there was that little bit of a quiver in her voice where she simply couldn't get quite enough air. Briar sat down next to him and held his hand, listening along with him. The woman before him was not the same woman he had known all these months. He watched her body move as she pulled in air enough to belt out each note until it nearly shook the glass of the windows. Most people could not sing like that. On his best days he could sing like that.

Only on his best days.

"I can't do this," he whispered, reality hitting him.

"I'm right here, Dad. Now go. Sit with her and let her sing to you," Briar said.

He gave her a weak smile fighting an urge to cry. It wasn't like him to cry, but with Alanna, he found himself doing it a lot more than he liked to admit. "When did you get so smart?"

"Just go," she said, and he forced himself to get up and walk over to the piano bench.

Alanna looked over to him as he sat down next to her, but she didn't stop what she was doing. She just kept singing, each word stabbing into him. In a complete reverse of their normal stance, he leaned his head down and rested it on her shoulder and placed his hand on her thigh. Closing his eyes, he breathed, slow and deep, savoring every beautiful note.

When the song was over, she didn't stop. She just went into another one.

"Hey, baby," she whispered, leaning down to kiss the top of his head.

"Hey," he whispered. "Sing for me?"

"Of course," she answered, and she did.

He wasn't sure how long they sat there as she went from one song to the next. Every one of the songs she sang was a powerful ballad of love, loss, regret, heartbreak, hope, and pain. Most of the songs he didn't know or had only heard here and there. Alanna knew a lot more music than he did. She had ventured much further outside of his usual stuff. It was impressive, and never once did she falter. Her voice was angelic, and he could feel how the songs released from her, easing something in her that he hadn't realized was there.

After what seemed like a lifetime, he started to hear the cracks, but when he looked, it wasn't her body growing weak. Tears streamed down her cheeks as she continued. He reached over and turned her to face him. Her fingers continued to play, but he wiped the tears from her. When that last song finished, Abe kissed her and pulled her close to him. It had been one of the most magical moments of his life, and he knew it would haunt him for the rest of his days.

"I love you," he whispered, holding her and kissing her softly.

"I know," she answered and kissed him back.

"Do you want to go to Vegas?" he asked, not even sure why he would be pushing more adventures on her. He could feel in his bones that something had changed, but he wasn't ready, and he was clinging to every moment he could.

"Yeah," she answered without hesitation.

A smile spread over his lips, and he kissed her again before getting up. "I'll go pack. You should get dressed."

"I'll be right up," she said, and he kissed her again before taking to the stairs.

"Briar! Do you want to go to Vegas?" he called out.

"What am I going to do in Vegas?" she asked back. Being nineteen meant she couldn't gamble, but there were other things she could do.

"I don't know. We'll go to some shows or something. Do you want to fucking go or not?" he asked again, getting into the room and pulling out a suitcase. He had more suitcases than he probably needed, but they came in handy. Single minded focus, he tossed some of his things into the bag, he would wait for Alanna before he put any of her stuff in.

"Yeah, I'm packing now!" Briar called from down the hall after a few minutes.

He was nearly dressed when Alanna walked into the room. She had a strange look on her face like she was lost in very deep thought. Maybe she was. Whatever she had been doing all morning had certainly been just as much mental as physical. He could feel it radiating off of her. With one of those brilliant smiles resting on her lips, she went about getting dressed and helping him pack.

They made arrangements for one of the nurses to go as well, and then he called one of the hotels to set the rooms.

"No, I want two rooms, one across the hall from the other," he explained to the clerk on the other end of the phone as he started taking bags down the stairs.

Briar walked with Alanna, and he worked on loading up the car. They were going to take one of his fancier cars because Alanna had expressed wanting to ride in one.

"No, across the hall not next to each other. I don't want to hear what is going on in that room, and I'm sure she doesn't want to hear what is going on in my room."

It took another ten minutes of arguing with the desk clerk before they agreed to what he was saying. Then they were on their way. He had a feeling there would be a secondary argument when he got to the hotel, but for now he just wanted to get on the road. He set up the nurse with her own car and some money for expenses, and then they headed to Vegas.

"It is so strange to me that someone was just wandering the desert one day and was like, 'You know what would be great here in the middle of all this sand? A bunch of hotels and casinos.'" Alanna said as the city drew near.

Abel burst out laughing, but she did have a point. "Yeah, well I don't think he is still around to ask, so we will just have to enjoy what he left behind," Abel answered.

As expected, when he got to the hotel, he once again had to explain what he wanted to the desk clerk, but they were finally able to get to their rooms. Alanna was tired, which he expected since she had gotten up before anyone else in the house, so he got her settled and then asked Briar to sit with her.

"Hey, can you sit here just in case? I need to run an errand," he said as he gathered up his wallet and keys.

"What kind of errand do you need to do in Vegas?" Briar asked, giving him a curious look.

"I just have an errand. I won't be long, and by then maybe Alanna will be up, and we can go catch a show or something before I go blow all my money," he answered, giving Briar a quick kiss on the cheek before he left.

As he drove, he had made another call when no one was around. He had been to a jewelry store there a few times for various pieces. This was different, though. This was something he had never done before, and his head was racing with how crazy the idea even was.

When he stepped into the store, a woman smiled at him from behind one of the counters. "How can I help you?"

"I'm Abel Sharp. I called ahead about a ring," he said and pulled a small string out from his pocket. He had used it to measure Alanna's finger when she had fallen asleep. "This would be the size. I hope this is helpful."

"It is. I think Gary has already pulled some options for you in the back if you want to follow me, Mr. Sharp," she answered and held open a section of the counter so he could follow her to the back of the store.

An older gentleman was sitting at a table with a black velvet case in front of him. Several diamond rings were placed on it, and Abel's heart pounded as he made his way to look at them. The woman took the string to measure it and then let the man, who Abel assumed was Gary, know the size.

"Abel Sharp, now this is certainly a surprise. My partner Matthew said you have been here a few times but never for a diamond ring. Are you planning on asking that girl everyone is talking about to marry you?" he asked, getting up and shaking his hand.

"No, I just want a ring is all," Abel answered, his chest growing tight.

"Well, she has a very tiny finger, but these should be some good options. They are of the highest quality and clarity of anything you will find in Vegas," the man answered.

Abel took his time looking over each ring until he found the one he wanted. It had a single diamond with three smaller diamonds surrounding it. In his mind he saw those smaller ones as Briar, Hannah, and Lacey, the three most important girls in his life. The larger one of course was Alanna. It was perfect. She was going to kill him, but it was perfect.

"I'll take this one, now," he said. After spending a small fortune, he left the store and went back to the hotel. He was sure Alanna was ready to get up and have fun, and all he wanted to do was give that to her.

CHAPTER TWENTY-SEVEN

ABEL

Their night started with them attending one of those circus style shows, and then Briar went to find something to do while he took Alanna into the high roller part of the casino. If he was going to gamble, he was going to do it in style. They had dressed up nicely, and Alanna wore a huge smile.

"I think I have only been gambling one time, and that was a very long time ago. I have no idea what to do in a place like this," she said looking around at all the tables and machines.

"There is only one thing to do. Go spend all my money," he said, holding his card out to her so she could take it.

"I can't do that. I will just lose it all," she answered, giggling.

"Then go lose all my money. I'll make more," he answered.

He knew she had an idea of how to play cards as they had played with the band in Florida. So, he guided her to a blackjack table as their first game and got them both a lot of chips to bet with. Before they got started, he leaned over and explained how to play at the table and then they were dealt into the hand. She was reserved at first, but after winning the first two hands, she got a little braver.

"Blackjack is cool because you have higher odds, most of the time," he explained, pushing more chips into the betting circle.

"This whole thing has my heart racing. It's so exciting," she said and squealed when she won another hand.

They stayed there for a little while longer, letting her build up her own little pile of winnings, before he took her to play more risky games. She seemed to have just as much fun losing as she did winning, laughing and carrying on as she tried to understand the game. After a while, she asked him to just play, and she stood with him to be his lady luck. He knew it was her way of saying she was too tired to keep up with the game, but he liked the idea of her being his lucky charm.

Hours went by, but he saw her starting to fade and knew she needed medicine and rest, so they packed up their chips and started to head off of the casino floor to their room. They were about halfway across the floor when Alanna stumbled and fell to the side a bit, ending up bumping into a man who was making his way toward one of the back tables.

It caused him to drop some of his chips, and he spun on her and yelled, "Watch where you're going, you fucking drunk bitch!"

Abel wasn't really sure what happened in that moment. He saw red, and the next thing he knew, he had the man on the ground punching him. Security rushed over and pulled him off of the guy, but he fought the whole time, pulling against arms and hands trying to restrain him as he screamed every profanity he could think of.

Distantly he could hear Alanna screaming for him to stop, but he couldn't. Before long he was being escorted to a police car and placed inside. From the window of the car, he saw Alanna standing there, a worried look on her face. What the fuck had he done?

"My name is Alanna Merrick. I'm here to pick up Abel Sharp," he heard her say from down the hall. He stood up and went to stand close to the door so he could gauge just how upset she might be. It had been so long since he had really lost his temper. Sure, he had punched Derrik, but the punk had it coming. It had been one punch. Usually, he kept his temper under control. The way that man spoke to Alanna caused him to snap, and he was not backing down.

After a couple of minutes, he saw her walking with the cop toward the holding cell. "Hey, baby," she said from the other side of the bars, that sweet and sexy smile resting on her face.

"Hey," he said, grinning back at her.

"They didn't kick us out of the hotel, but they aren't happy," she said as he walked out of the cell and toward her.

"You came to get me?" he asked, not caring about what the hotel had to say. He leaned down and kissed her, breathing in her sweet strawberry scent.

"Yeah, I came and got you. You left me this after all," she said holding up his Amex Black Card. "I had to take a cab, though, which was not fun."

"Is Briar pissed?" he asked.

"She doesn't know. I didn't tell her. Honestly, she probably thinks we are still playing the games," Alanna answered. After getting his stuff back from the desk and shoving it in his pockets, he took her hand and started to walk out.

He would deal with any legal ramifications later. All that mattered was his woman and getting her back to the fun time he promised. They got outside and into the cab, which had waited for them.

"She probably knows, and I will hear it when we get back."

"Abel?" Alanna said his name like a question, and he turned to look at her. "Do you remember that night we sat outside and looked at the stars and ate smores?"

"Yeah, I do," he answered. Abel remembered everything.

"You told me you used to drive out to the desert and lay on your car and do that. You told me one day you would show me," she said, her eyes looking out the window at all the twinkling neon that Vegas had to offer.

"Then that is what we will do," he answered.

When they got back to the hotel, he requested his car and drove her out of town as far into the desert as he could until the lights of Vegas were a faint halo in the distance. Once there, he parked the car and walked around to help her out. She smiled as he helped her up onto the hood of the car. When he had done this in the past, it had not been on the hood of the most expensive car he owned, but he didn't care. Scuff, scratches. None of that mattered. Alanna wanted to see the stars, so they went to see the stars.

"It's easier to breathe here," she whispered as he lay down next to her and reached over to hold her hand.

"I know. You live in a swamp over there," he teased.

They lay there in silence for a long time, and he just listened to the sound of her breathing next to him. She looked so beautiful lying there under the stars. Her dress billowed around her, and she wore a soft smile, the same smile she'd worn since the moment they landed in California. It was like she was taking in every single moment.

"It's so beautiful out here. I don't know how anyone can stand to live in a city and miss out on all of this," she whispered.

Lifting up on his elbow, he shifted and leaned in to kiss her. It was a soft kiss, not one to ignite any kind of passion. There was no way he was doing that again. His head was still swimming from the guilt of hurting her, regardless of what she had said. "Alanna, I need to do something."

He felt his body start to tremble as he slid off of the car hood and pulled her up so she was sitting in front of him. She had a curious look on her face, but that soft smile was still there.

"Baby, I... well, I love you," he said, trying to find the right words. All his life he had been able to come up with words. His songs were filled with lyrics telling the world everything that had ever happened to him. Words that he had needed to express to free his soul, but in that moment, he wasn't sure he would ever have the right words.

"I know," she answered.

"Look, I'm not going to ask the question, because, well, I'm not that stupid. I know there isn't any point. And honestly, I don't want to hear you say no. But..." He took a deep breath and pulled the ring out of his pocket. He didn't get down on a knee. He just leaned in closer to her until his head was resting against hers. "I won't ask the question, but will you please wear my ring? You don't even have to wear it on that finger. Just, until... well, will you please wear it for me?"

The pause was too long, which made everything hurt. She hadn't said a word and was barely breathing. For a second, he thought he had lost her in that very moment, but then she reached up and cupped his cheek. "I can't say them. I just can't. I'm so sorry, but you have to know."

"I do," he said. He knew. If he hadn't known before, he certainly did after hearing her sing for him all morning. The night air was cool, something about the desert always made it that way, and he was starting to worry she would get too cold.

"You have been the greatest joy I have felt outside of Hannah and Lacey. You have been the only man to make me feel the way you do. To give me happiness. You made every dream in my life come true, and in such a short amount of time. But saying those words. Saying..." Tears filled her eyes, and he leaned in to kiss them away. "They just hurt."

"I know. I know they do," he whispered. They hurt when he said them too, but he couldn't not say them.

"But, yes, I will wear your ring," she whispered, and a wave of relief rushed down his spine. His heart warm, he slid the ring on her finger, knowing what it meant and knowing that neither of them were stupid enough to do anything else. Their whole relationship had been stupid. Dangerous. A torture leading to a terrifying end. Yet nothing had stopped him from continuing with it.

"Thank you," he said and held her to him.

"It's beautiful," she said and turned her face to look up at him.

"You're beautiful," he said and kissed her again. He let himself feel her and take her into him. As much as he wanted more, he held himself in check and just enjoyed kissing her and holding her there under the stars. They were alone, away from the cruel world that beat them down every day. In that moment, they were the only two that existed, and he wished with every fiber of his being that he could make that moment last.

They didn't stay much longer. It was too cold for her, and he didn't want her feeling uncomfortable or getting any kind of illness on top of what was already there. When they got back to their room, Briar was there waiting for them. She had an angry look, and he knew she had found out about his quick detour to jail.

"Later," he said as he walked with Alanna to the bedroom. The nurse came in to get her fixed up, and then he would help her get ready for bed.

While the nurse worked, he went back out and wrapped his arms around his daughter, just needing to hold her and let her know that he loved her. "Dad, what's going on?"

"I got in a fight because someone said something mean to Alanna. I know it was stupid. I will deal with it," he explained.

"That's not what I'm talking about. What's up with the ring?" she asked, and he looked down at her confused. In that short amount of time, she had noticed it.

"It's just a ring, nothing else," he answered. It wasn't the full truth, but he knew what his daughter was asking, and that was the most truth she needed.

CHAPTER TWENTY-EIGHT

ABEL

"Yeah, I'll be back tomorrow, and we can go over that. I'll sign the paperwork, and we will start recording as soon as, well, I'm done dealing with this personal stuff," Abel said over the phone.

Mason needed him to come back and take care of business, and honestly, he knew Alanna wasn't going to be able to handle much more of Vegas.

She had slept in later than usual, and he kept going in to check on her, but when Mason called, he went out to the main part of their room so as not to disturb her. Turning, he saw her walking out of the bedroom area, and a smile spread over his lips. She still looked tired and a little weak, but she was still the most beautiful woman he had ever seen. He wasn't sure he would ever see her any other way, and it was something he was grateful for.

"Abel," she whispered and reached out to stabilize herself on the back of the couch. Slowly she inched her way around it, and he hung up on Mason so he could go help her.

"What's wrong?" he asked, feeling a knot form in his stomach.

She took a couple of deep breaths and then lifted her hand to press it against his cheek. It took more effort, but she gave him that soft smile again before speaking. "I think I need to go home."

"Okay, then we will go home. I'll have the car brought right away," he said and started to get up, but she grabbed his hand and tugged for him to stay.

"No, I think I need to go home," she said, and he knew exactly what she meant. He didn't want to know it, but he did. "I still have things I need to do."

"Okay, then I'll get you home. I have to do something in LA, but let me get you on a plane and then I will be right behind you," he said.

Fuck he knew he should just call Mason back and tell him to shove it, but he had promised not to let this relationship with Alanna fuck things up with the band, and the contract had to be signed. Maybe it could be faxed. He wasn't sure.

"BRIAR!" he screamed, not sure if she would hear him from across the hall.

The nurse rushed over to check on Alanna, and he brushed her away. "Go tell my daughter to come here."

"Alanna, look at me," he said, seeing her eyes go a little distant. She blinked a couple of times before focusing back on him. "You need to hold on for me, baby. Can you do that? Two days?"

"I don't know. I can't promise that," she said, and her jaw started to quiver.

"You can. I know you can. Come on, baby. Let me get you home, but you have to hold on for me. Okay? Please," he said. He knew just as much as she did that she couldn't make any promises. Frantic and full of fear, he called Mason again.

"I need a flight to Birmingham now," he said without even letting Mason say anything.

"I'll see what I can do," Mason said from the other side of the line.

"No, make it happen. I don't care what you have to do. I need a flight, and I need it now," he demanded before hanging up and shoving the phone in his pocket.

"Dad," Briar said and knelt down next to him. "What do you need me to do?"

"Get my car. Go back to LA," he said. "Get our stuff and just go back to the house, and I'll see you when I can."

"No, I'm going with you," Briar demanded.

He turned to look at her. Her jaw was set, and she had the same stubborn look that he often got.

"No, not for this. Not like this," he said. It was already going to break him to do this. He didn't want to drag his daughter into it as well.

"Look, you need me. I'm going," Briar said.

Alanna fell forward and he caught her, pulling her into his arms to hold her. Her breathing was so shallow, and her skin was clammy.

"Call Hannah and let her know that we are getting her there as soon as possible. Tell her to be ready," he told Briar and nodded toward his pocket.

She fished the phone out of his pocket and scrolled for the number. "Hi, this is Briar. I'm Abel's daughter. Look, we are looking for a flight now, but we are on our way back with your mom. He told me to let you know to be ready."

In that moment he couldn't have been prouder of his daughter. He should have never dragged her into all of this, but he couldn't have been more grateful in that moment to have her. When the phone rang again, she answered it. "I don't know. Let me give you to my dad. It's Mason."

"I got a flight, but just for her. I can't get you there for another few hours," Mason explained.

"That isn't good enough," he nearly yelled. That made Alanna jump, and he took a couple of deep breaths to try and calm down.

"It's the best we can do on such short notice. I already booked it. I'll get you on the very next flight," Mason said. "They are aware of the situation, and she will be taken care of the whole time."

"No, no, no, no, I can't abandon her like that," Abel said, his breath shaking.

"Baby," Alanna whispered, and he dropped the phone to turn his focus back to her. Briar snatched the phone, but he turned his full attention on Alanna. "Just get me home."

"Mason can't get us a flight together," he said. He had to be there. He wouldn't abandon her.

"I'll be fine. I'll hold on for you," she whispered. "I promise."

He knew it was a lie. She couldn't make that promise any more than she could heal herself. It was a little lie, and her way of telling him that getting her home was more important than him being next to her. It broke his heart, but he couldn't keep her from Hannah and Lacey just so he could selfishly stay by her side. "You swear it?"

"I swear. I still have something I need to do," she said. She had said something similar before, and he had no idea what she meant.

"I will be right behind you. Do you understand? I will be right behind you," he said next and kissed her.

"I know," she said and took a shaking breath.

"Mason said it is a medical flight, but he can get us booked two hours after. We won't be far behind," Briar explained. "We need to head there right away, though."

"Okay, let's go. We will deal with this shit later," Abel said and lifted Alanna in his arms to carry her out of the room. Neither of them was really dressed, but it didn't matter.

The car had already been pulled up front, and he got Alanna buckled in before going around to drive. Briar was buckled into the back seat, and he put the car in drive, speeding out of the hotel like hell was chasing him. It was.

Alanna reached over and turned up the radio, softly whispering the words of the song that played. Oh, how he wanted to hear her sing for him again. That powerful voice vibrating out of her. It would make everything better. He slammed on the breaks as he pulled up in front of the airport, and then slammed the car into park before rushing to get Alanna out.

"Sir, you can't park there," a security officer said, trying to stop him.

He didn't stop or even look back. Instead, he called over his shoulder. "Tow it!"

Briar was rushing by his side, but his focus was solely on getting Alanna to her flight. "We need to go this way," Briar said, pointing them in the right direction.

She provided all of the information as Mason had given it to her, and he carried Alanna. The process of getting through security was torture, but they managed to get Alanna a wheelchair so he wouldn't have to continue to hold her. Not that he really wanted to let her go.

"Hold on for me, baby. I'm going to get you home," he said as they weaved through the airport until they made it to the proper gate.

The staff explained that they had people on flight to help take care of her and that she would be given directly to Hannah on the other end if not transported directly to the nearest hospital. Alanna was in and out of consciousness the entire time, but when she was awake, she would look up and smile at him, and it would take the pain away for just the shortest moment.

"Baby, I'm right behind you. Mason already sent my flight info. I'm not going home to get my stuff. I'm waiting here until they get me on that plane then I will be right behind you. Can you hold on for me?" he asked as the flight attendant took hold of the chair to take her away.

"I'll see you soon, baby," she whispered and cupped his cheek. Her movements were so slow and weak that it almost hurt to see.

"I love you," he said, kissing her with everything he had.

If it was his last kiss, he was going to make it the best kiss of his life. He held her to him, savoring every single moment of it until he had to pull away.

He stayed there, staring at her until she disappeared from view, and once she had, he fell apart. His body collapsed to the ground, and he started to cry and scream. It didn't matter that he was in the middle of an airport. It didn't matter that people everywhere knew who he was. He had just put the love of his life on a plane, and he had no idea if he would ever see her alive again. It tore him apart, and he couldn't hold it in anymore.

Briar wrapped around him and held him to her. "I got you. I got you, but we need to go. We have another flight to catch. Come on, Dad. I'm with you, but you have to stay strong for a little while longer."

He could tell she was crying too, but she was being strong for him. She shouldn't have to do that, and in that moment, he realized she really was just like him. He didn't have to be there for Alanna. He didn't have to keep going back and spending time with her. He didn't have to keep giving her things and sharing in her life. But he did.

Briar shouldn't have to be his rock. His light in the darkness, but she was. She always had been, and he would be eternally grateful for her. His daughter had saved him nineteen years ago just by existing. Now she was helping hold him up when he wanted to completely fall apart. Once he regained some of his strength, he got to his feet and walked with her so they could find their flight.

"I can't do this," he whispered as he sat on a chair at the gate.

"Yes, you can," Briar said and leaned against him.

"Hold on for me, baby," he prayed, hoping with all he had that she would still be there when he got to her.

CHAPTER TWENTY-NINE

ALANNA

It was a strange sensation that she simply couldn't describe, but she could feel it coming for her. It had creeped its vines around her and was starting to press in. All she wanted was to be home. She needed to be with Hannah. Her daughter needed her. Alanna's heart broke when she had to leave Abel behind, and she kept looking down at the ring on her finger. In her mind she kept chanting that she had a couple of things left to do. It was her own secret prayer to keep her going a little longer.

Her body was failing. She had known it that morning when she sat there and sang to Abel. She had woken up knowing she had reached the end of her clock, and every moment since had been borrowed time. She still had a couple of things left to do, and she prayed with everything in her that she had time to do them.

The staff on the plane were very nice and kept her comfortable the entire time. How she held herself together, she wasn't sure, but she sat there, watching the world go by below her and wondered if that was how things would look when she left. Alanna had never really thought about what would happen to her when she died. She wasn't terribly religious, but suddenly she had all of the questions. Did everyone have those questions when they were at the end, or was her own lack of seeking out answers bringing them on now? Not that any of it mattered. She would find out soon enough.

Something else she had always thought was that she would be afraid. Instead, she just felt peaceful. Her life had not been a good one. Her childhood had ended abruptly, and she was thrust into being a single mother. Then her mother abandoned her, followed by a ten-year relationship with an abusive asshole. Her entire adult life she had fallen into line, just an ant in the machine of life instead of following her dreams. Even in the small band she had, she knew it was just playing at a dream she would never have.

Abel had given her that dream. She closed her eyes remembering singing that one song in front of twenty thousand people. For five minutes she had been a star, and he had made that happen. He had given her everything when he didn't have to. The only thing she was giving him was a broken heart. It really wasn't fair.

"Miss, we are about to land," the flight attendant said, and she looked out of the window to see the city of Birmingham coming in closer. Home. Well, close enough to home.

He hadn't wanted to let her go, but he did, knowing that she needed to be home. As much as she loved the idea of just leaving the world there in his beautiful home, she needed to see her girls one more time. Once the plane was parked, or whatever it was called when a plane stopped moving, someone came to take her to where her daughter was surely waiting for her.

God her daughter was so beautiful, and she couldn't have been more proud of her if she tried. Despite all of her flaws, she had managed to raise a very smart, beautiful, and compassionate woman. Hannah rushed over to her and knelt down to wrap her arms around her. "Mom, oh god."

"I want to go..." she didn't finish the last word before she passed out.

CHAPTER THIRTY
ABEL

"Alanna Merrick," Abel asked at the circulation desk a moment before Hannah called for him.

The moment he saw her, he rushed toward her and wrapped his arms around her. He didn't have it in him to ask just yet. Once they had landed, he got a car and raced toward the hospital, not even bothering to call. Hannah had already told him Alanna collapsed at the gate of the airport. All he could hope was that he made it in time. With a couple of deep breaths, he stepped back. "Is she still?"

"Yes, she actually just woke up," Hannah answered and showed him toward the room where Alanna was lying in the bed.

Behind him, he heard Briar and Hannah introducing themselves to each other, but his focus was to check on his woman.

"Hey, baby," he said, moving into the room and leaning over the bed so he could kiss her. Then he let down the guard rail on the side and told her to scoot over so he could join her. Of course, he didn't actually make her move, but he did crowd her so he could be near her.

"Hey, baby," she whispered and leaned her head against him. "You made it."

"I told you I would. You waited for me," he said and kissed the top of her head again.

"Yeah, I told you I would. I promised, and I couldn't break a promise," she answered and then took another couple of deep breaths. "Baby, I want to go home."

Those words hit him, and he knew in that moment that she was asking him to make sure that what she wanted happened. "Okay, let me get the doctor."

He got up and went to find Dr. Carter, remembering her from the appointment he had accompanied Alanna on before they went to California. She was at the circulation desk going over charts but smiled up at him when she saw him.

"Hey, I wasn't sure if we would see you," she said and stood up to shake his hand.

"I'm not leaving her," he answered. "Doc, she wants to go home. So, ummm, I'm taking her home."

"No, you aren't. She needs to be here," Hannah interrupted, pulling back on his shoulder to make him look at her. He knew out of everyone there, she was hurting the most, so he kept himself in order, but he would do what Alanna wanted no matter what anyone else had to say about it.

"Actually, I think that's a great idea. Look, let's go talk in private for just a moment. Follow me," the doctor explained and motioned them toward a small office-like room. It was a counseling room, and he couldn't help but wonder how many times this doctor had to go in this room and give families the worst news of their lives.

"We can't take her home. She needs care. She needs you," Hannah protested.

"Hannah, there isn't anything else I can do. You know that as well as anyone. Alanna certainly knows it. She has known it from the start. Now, listen to me, I have no idea the timeline at this point. When patients get to this point, it is literally up to them. It could be hours. It could be days. I have no idea. I'm not even going to try and guess. But I will say this. No one should have to die in a hospital. They should be at home, where they are comfortable and surrounded by the people they love. This is the furthest place from that there is. So, if she wants to go home, I say you take her home. She is already set up to have nurses there, and they will stay until the end," the doctor explained, and Hannah started to cry.

Abel reached out to comfort her, but she pushed him away and left the room, leaving him alone with the doctor.

"When I talked to her earlier when she had a small spell of being awake, she told me that you have given her the happiest end she could have ever asked for. I see hundreds of patients, and I can tell you that I have never seen someone look so happy and be this close to the end. Thank you for making her life special, even if it was just for a little while."

"You don't need to thank me. But I do need to go get her and take her home. Thank you for all you did. I know you did the best you could," he said and left the room.

Hannah was crouched down outside her mother's room, her face a mess of emotions. "Briar, can you help Hannah with whatever she needs. I'm going to get Alanna, and we are going to get her home."

"Okay," his daughter answered, and she knelt down to talk to Hannah.

Abel paused for a moment and looked at the two women and knew that this was not the end of them being in his life. He wasn't letting go of Hannah any more than he would let go of Lacey. He had done all he could for Alanna, but she had done a lot for him too. She had given him a new family.

"Hey, baby," she whispered when he walked into the room. Such simple words that always meant more than they seemed. He was sure the sound of her saying them to him would haunt him for the rest of his life.

"I'm going to take you home," he said.

They had to wait for her to be officially released and disconnected from everything, but as soon as she was, he took her and carried her out to Hannah's van. Abel got her settled, then climbed and pulled Alanna into him so he could hold her all the way home.

For a second, he started to chuckle, and she looked up and asked him what was so funny. "I'm just leaving a line of cars in my wake. I told them to tow my Maserati at the airport in Vegas, and now I just abandoned my rental car here."

She giggled, and it filled him with joy. That is what he wanted. He wanted to make her laugh and smile and fill these last moments with joy, just as he had done since he met her.

"That is going to be expensive. You know, getting your car back."

"I don't care," he said and brushed his finger over her face. In the front, Hannah and Briar were talking, but his whole focus was on Alanna.

"Thank you," she whispered.

"For what?" he asked. He would just keep her talking.

"Everything," she answered.

Once they got to Alanna's, he got her settled in bed then moved in to sit next to her. "What do you want to do?" he asked as the nurses started to set a few things up. He wasn't paying attention to any of them.

"I want to watch you," she whispered, her voice weak and full of air.

"Okay," he answered and turned on the television.

Some of his old concerts were on YouTube, so he navigated there and turned one on. She nuzzled into him, and he held her close as the concert started. As he watched and heard some of the stupid shit he said, he laughed.

"Damn, I can be such an asshole."

"I like it. I used to say that stupid shit all the time on stage," she answered.

"I know. I've seen your show," he said laughing.

"Grandma! I missed you!" Lacey exclaimed, running into the room.

"My girl! Look at you. I missed you too!" Alanna said and gave the child as strong a hug as she could muster.

"Hey, Lacey, no love for me?" he asked, and the girl came around to give him a hug. "You see that pretty girl over there. That's my daughter Briar. You want to show her around?"

"Yeah, I can do that!" Lacey responded and hopped down. Briar took the small girl's hand and went with her. Abel wasn't really sure what Lacey was going to do with her, but he knew Briar would help keep the child occupied.

Hannah pulled up a chair and sat with them, watching the show. For the most part, Alanna kept her focus on the TV, but now and then she would look around at them. He kept his focus on her, and watched every smile and every expression. A smile crossed his lips as he took in the way her mouth still moved to every word as if they were imprinted on her soul. He refused to miss a single moment.

"Hannah, can you go check on Lacey and Briar?" Alanna said, and her daughter gave her a curious look.

Abel shrugged, not knowing what Alanna was up to either.

"Yeah, I'll be back in just a second," she answered.

The moment she was gone, Alanna turned toward him. "Abel, I need you to promise me something," she said, and suddenly she seemed to have the energy in her to speak.

"Anything," he said and held his breath to take it all in.

"It's always just been me and her against the world. I can't leave her alone. I just can't. I need you to promise me that you will take care of her. You will take care of her and take care of Lacey. Please, promise me," she said, and tears started to fall down her cheeks.

"You don't even have to ask. I had already decided that a long time ago. Hannah, she's my daughter now, whether she likes it or not, and Lacey already agreed to be my grandbaby. They will want for nothing for the rest of their lives, and I will protect them with everything I have in me. I swear it," he answered, lifting her hand to kiss it.

"Thank you," she said and leaned in and kissed him. Then she turned back to the concert on the screen, her body relaxing in relief.

She had things to do. That is what she had kept saying. Was this part of that? He had a feeling it was. There was a commotion outside, and it drew his attention away from Alanna and the concert. "Hold on, baby. I'll be right back."

When Abel stepped outside, he heard Lacey crying, and Hannah and Briar were yelling at someone. He wasn't sure who it was, and he really didn't care. If they were upsetting his girls, he would take care of it.

"Get the fuck out of here, John. Now is not the time!" Hannah yelled, throwing something at a man who was standing in the driveway.

"Briar, take Lacey inside and call the cops," he said as he moved past.

He knew exactly who John was. He had wanted to kill him the moment he had found out about him and what he had done to Alanna.

How dare this man show up today of all days? "You need to fucking leave."

"Who the fuck are you? I'm not going anywhere until I see Alanna. I gave that bitch ten years of my life. I'm going to see her," the man yelled.

It was the last thing he said before Abel punched him so hard, he fell to the ground. Abel laid into the man, punch after punch, taking out more than just his initial anger. He took out his anger at the whole situation on the man.

"Dad!" Briar called from the porch. "Dad, get in here now!"

It wasn't the scream of her trying to get him to stop fighting. He heard an urgency to her voice. He could hear sirens in the distance, and he knew that they were on the way. Abel got up and kicked the man in the stomach one more time for good measure before he and Hannah headed into the house. They locked the doors, and he told Briar to keep Lacey in the living room. He didn't know where Brandon was, but he wasn't happy with that man either.

When they got into the bedroom, the TV was off, and Alanna had curled up with the blanket in the dark. "Baby, you turned the show off."

"I hurt," she said, and he knew what was coming. It was there, in the room with them. And that was one being he couldn't fight off.

CHAPTER THIRTY-ONE
ABEL

"Okay, well let's do something about that then," Abel said, kneeling down on the floor next to the bed. The nurse had already run off to get the necessary medication for her pain.

"Brandon is on his way to deal with that situation," Hannah said before putting her phone in her pocket and sitting in the chair. She reached out and took her mother's hand, and he did the same with the other one.

"Hannah you were the best thing to ever happen to me. I'm so sorry I couldn't give you a better life," Alanna said between ragged breaths.

"You are the best mom in the world. I love you so much," Hannah answered, trying with everything in her to hold on to her composure.

"You deserved better, but I promise, I'm not leaving you alone," she whispered and gave her daughter a gentle squeeze before turning to look at him. "Hey, baby."

"Hey," he said, his breaths coming hard and deep, but helping to keep him steady and focused on her.

"I hurt so bad," she said as a tremble raked down her body.

"Hold on. It's coming," he said, and he wasn't sure if he was talking about the medication or death. In all honesty, they both were, and he knew it.

The nurse came in with the needle and went to put it in Alanna's port, but he stopped her. "Sir?"

"Let me do it," he said and reached for it.

"I'm not allowed to do that," she said and started to move in.

"Stop me then," he growled and snatched it from her.

The nurse gasped and backed up, but she didn't go to take it back from him. "Okay, baby, I'm going to make the pain stop. Okay? I'm going to help you."

He was shaking as he put the needle into the port and slowly released the medication into it. "Her eyes closed for a moment before she let out another jagged breath.

"Remember what you promised me," she whispered, reaching up and brushing hair from his face. He had let the needle fall to the floor, forgotten as he took in these last moments.

"Always," he said, biting the inside of his cheek.

"Remember that it's poison. You don't want poison," she said next, and he smiled.

"I don't. I never will," he answered, though his mind was screaming for it. It would certainly make his pain go away.

She gave him another smile and then looked over to Hannah again and gave her a smile. "I love you, Hannah."

"I love you, too, Mom," she said, but she had broken, tears streaming like rivers down her face.

When Alanna turned back to him, he noticed she was barely breathing. She was fighting. Even in those last few moments, she was fighting with everything she had to hold on, and it made him so proud.

"Hey, baby," she said again, and he wondered if she even knew what she was saying.

He leaned in closer and softly kissed her. "Hey, baby. I love you."

"I love you," she whispered against his lips a moment before her body shuddered.

She didn't say anything else. She didn't move. She didn't breathe. He felt his heart shatter, but just when he thought he was going to lose it, Hannah screamed.

"No, no, Mom, no! I'm not ready. No!" she screamed over and over, and he knew what he had to do.

Without a second thought he pulled Hannah into his arms and wrapped himself around her. Arms and legs held her, and he rocked her as he petted her head.

"I got you. I got you. I'm not going anywhere. I got you," he said over and over.

His body shaking, he held this woman who had never had a father. Who had just lost her mother and became the father she had always needed. It was natural and easy and gave him the strength he needed to push past his own pain.

"I'm not going anywhere. I swear to you. I'm right here. I love you. I love you and I have you," he continued as Hannah screamed and cried in his arms.

From the other room he heard Lacey say as calmly as only a child could be, "Grandma went to sleep now. Didn't she?"

"Yeah, she did," Briar answered. She had been right. He had needed her there.

The nurse was moving around the room, and he reached out and patted her leg. His own demons were screaming, fighting with the sweet words Alanna had said to him. "I need you to get that shit out of here. I need it gone. I don't trust myself right now."

"I'm getting it now," the nurse said, and he turned his focus back to Hannah.

In his mind, he heard those words again. She had never said them before, but she did, in that last moment. He heard her say them. He wasn't even sure if she knew she had, but he heard them, and it had been the most beautiful thing he had ever heard in his life.

He sat on the stairs of the porch, needing some air and a moment to process. The police had taken John away, and the coroner had already come to get Alanna, which had been harder to see than he expected. Hannah had managed to pull herself together and had gone into some sort of mode needing to do anything other than think. She was calling people and going through paperwork, and he realized he was just in the way. He figured everyone processed things differently.

There was a motion next to him as Briar sat down on the stair next to him. She rested her head against his shoulder and wrapped her arm in his until she was holding his hand.

"How you doing, old man?"

"Strangely better than I thought," he answered. "I had this second where I thought I was going to lose it all, but then Hannah needed me. I couldn't fall apart because she needed me."

"I'm so proud of you. This whole thing was crazy, but I have never seen you like this. You loved that woman with everything in you, and you did right by her," Briar said next.

"I love her, not loved. There is no past to it," he said and kissed the top of her head. "When did you get so smart?"

"I learned from you," she answered. "Now come on. Hannah said she needs to talk to all of us."

He wasn't sure he was ready to talk to anyone, but he got up and went inside to see what was happening. Hannah was sitting in a chair in the living room with Lacey on her lap. Apparently, they were both getting comfort from their daughters. There was an envelope in Hannah's hand with some words written on it, and Abel took a seat on the couch near her to waiting to find out what it was.

"I found this when I stripped Mom's bed. I don't know what it is," she said and handed the envelope to him. Tears formed in her eyes, and she leaned her head back as if to blink them away.

His eyes looked down at the envelope, and he saw the words *To My Girls* written on it. There were some lumps inside, and he turned it over to open it. Inside there was a sheet of paper and three rings.

She had things she needed to do.

"Do you want me to read it, or do you three want to read it together?" he asked. It seemed like something they should do, but he would read it for them if they wanted him to.

Briar reached over and took the letter. "I'll read it," she said. He opened the envelope bigger and let the rings fall into his hand.

To my three beautiful girls,

I wish so much that I could be there to see all the wonderful things you have coming in your life. I know you are all going to be incredible, and I want you to know that even if you can't see me, I will always be there for you. I don't have a lot to give any of you. Try as I might, the most valuable and wonderful things in my life were you. So, I'm going to give you something that represents something I treasure almost as much as you.

Briar had to take a couple of deep breaths. She apparently hadn't expected to be included in such a personal letter. Abel reached out and took Hannah's hand while holding the rings in his other hand. He held his palm open so Briar could see them. He knew what two of them were. The other he had never seen before, and Briar continued to read.

Briar, you are my newest girl, but that does not mean I love you any less. Don't let your dad bully your boyfriends. Deep down, he just wants you to be happy. Derrik is a good kid, whether your dad likes it or not. And even if he isn't the one, you better have a good time. Drummers are always the most fit in the band. You're young. Enjoy that.

The group burst out laughing, and Abel found himself blushing. Damn that woman.

In Vegas, your father gave me a ring. Well, I don't believe that people can take things back once they give them. So, it's my ring, and I will do what I want with it. I'm giving that ring to you. When you find that special person, you lock him down. Don't wait on a man to ask. You are better than that.

Abel lifted the ring to his lips, kissed it, and then handed it over to his daughter. She took it and then reached over and hugged him. He could feel the sting of tears in his eyes, but he did his best to fight them.

Hannah, you are my world. You made me a mother and gave me the best friend anyone could ever have. You put up with your wild mother through it all. I don't know if I would have survived as long as I did if it weren't for you. There are not enough words in the world to tell you how much I love you. It was always just me and you, kid, but I couldn't leave you alone. So, I made sure you wouldn't be. Look around. You have a family. You have a sister, you have a daughter, and you have a man very much willing to be a father, which is more than any other man I have ever known. He isn't perfect, but he will defend you to the end of the Earth. Just ask Derrik about his black eye. I'm leaving you my grandmother's pearl ring. It is the only thing I have that is from our family. How I managed to get it from my mother, I will never know. But it is yours now.

Like he had with Briar, he kissed the ring then handed it over to Hannah who slipped it onto her finger. He looked down and noticed her wedding ring was absent, and he made a note to talk to her about it later.

Lacey, my sweet magical girl. If you aren't a carbon copy of this old lady, there never was one. Oh, you are going to give them all hell, and I love it. Don't let anyone tell you that you can't do exactly what you want. I let people tell me, and it took finding the end to see exactly what I should have been doing all along. Be that bad ass bitch I know you have inside of you.

Briar paused and started to laugh before going back to the letter.

Don't let any of those mother fuckers tell you that you are less than amazing. Remember every song you sing should have meaning, even if other people don't like it. Keep that fire burning bright and be the star you already are. The ring I left you Grandpa Abel gave me in Florida. He told me he used to wear it on stage to give him confidence. I'm not sure that man was ever lacking in confidence, but if this ring brought him strength, I know it will you too. So, when you go on stage, you wear it and remember that I'm also there giving you strength, and that you have the grandma pass on all the naughty words.

I wish I had more time, but at the same time, I know I'm leaving you with a strong and loving family. Take care of each other. Lift each other up. Don't cry that I'm gone. Sing for me and let me hear you from wherever it is I have ended up. Be warriors. Be lovers. Be friends. Be bad ass bitches. Be Women.

With all my heart,

Alanna

PS. Take care of your dad/granddad. He might be strong right now, but he is going to need to let go too. And when he does, just let him. And if he loses his way, remind him. It's poison, and he doesn't want poison.

Briar set the letter down on her lap, and Abel picked up the last ring that still had the chain attached to it. He kissed it then fastened it around Lacey's neck before kissing her cheek. "Beautiful."

CHAPTER THIRTY-TWO

ABEL

There was a heavy weight on his chest when he woke, and he looked down to see a little blonde five-year-old lying on him. Smiling, he laid his head back and remembered when Briar would do that. He was gone so much that when he was home, she didn't want to leave him alone.

They were on the couch in Alanna's living room, and the world was quiet. That wasn't normal for her place. Music almost always played, and it made everything feel eerie. He dug his fingers into his pocked to pull out his phone and did his best to fumble through until he connected to Alanna's speakers and turned on some music. Silence made the demons louder, and he was still having a lot of trouble pushing them back. Despite what he had said, every fiber of him wanted to give in, give up.

Lacey wiggled a bit and then rubbed her nose on his shirt before blinking awake. "You turned on the music?"

"Yeah, it was too quiet," he answered, and they shifted so he could sit up. "You hungry?"

"Yes," she answered.

He wasn't much of a cook, but he had no idea where Hannah was. If she had managed to get to sleep, he certainly wasn't going to wake her just to feed a kid. They had been awake until almost sunrise, and he still wasn't sure how he had fallen asleep or ended up with a child. There was a box of pancake mix in the cabinet, and he figured that was something he could handle. He found a bowl and some measuring cups and pulled up a chair so Lacey could help. She stirred while he put the ingredients in and started the pan so it would get hot.

By the time the cakes were cooking, he and Lacey were singing along with the songs playing over the speakers. He loved that she knew the words to the harder rock and now and then would try out being rough. When she got a bit older, he would teach her how to do it for real.

"Are pancakes vegan?" she asked as he poured some syrup on her plate.

"I don't know. Let me look at the box," he answered. "Well, not these ones. They have milk in them."

"Oh, then hold on," she said and went into the cabinet. She grabbed the bread and some peanut butter. Then she used a spoon and proceeded to make him a sandwich. Task complete, the girl put it on a plate and handed it to him before they went to sit down at the table.

It was a lot of peanut butter, and he didn't have a drink. But he did his best to get down a couple of bites before just getting up and getting them both some soda. No one had been able to get groceries, so they were making do with what was there. "Mommy doesn't let me drink soda in the morning."

"Well, Mommy didn't make breakfast," he answered. When they were finished eating, he cleaned up while Lacey drew at the table. "Hey, Lacey, I'm going to be outside. Okay?"

"Yeah, I will be here," she answered and turned back to her drawing.

He went outside and then to Alanna's music room. He stepped inside and then closed the door. She loved that room, and just being inside of it, he could feel her there. There were boxes in one of the corners labeled "Lacey," and when he looked inside, he saw all the shirts and things she had gotten with him in Florida. Taking his time, he looked at all the memorabilia she had scattered around the room, just like he had the first time he had been there, but this time he saw it all with different eyes. This time, he saw the woman he loved and how these things meant something to her.

"I wish I had known you better when I signed this. I wish what I know now had hit me in the head then," he said, looking at the shirt and photo from his concert she had gone to. Before they had met. Before she knew she was sick.

Making his way around the room, he ended his trip staring at the photo of her on the wall. She was wet and sexy and screaming out with everything in her. His mind could almost hear it. She wasn't afraid to lay it all out on the stage. A true musician. A true artist. Closing his eyes, he could hear her singing to him. That last day in California when he had been woken up to go listen to her had been both magical and painful, and he had let it sink into him and brand a place on his soul.

"I wish I could have sung with you for the rest of eternity. I didn't get enough time," he whispered, reaching out and tracing the photo with his fingers. "I wish I had time to write us a song to sing together. There just wasn't time. I tried. I tried so many times, but I couldn't do it."

A shiver ran down his spine, and he stepped back to lean against the desk. He had been forcing himself to stay strong for the girls. They needed him to be strong so they could fall apart. Especially Hannah. She needed him more than she even wanted to admit. He would get her through the hardest part, and then he would break down, but not before.

"I've got her, baby. I've got her, and she is going to be fine," he whispered.

He heard a loud noise outside and went to the door to see his tour bus pulling up outside. "What the fuck?"

Hannah was also walking out when the bus came to a stop, and Mason stepped off followed closely by the rest of the band. He hadn't expected them to show up. Hell, he hadn't even had a chance to call them, though he had a feeling Briar had let them know what happened.

"What are you doing here?" he asked, giving Mason a hug.

"I got a letter and thought it would be rude not to give a dying woman her wish," he answered and held up a piece of paper. Taking it, he read what it said.

Mason,

I know you guys have to be getting ready for recording. Abel had mentioned it, and I heard him frustrated with trying to balance his career and everything going on with me. I do want to ask a favor, though. I know this is the end. Abel doesn't, not yet, but I do. I'll be lucky to see the end of the week. He is going to need you guys more than he will ever admit. More than that, he will need to let go. I don't want a sad funeral, so get the guys and bring the music. Let him scream it out the best way he can.

Alanna

She had certainly been busy those last few days. He had never even noticed her writing letters, and now he had found two. What else had she done?

"She is so right."

"Yeah, we got everything. I don't know what the plans are, but maybe we just rock out for everyone here," Trey said, patting Abel on the back.

"She was an awesome chick. The world is missing out for sure," Derrik said, reaching out a hand to him.

His eye was still discolored from the punch, and it made Abel smile.

He pulled Derrik in for a hug, "Yeah, she was. Sorry about the eye."

"It's fine," he answered.

"What is going on?" Hannah asked, her eyes red.

Abel reached out and pulled her into him. "Your mother planned everything. Didn't she?"

"I wouldn't put it past her. Why?" she asked.

He passed the letter over to her and then went to help get stuff off of the bus. Lacey rushed over to help, and he handed her small stuff so she could feel of use without getting hurt or breaking anything. As she carried a symbol over to Derrik, he laughed hearing it clatter in her hands.

"Hey! I know you! I have your picture on my wall!" Lacey said when she saw Derrik.

"Do you now? Well, I feel honored. Usually all the pretty girls have Abel on their walls," he teased.

"You got my tattoo!" Lacey said next and he turned to show it to her. "That is so silly."

"I like it," he answered and then handed her a stick. "Come here, let me show you how to do this."

The kit wasn't fully put together, but he sat down and showed Lacey how to hold a stick and strike a drum. Abel stood there watching as the little girl picked up on it with a sharp quickness. Oh, she was going to be talented and given a better environment to let it thrive.

"So that's the boyfriend?" Hannah asked, leaning against him as he wrapped an arm around her.

"Yeah, I guess. To be honest, I didn't ask a lot of questions," he answered.

"I agree. He's sus. I'll keep an eye on him," she teased.

But when Briar went over to Derrik, and he hugged her, Abel realized he had overreacted.

He didn't really want to talk about the funeral, but seeing as his band was already there setting up, he figured he needed to. A shuddering breath escaped him, and he took Hannah's hand to lead her inside. The guys could get everything set up while he talked to his newest family member about what they were doing. "I don't know what to do right now, but I figure we should talk about this."

"Mom wanted what she wanted. She didn't want to be buried, so we don't have anything like that to do. She will be cremated, and then I guess we can figure out what we want to do from there whenever we are ready to face it. Apparently, she didn't want a funeral either. I was reading her paperwork, and she said it in there too. Paperwork she wrote out before she ever met you. All it talks about is wanting a day filled with music and living life, so I think that is what we should do," she explained.

"Then that's what we do. Now I have another question," he said and took her to sit down in the living room. He picked up her hand and rubbed his finger over where her wedding ring used to be. "What happened?"

"Now is not the time," she said, her lip quivering on the verge of tears.

"I've got a hairpin trigger right now, so now is either the time or you can ask Derrik what happens when someone messes with one of my girls," he said.

She took a shaky breath and closed her eyes for a moment. "Things have been over for a while, but we were trying to make things work while I dealt with my mom. But then, I don't know. We couldn't stop arguing. It wasn't bad. Nothing like what Mom went through for sure. We just want different things, and I think I was just too young. I lived my whole life without a father and without seeing my mom in love that I just wanted love. Brandon is great, but I think I was more in love with the idea of him than actually him."

"Okay, then, if this is what you want, it's what's going to happen. Now, I want you to think about something. Don't answer right now because there is just too much going on, but I want you to think about moving to California with me and Briar. I can get Lacey in the best schools, and I can be more involved," Abel explained.

"I don't know," Hannah started to answer.

"Just think about it," he said next and then hugged her. "Well, I guess we have a concert to do."

CHAPTER THIRTY-THREE

HANNAH

He had told her that if he was going to do it, he was going to do it right. They didn't just set up their instruments so they could do an impromptu show. They made it a real concert. Mason ran around like a crazy man prepping like he would for any other show. All of the guys worked through the whole day to set up, but they decided to wait for the show to be the following day, giving Hannah time to let friends know about it. She told them it was her mother's wish to do this in lieu of a traditional funeral, and while some of them felt it was strange, one thing she had learned from her mother was not to care what other people thought.

They had erected a large screen behind where the band was set up so they could project photos of her mom. They had catered food and set it up around the pool along with some rented chairs and tables. Abel had pretty much taken charge of funding the whole thing. He was doing his best to make things perfect for her mom, and it meant the world to her.

He hadn't cried, at least not where she had seen. Since the moment Hannah's mother's last breath escaped her, Abel had pushed away his own feelings to be there for everyone else. As she sat on the porch watching him order people around, she could see the tension in him. Any minute she expected him to break, but still he kept going.

Briar was sitting in one of the chairs by the pool doing Lacey's makeup. Lacey had insisted on getting the full rock start treatment, so Hannah let Briar take control. She had really taken to Briar and was thankful for how much help she was being, especially with Lacey. Everyone was in black, but in truth, most of them wore black on a daily basis. Abel was still in his pajama pants, though, and Hannah was curious what his plans were.

People were starting to show up, and when their cars made their way toward the house, Abel came toward her. "I'll be back. I need to get changed," he said, quickly kissing the top of her head before disappearing inside.

"Lacey, come here!" Derrik said from over by the drums, and Hannah watched her little girl run over to him. Lacey didn't really know how to be sad. While she knew her grandmother was gone, she didn't fully understand what that meant. Instead, she was a little light in the darkness that had fallen around everyone.

Derrik pulled her up on his lap and then handed her a pair of sticks. "Okay, do you remember what I showed you?"

"Yeah!" she answered and started to play. It was messy and silly, but she beat on the drums for a bit while he worked the kick petals, and Hannah couldn't help but laugh.

"Okay, when I call you, I want you to come over and play a song with me. It's going to be a hard and fast one. You think you can do it?" Derrik asked.

"I got you!" Lacey answered then gave him a hug.

The whole band had taken to Lacey, and Hannah realized that her daughter hadn't just gotten a grandfather figure in Abel. She had gotten a whole group of men who would probably do anything for her. It seemed strange that just a few months ago none of them knew each other. Now it was like they had known each other their whole lives.

Abel walked out of the house a few minutes later. His hair was down and wet, and he was dressed in black leather pants and a black shirt that was a bit tight on him. She had seen pictures of him in similar outfits and she shook her head. Yes, he was taking this seriously. Some of the people who had come for the "not funeral" looked at him funny, but no one said anything to him. Hannah wasn't sure if it was out of confusion, fear, or sensing the volatile energy radiating from him. Regardless, they kept any thoughts they had to themselves.

Getting up, Hannah knew it was her turn to address the crowd. As she walked across the yard toward the stage area, people would stop her and tell her they were sorry for her loss—empty words that everyone said in times like this. They weren't what she wanted to hear. She wanted to hear something real, and she knew only one other person there could do that for her.

When she got to the microphone, she saw Briar get up and turn on the camera they had set up. Then she clicked a button on a computer. Hannah didn't have to turn around to know a picture of her mother was on the screen behind her.

"I want to take a moment to thank everyone for coming. I know there aren't many of you, and you are probably really confused, so I thought I would say a few things first," Hannah started, and she had to take a few breaths to keep going forward.

Abel came over and took her hand, which helped.

"Gosh, my mother was not a conventional woman at all. She wasn't really religious, and she never cared what anyone thought of her. When she got pregnant with me, she took that challenge full force. The only other thing she ever loved was being on the stage. I spent most of my teenage years watching her perform, and it was the only time I ever saw her happy. She fought every day to take care of me."

She had to take another couple of breaths, and everyone just stood there staring at her. Tears formed in her eyes and started to trail down her cheeks, but with a voice cracking in pain, she continued. "About six months ago the doctors told me I would lose my mother. Then something amazing happened. Something no one expected. This very strange, very unconventional man came into my mother's life. For the last few months of her life, my mom got every dream she ever had because of him. She got to meet her favorite bands. She got to sing in front of twenty thousand people, but more than that, she got to finally have the love of her life. The love she deserved to have all along."

She heard Abel take a shaking breath next to her, but he didn't step in or say anything. "My mother didn't want a funeral, so we aren't giving her one. What she wanted was this. She wanted the man she loves with all of her heart to sing his songs. So, instead of a funeral, you are all getting treated to a free concert by one of the greatest bands in the world. She didn't want sadness. She wanted power. She wanted ferocity. She wanted music that meant something. She used to tell me and my daughter, Lacey, to never sing a song that didn't mean something. She never sang silly songs to Lacey, and I have a feeling this man never will either. So, I'm going to let him take over from here. Enjoy the food. Enjoy the drinks, and enjoy the music."

She turned, and Abel pulled her into him. "I love you, kid. Thank you."

"I love you too, and no, thank you. You really did those things," she answered and then kissed his cheek.

Hannah took a seat next to Briar who reached over and held her hand as the band started playing some notes as if getting warmed up. Maybe they were just letting Abel get ready. He ran his fingers through his hair and Hannah watched as the man she had grown so familiar with faded away, and the rock star he really was came out. It was just like when her mom would step on stage. They became different people.

They had put headphones on Lacey to protect her ears, but she was up there with them dancing around as the band went from playing random notes to beginning the first song. Tears formed in her eyes as she realized what he was doing. Looking up to the screen, she saw what they were playing. While the sound wasn't coming through, it was the concert that her mother had done at the fair just over five years ago. He wasn't just doing a set. He was doing her set.

A fierce cry screamed out from him and a rush of warmth ran through her heart as he began to perform. "This is certainly not what I expected," Missy said, sitting down next to her.

She worked at Lacey's school, the same school where Hannah had been working. "Well, you knew my mom, and that man up there was determined to give her everything she wanted."

"Well, while I'm sad for the reason for it, I'm not sad to get the free concert," Missy said with a bit of laughter. "So, will you be coming back to the school next year?"

Hannah thought about it for a second. Abel had asked her to move to California, which was a huge step. It was a lot to think about. "I'm not sure yet. I might have other plans in the works."

"Well, I know I would love to have you back," Missy said.

People were put off by things at first, but then they started dancing and enjoying the music. Many of them had seen her mother perform before but probably had never seen Abel. He was certainly out of place in Alabama, but like Alanna, he didn't care. She watched him as he continued, and then she saw it. She saw the moment it hit him. For a second the world stood still. No, he didn't stop performing, but something changed in it.

Hannah go to her feet and started to move toward him, but then stopped as he roared out a scream so loud it echoed to the heavens. It wasn't just the scream of the song; it was the scream of his own pain and agony. He had fallen hard for her mother. It didn't make sense. Their whole relationship had been crazy, but it had been real. Most people probably thought his screams in that moment were just part of the song, but she knew different. She felt them to her soul. The band just played the same runs over and over while he got it out of his system.

Lacey went over to him and started screaming along with him, and Hannah had to fight back tears. Taking Briar's hand, she went up to the stage and joined in. They all screamed over and over, getting out so many emotions in just a full-on cathartic release.

Like a true professional, once he had his breakdown, he went back into the song as if nothing had changed. Derrik called out for Lacey, and she rushed over to him. He handed her a drumstick as the final song of the set started to play. Hannah could barely hear over the loud music as they began to play one of the hardest songs they did.

"Just like I showed you," Derrik yelled out to Lacey, and she began to hit one of the drums at a very steady pace. Derrik lost his mind on the drums with Lacey's help, and the other band members shredded through the music as Abel sang and screamed that last song. His eyes were shut tight, and he was gripping to the microphone like it was his lifeline, but when the song ended, he collapsed to the ground, drew his knees to his chest, and buried his face in his hands. He didn't cry. He didn't do anything else. He just sat there, shaking, and Hannah desperately wished she could do something to help him.

CHAPTER THIRTY-FOUR

ABEL

It had been a week, and he was finally walking back into his own home. Hannah wanted time to think about his offer, which he understood, but he had to get back to his life. No matter how much he just wanted to wallow, his band needed him. His family needed him. He was tired of people needing him.

The house felt empty without her there. Briar was there, but he knew she wasn't going to be staying. She had her own life, too. No, he was alone, again, and for the first time he felt it. His body felt heavy and weak, and every day the shakes became more intense. His demons were still screaming in his head. It wasn't something he had talked to anyone about, but they were there.

Walking toward the back of the house, he realized they hadn't been back since leaving to go to Vegas. He had a mess to clean up from that whole trip, but it could wait. When the piano came into view, he closed his eyes and remembered what she looked like sitting there playing for him.

"Dad, was that there before?" Briar said, and he opened his eyes again to see what she was talking about.

Sitting on the bench was a video camera with a piece of paper under it. He went over to it and looked. The paper read "Watch Me." His heart began to race. What had she done?

"Do you want me to watch it with you?" Briar asked next to him.

Slowly he reached down and picked up the camera and the paper. "No. To be honest, I think I need some time alone. I'm sorry."

"Don't be. I'll be in my room if you need me," she said and kissed his cheek.

Abel could hardly stand; his body trembling as he made his way up the stairs to his bedroom. He passed the room that had been set up for Alanna's nurses, and he was almost sick seeing it. Maybe he should have had someone clean the place out before he returned, but he didn't want anyone touching any of her things.

Inside his room, he sat down on the bed. He wasn't sure if he was ready to see what was on the tape. It would just be another reminder of how real everything had gotten.

It was when he went to set the camera down on the bedside table that he saw it. The bottle was just sitting there out in the open. When she had come to visit, they had gotten a little careless about putting her medications away. Abel was so focused on taking care of her that he wasn't distracted by it. There were no distractions now, only heartache. His hand shook as he placed the camera on the table and grabbed the bottle. He didn't have to read the label; he already knew what it was.

Morphine

"Just one time," that old voice whispered to him.

He closed his eyes as his fist tightened around the bottle, and his hand shook making the pills inside rattle. More than one.

She had called it poison. She had told him he didn't want poison, but she had left him alone. Now he was alone in a house too big for just one man. His heart had shattered, and he wasn't sure he would ever be able to put it back together. There had never been another woman in his life that he had loved like he loved Alanna, and he was sure there never would be again.

He grabbed a bottle of water and went into the bathroom, slamming the door closed and locking it. His heart pounded so hard it had him dizzy. Water splashed all over the place as he broke open the bottle and slammed it down on the counter. He looked up at the mirror and felt nothing but rage. With his fist still wrapped tightly around the medication, he punched the mirror, letting it shatter just as his heart had.

The demons screamed at him. Take it. Just take it and all the pain would go away. He had given her the morphine, and it took her pain away. Then death had taken her from him. Before he could stop himself, he unscrewed the bottle and poured the pills into his hand. There had to be at least ten of them, but he was too dizzy and filled with so much desire that he couldn't focus enough to count. It would either take away the pain or kill him. Either way, he would be better.

He started to lift his hand to his mouth, and he shut his eyes tightly so he wouldn't watch himself actually give in. Then he felt something. It was faint, like a memory, but he swore he felt a gentle hand rest on his shoulder. He stopped with his hand just touching his lips.

"Hey, baby," he heard, and he knew it was only in his mind, but his broken brain swore he heard it in truth. Tears formed in his eyes and began to pour down his face, and he tried to shake off the memory. The pain was too much. "You promised me," the voice whispered next.

"I'm sorry. I'm a liar. I can't. I can't do it, baby," he cried out, but he stayed frozen.

Some of the pills were starting to dissolve in his hand where the water had splashed on him. Another tremor raked over his body, and he had to catch himself with his other hand to keep from falling over.

"Baby, that's poison. You don't want poison," her voice whispered to him again. It was just a memory, but it all felt so real.

"Right now, I do. I just want the pain to go away. I just want the pain to stop," he cried out.

The demons screamed. He went to take the pills again. But then stopped, and with a roar, he tossed them into the toilet and flushed. Turning on the sink, he washed his hands to get the residue off of him. Then he lost it. He threw things, smashed things, breaking anything that wasn't nailed down. He screamed over and over until he ran out of breath.

"I'm sorry. I'm sorry. I promised. I know I made a promise, and if I break it now I'll never see you again," he said.

Despite how much he wanted to just give in, he couldn't. The girls needed him. His band needed him, and he had made a promise to her that he would take care of all of them.

The demons inside of him continued to roar out, and he tore out of the bathroom and down the hall to the room they had set up for Alanna. He threw open drawers and tossed equipment across the room. There had to be more. He had made a mistake tossing the pills. There had to be more somewhere.

"Fuck! Fuck!" he screamed, ripping things open. "Where are you! Fuck!"

His fist punched a hole in the wall, and he kicked over a bin. Then he saw it. A rush of heat hit him as he snatched the bottle and needle. He stabbed it into the vial and drew out the drug, filling it far more than his body would be able to take. Another roar of agony hit him as he smacked at his arm. He couldn't stop it. He needed it. He needed her. She had left him, and he had to find her. The pain was too much, bracing the needle to his vein he could barely see as he took a ragged breath.

This time when he felt a hand, he turned and was instantly wrapped into the arms that had saved him more than once. She had saved him before she had even been born.

"Dad," she whispered as they collapsed to the floor.

The needle clattered away from him as Briar wrapped herself completely around him. Like he had done for Hannah, she held him as he screamed and cried and shook.

"I just want the pain to stop," he cried. "Fuck, make it stop!" He wasn't really talking to her, and he had a feeling she knew that, but she answered anyway. "It will. One day, it will."

"No, no, no. The screams are so loud. I haven't. I can't. Just one time, please god please," he cried, scratching at his arms and begging to anyone who would hear him. He couldn't see the needle. Where had it gone? He needed it.

"Dad, it's poison. Remember what she said. It's poison. You don't want poison," she whispered, rocking him like he was the child.

"Fuck! Fuck! Fuck!" he screamed again and again. He had held on to his control for so long, and now that it had broken, he just wanted to give up.

"I've got you," Briar whispered and held him. She held him until the tears stopped and the shakes subsided. She held him until he felt strong enough to move away.

"I wanted to so bad, baby. You have no idea," he whispered, trying to regain some of his sanity.

"But you didn't," she said, and he turned to look at her. Her breath caught, and he felt so guilty putting her through that. She should never have to be that person for him.

"No, I didn't. But fuck did I want to. No, I do want to," he said, because that was the truth. "I think I'm going to need some help for a little while."

"Then we get help, but I'm not going to lose you too, okay. There has been too much sadness going around for me to lose you too," she whispered.

He didn't have an answer for that because his emotions were too volatile to make any promises. "I'm sorry."

"We'll get through this, Dad. I promise," Briar answered.

He wasn't sure what happened to the vial and needle. Somehow, at some point while he was in hysterics, Briar had managed to hide them away. Whatever she had done made it easier for him to calm back down. The rage, the pain, the need was all still there, and he wasn't strong enough to fight it alone.

Briar and Derrik searched the rest of the house for any remaining hidden pills or vials. They found a couple of bottles in other places and disposed of them. His head was still screaming, but the temptation was gone, and he went back to his room to try and start again.

Her dress was still in a pile on the floor, and he remembered their last time together. He had hurt her. It had been an accident. Abel closed his eyes as the memory of her all but begging him to do it flashed through his mind. She had come so hard for him before the pain took over. It had been incredible, so he decided to only remember the pleasure and let go of the rest.

The camera was still sitting on the table, and he reached out to hold it. Again, he read the note that told him to watch it. "What did you do, baby?" he whispered, getting up and going to his TV.

He hooked up the camera and then went to sit on the bed so he could watch it. He wasn't prepared for it, but it was something she left for him. There had been no other letters, not that anyone had found at least. All he had was whatever was on this video.

She came into view as she fiddled with the camera a bit before taking a seat in front of it, and he felt a sharp pain in his chest. Maybe he would just die of a heart attack and could join her on the other side.

"Hey, baby," she whispered first, giving him that beautiful smile as she looked directly into the camera lens. She was dressed in a white silk nightgown with a silk and lace white robe on. It was what she had been wearing that morning when he found her playing, and he realized she looked like an angel.

"Hey," he whispered back to the screen.

"So, it's like four in the morning and everyone is asleep. I couldn't sleep, though. I hate to say it, but it's time. I can feel it, and I think every moment from this one on is just borrowed time. Hopefully I will have enough time to do all the things I still need to do. I'm sorry I had to leave you like this. I never wanted to break your heart, but as I sit here, I hate to say it, I'm a bit selfish because you giving me your heart is one of the best things to ever happen to me."

He leaned forward, wanting to get closer to her even though it was just a video. "I'd do it again," he said as if she could hear him.

"I know I can't say the words to you. The idea of it, well, it just hurts too much. You say them to me all the time, and I can feel them to my very soul. I'm sorry I couldn't say them to you when I was alive. You deserved better, but baby, I need you to know that I love you with every fiber of my being. You are the world I never knew I was missing. You didn't just make all my dreams come true. You showed me dreams I never knew I had. You gave me the best, well, everything of my life. The best music, the best fun, the best joy, the best sex, oh yes, the very best sex, and the best love. I wish I was braver. I wish I could look into your eyes and tell you this, but I can't. So, if you are watching this. Look into my eyes and believe me when I say, Abel Sharp. I love you."

"I love you too," he cried, moving closer to reach out and touch the screen. "I love you so much it hurts."

"I'm sure everything hurts right now. It does for me too," she said next, and he saw tears form in her eyes. "I don't want to leave you. I don't want to leave Hannah and Lacey and Briar. But I don't have a choice. I swear, it hurts more than the cancer killing me. If I only had more time. So, I'm going to do the only thing I know to do. I'm going to do the thing I know will show you and tell you just how much I feel for you. I'm going to sing for you until I can't sing anymore, and with my songs, I'm going to tell you just how much I love you and how much it hurts to leave you."

He began to pant in anticipation as he watched her get up and walk to the seat of the piano. She had recorded it. She had recorded the morning. He couldn't breathe as she began to play a song he had never heard before. It was something she had played before Briar had woken him up. It wasn't a pop song or something she had heard. It was too personal. It was a song for him. Unable to stop it, he cried as she sang her song for him. A song that told him she loved him. A song that told him how much it hurt to leave him. A song that meant something. It was the most beautiful song he had ever heard her sing before. Her last good-bye.

Her body shook as she finished it. Then she began to play another song. It was a song he knew, and he realized that was the song she had been playing when he went downstairs. Watching, he saw Briar coming into frame for a second before she raced up the stairs. A moment later he saw himself come into view. He watched and relived that morning.

When it got to the end of her little concert for him, and he left to go pack for them, she went back to the camera and picked it up. "I love you, Abel Sharp. This is only good-bye for now. I know we will see each other again. Take care of our girls and stay away from the poison." She kissed the lens then turned off the camera.

"She had things to do," he whispered. "Oh god, baby. I love you so much."

CHAPTER THIRTY-FIVE

ABEL—TEN YEARS LATER

"Dad, can you get Max!" Briar called from the kitchen. His grandson was screaming from the other room, and he went to pick the boy up. Instantly he knew what was wrong.

"It's like you know! I'll get him cleaned up!" he called out to his daughter as he took the boy for a diaper change.

"What can I say, it's a gift!" Briar teased.

"Dad! Lacey got in trouble again!" Hannah called out, coming into the door. He passed over Max. "Deal with her, and I will deal with him."

At least he got out of diaper duty, though angsty teen was probably more difficult. "Okay, kid, what happened this time?"

"They want to expel me," she answered, storming past him toward the back den.

"What do they want to expel you for?" he asked, turning her to look at him.

She was the spitting image of Alanna. The older she got, the more she resembled the woman he loved, and her attitude fell right in line. She was dressed in baggy jeans that were tight on her waist with one of the band T-shirts Alanna had left her, and his ring hung from the necklace around her neck. She had a lot of piercings in her ears, but at fifteen, they had managed to keep her from getting any other metal or ink so far. At least, that they were aware of.

"So, I may have punched this guy in the face for cheating on me, after I locked myself with my band in the audio-visual room and performed a fuck you song to him for the whole school," she said, rolling her eyes.

He had to bite his lip to keep from laughing. "Okay, well you certainly did your best to make it interesting."

"He also said your music sucks, so I was also defending the family honor," she answered.

"Well, as much as I want to thank you for defending my honor, I'm old enough to fight my own battles, and I really don't give a fuck what some punk kid at your school thinks of my music. He's probably not going to amount to anything anyway," he answered.

"It's not like it matters that I got expelled. Today was the last day of school. They said it might roll over to next year, though," she said and flopped down on the couch.

"Look, a hundred years ago, when I was young, I used to get in trouble all the time, and it started out just like this. First it was just getting into fights with guys at school for stupid shit. Then I started getting into bigger fights and doing other stuff that I shouldn't have done," he started to explain.

"Like the drugs?" Lacey asked, and he nodded.

"Like the drugs. It's a slippery path, and it landed me in prison, Lacey. Trust me, you don't want to go there," he explained.

"But everything worked out for you in the end," Lacey said as if that made all the bad stuff he had done right.

"I was very lucky in that. Most people, like almost all people, are not so lucky. Now, I know you are all full of fire, and you took your grandma's letter to heart, but sometimes we have to redirect our fire to more constructive avenues," he said, hoping he would be able to get through to her.

Lacey looked up at the portrait of her grandmother that was hung up behind the couch. It was the one that used to hang in Alanna's music room so long ago. "I don't understand how I can miss someone I barely remember," she whispered and then got up and left.

"Today is always hard on everyone. You know that," Hannah said and took a seat next to him.

"Yeah, and she doesn't make it any easier," he said. "Alanna called it. That girl is giving us all hell."

"I blame you," Hannah said with a laugh.

"Me! No, your grandma did that," he protested.

"She only had five years with the girl, and most of that time she was a baby. No, this is all you." She laughed, and then her tone turned serious. "It's hard to think it's been ten years. Sometimes it still feels like it was yesterday."

"Yeah, it does," he agreed.

"You know, I wanted to hate you for a while there. It was like, how dare this man come in and steal all that time from me," Hannah began. She had never told him that before, and he had never thought of it either. He had been so consumed with his love that he hadn't thought about what it had done to the other people in Alanna's life. "But I couldn't because no one else could have done what you did for her. I just couldn't be angry at how happy you made her. You know, this is probably a stupid question that I probably already know the answer to, but I never asked, and it's been ten years so I'm going to."

He got nervous and prepared himself for whatever she was going to ask. "Okay, what do you want to know?"

"So, I know you guys loved each other," she started.

"Love. We love each other, but go on," he corrected. He always corrected people when they put his feelings in past tense because his love had never faded, and he was sure it never would.

"You two love each other, but well, she was really sick and in pain all the time. I mean, I know she pretended like she wasn't, but she was. So, did you guys actually ever, you know, hook up?" she asked, and he could see from the look on her face she regretted it right away.

He burst out laughing, unable to hold back. How she had managed to keep that level of denial up for ten years, he would never know. "Do you seriously want me to answer that?"

"Oh god that means yes," she protested, laughing along with him. "But how? I mean, seriously, and when?"

He felt like she was digging herself into a hole of questions and answers she didn't really want. "Well, you have a kid and have been married, so I'm pretty sure you know how. When, well, it started in Florida and ended here, right before Vegas."

"I really never knew. I suspected. I mean, figured something was happening, but my brain could not wrap around how," she said. "Dear god, that woman was wild until the end. Crazy."

"It's what made her special," he said. "Now I have to ask you a question. I have a friend. Well, a little more than a friend who I have been seeing for a little while. You know how hard it has been for me since your mom and all, but this one seems to understand. So, I invited her over tonight, but I told her it was only if you were okay with it."

"Oh, you're bringing a girl home. Now that is something," Hannah said and reached over and took his hand. "It's been ten years. I think we are fine. It's not like you haven't been dating."

"This is different," he said and looked down. "I really like this one."

"Good, you shouldn't be alone," she said and kissed his cheek. "I look forward to meeting her. Now, Lacey might think differently."

Every year on the anniversary of Alanna's death they all gathered to celebrate her life. It had been a tradition since the funeral, and something they never faltered from. Sometimes friends would come, but most of the time it was just him, Hannah, Lacey, Briar, and Derrik. This would be Max's first year participating, but he got a pass since he had just been born a few months before.

It was always the hardest day of the year for him, and every year, the week after the anniversary of her death, he held a benefit concert in her honor. All of the money earned from the show went to cancer treatment and research, and it was the single most important show of the year for him.

Everyone was already in the living room for the viewing when the doorbell rang. Abel went to answer it, knowing who it would be. When he swung open the door, he smiled at his current girlfriend. She was taller than Alanna had been, and obviously bigger considering the situation. She was slightly curvy and had deep green eyes. Her hair was dark, and she had a bit of a tan. Everything about her was different, which had been part of what drew him to her. It made it easier for him.

"Hey, you are just in time," he said, leaning in and giving her a quick kiss. "You sure about this?"

"Yeah, I'm sure. Look, at our age, I get it. We all have a past, and I'm perfectly fine with it," Teresa answered. There hadn't been anyone serious since Alanna, but he was getting older and tired of being alone. He knew she would understand.

"Alright, well let's get to it. I promise, most nights aren't like this one. This is literally the hardest night of the year for me, so I'm sorry if I'm not myself," he said, leading her toward the den where everyone was waiting. Snacks littered the place, and the TV was paused on the opening shot of the concert. "Everyone, this is Teresa. She is my girlfriend. Be nice to her."

Everyone welcomed her, but Lacey stared at her as if sizing her up. His granddaughter was very possessive of him, and he was sure she would have something to say later when they were alone. Once he was settled on the couch with Teresa next to him, they turned on the show.

It started out backstage. Alanna was dressed in those low-cut pants, bra top, and a long jacket. Rain was pouring down in the distance, but there was a huge smile on the woman's face.

"Do I look okay?" she asked the camera.

"Mom, seriously! I can't answer that," Hannah said from behind the camera.

"Fine, be that way. Now wish me luck," she said before walking out to the stage, Hannah's camera following her the whole way.

She was soaked before she even made it to the microphone and lifted her hands in the air with her horns held high. Abel found himself lifting his own hand and doing the same as he often did.

"Fuck, y'all! It's wet out here and not in the good way! You ready to have a good time!" she called out into the microphone, and the crowd erupted in cheers.

The music started to play, and as if on cue the living room exploded into a party.

"Oh my god, she is so beautiful," Teresa whispered next to him as she stared at the screen oblivious to the fact that everyone else in the room was dancing and singing along.

"Yeah, she is," he answered and pulled her closer to him. His body began to shake, and he took a deep breath.

The concert went on, and the room got more and more crazy. Lacey especially got into it, climbing on the furniture and belting out song after song. She knew every word, every note, and sang it as if Alanna was speaking through her. It was eerie sometimes just how much like Alanna that girl was.

"Hey, Lacey!" Abel called out and she turned toward him.

"This year is the year. Right?" he asked and watched as a huge smile spread over her lips.

"Really? You think I'm ready?" she asked.

"I think you are more than ready," he answered.

She rushed over to him and wrapped her arms around him. "Thank you!"

CHAPTER THIRTY-SIX

ABEL

"It's been ten years since you started putting on this benefit, but you said this year is special. Why is that?" the reporter asked Abel as he sat for his interview.

"Because this year I have a very special guest who will be joining the show, but I don't want to give away the surprise," he answered. He and Lacey had worked all week getting her ready for the show. She had picked a couple of the songs from Alanna's concert and had practiced until she felt confident that she had it right. He had offered to go on stage with her, but she had said she could do it on her own.

"Well, that is very exciting. You know, you had a pretty notorious history for a long time, but you never talk about what changed," the reporter said next.

"It's hard to talk about, so I sing about it. If you pay attention to the music, you'll figure it out," he answered. Through all that time, he had never openly talked about his relationship with Alanna, even when asked about the mysterious woman he had been spending time with.

The press had figured out enough. They knew her name, that she died, and that not long after he set up the first benefit. The rest of the story was really no one else's business. Maybe one day he would write a book and tell all, but for now, he liked that his love story was just between him and Alanna. No one really knew all of it, not even the kids, and that kept it special to him.

"Well, as always, we are looking forward to the shows. It was great to talk with you. Abel Sharp, everyone," the reporter said, and then he was able to leave.

Bands were already playing, and the place was packed. It was a huge event every year and had only grown over time. He hoped that eventually Lacey would take it over because he certainly couldn't do it forever.

"Abel Sharp," a woman's voice said from behind him, and he turned to see Leia Rice standing behind him. She had been at every one of the shows. It was something he always appreciated since she had been Alanna's other favorite singer.

"Leia," he said and went to give her a hug.

"So, it's been ten years, you ever going to tell me the story?" she asked.

"Nope, but I will once again let you know that I won," he teased remembering how Alanna had claimed to be willing to marry the powerhouse front woman before him.

"Only because I didn't try," she teased back before giving him a hug. "I know this is always hard for you. Thank you for letting me be a part of it."

"Thank you for being here," he answered, and she went to get ready for her set. He always closed out the show. It was his show, after all, and it was all for Alanna. She would want him to bring the house down, but there were always incredible bands there.

With a deep breath, he went to go check on Lacey, who had been getting ready the last time he saw her. She had told him that she had a plan and had even made Briar take her shopping. He was not looking forward to the girl getting her license. There would be no stopping her then. With a tap on the door, he waited for Lacey to say it was clear for him to come in before walking through.

Then he froze. For at least ten full seconds he thought she was there. It was like he was seeing Alanna there in the flesh, but it wasn't her. Lacey had done her hair just like her. She had gotten leather pants that thankfully were not cut as low as Alanna's had been, but still lower than he wanted her to go on stage in. And she had on the same style top with gold embroidery. She was shrugging on the jacket when he walked in, and she turned to look at him.

"What?" she asked as if she hadn't just given him a heart attack.

"You can't go out there like that," he said, blinking several times to shake off the shock.

"Why? It's what she wore," Lacey said.

"You're fifteen. She was like in her thirties," he answered.

"Performers my age go out in less all the time. This whole thing is for her, so that's what I want to do," she said.

He realized he was probably overreacting. After another look, he realized that the top, though similar, did cover more, though not much, and the pants were closer to her belly button for sure. Lacey had a point. Lots of girls her age would wear a lot less.

"Does your mom know?" he asked next.

"Nope, and I don't want you to tell her. I want it to be a surprise," she answered before picking up the necklace with his ring.

He walked over and helped her put it on. "You look just like her, you know."

"Yeah, all of you tell me that all the time," she answered. "So, I assume I have the grandma pass tonight. Right?"

He laughed, remembering the joke from all those years ago.

"Yeah, you have the grandma pass, but if your mother tries to kill me, you have to help defend me," he answered.

"Didn't you just tell me that you were old enough to fight your own fights," she teased back.

"Oh, I will never be able to fight your mother. She is mean." He laughed. "You sure you don't want me to go out there with you?"

She thought about it for a moment. "No, I got it."

"I know you are all amped up and ready for my set, but you are going to have to wait just a little bit longer. Before I come out, I want to introduce someone very special to me. She is going to be singing lead while my band plays. This girl came into my life during a very crazy time, ten years ago. She is my granddaughter, and you better fucking cheer for her," he called out to the crowd. He was already dressed for the show since he would go on right after her. "So get your fucking hands in the air for Lacey Grace Sharp!"

They had agreed she would use his last name on stage, and it filled his heart with pride. The crowd cheered, and he walked off the stage to go stand with Hannah. She was standing there with her hands folded together, nervous for her daughter.

Then Lacey walked out from the other side of the stage. She didn't just walk out; she marched out with every ounce of fire that filled her soul. The echo of her boots against the stage rang out with every step, and her face was hard.

"Oh my god, she looks just like her," Hannah gasped and reached to grab his hand. "She's so beautiful."

Once at the microphone, she tossed off the jacket and raised her hands in the air. Unlike her grandmother, she didn't raise her horns.

No, he had corrupted her too much, so she flicked off the whole crowd.

"Alright, mother fuckers! Let's do this!" she called out to the crowd, and all thirty thousand of them roared out in excitement for her.

If Alanna had been a fire, Lacey was an inferno, and he was terrified and proud of the woman she was becoming. Hannah gripped his hand tighter as the music started hard and fast. This wasn't girl pop. This wasn't even soft rock. No, Lacey was as metal as they came on stage. Her hand gripped to the microphone stand as she began to move and head bang to the music, letting the crowd really get into the song.

He held his breath and smiled the moment she lifted up and screamed out that first note. It was fierce and cathartic just before the song fell into a more melodious tone. She sang with intensity and passion. She felt the song deep down just as her grandmother did. Just as he did. Every word ignited an emotion, and she blasted it out to the crowd who ate it up.

"She's a fucking star," he whispered as he watched her perform.

"Yeah, she is," Hannah said. "Mom would be so proud."

He heard the break in Hannah's voice, and he leaned over to hug her. "She is very proud. I know it."

Lacey only sang three songs, the last of which he did join her for as he took over the set. He couldn't have been prouder of the girl, and the pride inside of him for her was beyond anything he could ever express.

However, when it came time for him to sing, it was different. This show wasn't for him. It wasn't for the fans. This show was for her. Alanna. The woman he never stopped loving, and just as he had done at her funeral, he sang to her. He screamed to her. He put every shattered part of him out on the stage and gave her the thing she loved most.

She was a beautiful woman who lived a not so beautiful life. He had been a broken man who had been given more chances than anyone had a right to have, but Alanna had given him something he had never thought to have. She had given him love. She had given him strength. She had filled his house with a family he wouldn't trade for the world. While their love story had ended in tragedy, his love for her never died. It would never die because even when he died, he would be taking it with him to find her on the other side.

About the Author

Vanessa Rose is a Contemporary Romance author currently residing in Tuscaloosa, Alabama. She can often be found at a coffee shop working on her books and refers to these trips to town as "Going to the Office". She credits her friends and family with inspiring her and being a sounding board as she plots out her next book. To read her Paranormal Romance works, look for her under the pen name Cherron Riser.

For more from Vanessa Rose, go to her Linktree: https://linktr.ee/author.vanessa.rose

https://linktr.
ee/author.van
essa.rose